TOTAL REPRESEN
A New Electoral System for Modern Times

To Michael and Bridget Smith
With best wishes
Feb. 2010
Aharon Nathan

Aharon Nathan – Ivo Škrabalo

TOTAL REPRESENTATION

A New Electoral System for Modern Times

Introduction
Dr Ken Ritchie
Chief Executive: Electoral Reform Society

Commentary
Professor Gideon Doron
President: Political Science Association, Israel

Editor
Stephen Cviic

ISBN: 978-184426-696-8

PUBLICATIONS

ERS Publications, London, 2009

Copyright © Aharon Nathan & Ivo Škrabalo

This book is published on the authority of its writers and contributors and it does not necessarily represent the views of the Electoral Reform Society. The ERS does not accept responsibility for its contents.

All rights reserved. No part of this publication may be reproduced, stored in a retrieval system, or transmitted, in any form of by any means, electronic, mechanical, pthotocopying, recording or otherwise, without written permission from the authors.

ISBN 978-184426-696-8
A CIP catalogue record for this book is available from the British Library

Printed by
www.printondemand-worldwide.com

CONTENTS

Acknowledgements	7
INTRODUCTION Dr Ken Ritchie, Chief Executive, Electoral Reform Society	9

PART ONE   Aharon Nathan
THE IDEA OF TOTAL REPRESENTATION

1 Total Representation – system and context	19
2 Applying Total Representation	28
Fixing the boundaries	28
The electoral commission	29
An electoral simulation	31
Electing the party leaders	33
3 The advantages of TR	36
4 The theoretical background to TR	40

PART TWO   Aharon Nathan
ELECTORAL REFORM – THE UNITED KINGDOM

5 The House of Commons	49
Background	49
Imbalanced representation in the House of Commons	50
Grafting TR on to the present House of Commons – two solutions	59
Boundaries – and a simulation of TR based on the 2005 election	63
6 Applying TR to the House of Lords	67
Background	67
Implementation	70
7 Applying TR to the Scottish parliament	74
8 The UK, the European Parliament and its electoral system	89

PART THREE   Aharon Nathan
ELECTORAL REFORM – ISRAEL

Commentary on TR: Professor Gideon Doron, President of the Association of Political Science in Israel	99

9	The crisis of democracy in Israel	105
10	Attempts to reform the Knesset from the 1950s onwards	114
11	The President of Israel's Commission (2005-7)	121
12	The Electoral Draft Law in the Knesset (2008-9)	130
	Suggested changes to the Draft Law	131
	Supplementary measures and regulations	136
13	Analysis of future voting trends	141
	Electoral simulations – Knesset: 2003, 2006, 2009	145

PART FOUR   Professor Ivo Škrabalo
CROATIA – THE HISTORY OF ELECTIONS

	Commentary – The power of elections: Chris Cviić, OBE	163
14	The historical background to Croatian democracy	170
15	Electoral systems: 1990-2007	178
	1990: Parliament of the Socialist Republic of Croatia	178
	1992: Chamber of Representatives – a combination of first-past-the-post and proportional representation	183
	1995: Chamber of Representatives – a revised combination of first-past-the-post and proportional representation	188
	2000: Chamber of Representatives; 2003 and 2007 Parliament – proportional representation	195
16	Croatian expatriates: their right to vote and special representation	202
17	National minorities and positive discrimination	210
18	A brief history of the Croatian bi-cameral Parliament	221

PART FIVE   Professor Ivo Škrabalo
CROATIA – ELECTORAL REFORM

19	TR and the Croatian electoral system	229
20	Why TR in Croatia? Points for discussion	245

Key to abbreviations in the text (for Croatia)	259
NOTES ABOUT THE AUTHORS	261

ACKNOWLEDGEMENTS

We would like to record our gratitude to all those who read the drafts of this book at various stages of its progress and helped us with suggestions and feedback.

In particular, we want to thank: Dr. Ken Ritchie, chief executive of the ERS, for the penetrating introduction he provided to present TR to the British public; Professor Gideon Doron and Christopher Cviić, OBE, for contributing critical evaluations of the TR system; and Lewis Baston, ERS director of research, for his review and analysis of the UK chapters.

In Israel, we greatly appreciated helpful comments on TR from Professor Shimon Shetreet of the Hebrew University, Professor Zeev Segal of Tel Aviv University and Jamal Majadle of Baqa El Gharbia. We are also grateful to Dr. Fany Yuval of Ben Gurion University for conducting the simulations for the last three Knessets included here.

In Croatia, we would like to thank: Slavko Goldstein and Sanja Petrušić Goldstein of Novi Liber; Denis Stankov and Studio DiM of Zagreb for permitting us to use the design and parts of the content of the book on TR published by them recently; Boško Picula for reviewing the Croatian parts; and Davor Stipetić for his translation of the Croatian chapters.

We would also like to express our appreciation to Stephen Cviić for his skilful editing and Vladimir Pavlinić for his help, advice and work on every aspect of the book's design and layout. Michael Nathan accompanied the preparation of this book at every stage of its writing and publishing.

We are deeply indebted to all of them. However, much as we value their contributions, we alone are responsible for the contents of this book.

Aharon Nathan,
Ivo Škrabalo

August 2009

INTRODUCTION
DR KEN RITCHIE
Chief Executive – Electoral Reform Society

The number of voting systems that one could devise is almost infinite, and we are certainly not short of well-intentioned reformers who have discovered what they believe to be the right medicine for our troubled democracies. The Electoral Reform Society attracts many of these systems inventors: some of their letters are interesting and s ome are fanciful to the point of being entertaining, but very, very few offer ideas that are new, relevant and practicable.

When Aharon Nathan contacted me to talk about a new voting system, 'Total Representation' (TR), that he had developed, my natural reaction was one of scepticism and with a sigh I resigned myself to writing yet another "thank you for your interesting idea but..." letter. However, it did not need more than a quick look at Aharon Nathan's proposal to see that this was something quite different.

Two things were apparent from the start. Firstly, the idea behind TR is so attractively simple that it leaves us wondering why no-one thought of it before. Secondly, the idea was not the work of an amateur mathematician concerned solely with the formulae for converting votes into electoral outcomes, but came from someone who has been involved in politics and with the consequences of political decisions for more than half a century. TR was not being advocated as a result of any theoretical discussion about the nature of democracy, but as a possible solution to some of the serious problems faced by many of today's democracies.

Aharon Nathan has approached voting system design with experience from two countries – Britain and Israel – which are at opposite ends of a spectrum in terms of electoral systems. Britain's first-past-the-post system uses single-member constituencies and pays no heed to the concept of proportionality, while Israel's list system treats the entire country as a single electoral region, providing about as much proportionality – at least in the sense of proportionality by party – as is possible. Neither of these systems is performing satisfactorily and in both countries the electoral system is increasingly becoming a matter for debate.

The demand for electoral reform in Britain has intensified since the 1970s. The stranglehold that Labour and the Conservatives had had over British politics for much of the twentieth century has been breaking down with the emergence of the Liberal Democrats as a significant third party, while the nationalist parties have been gaining ground in Scotland and Wales. But with first-past-the-post, general elections have remained a two-horse race, with Labour winning a comfortable majority in 2005 with little more than a third of the votes. Governments take power with a minority of the votes, but without a parliament that can effectively hold them to account. Elections are won or lost on what happens in a small minority of marginal constituencies, and it is only in these constituencies that election campaigns are vigorously fought. Elsewhere, who wins is usually a safe bet and the votes of a majority of voters have little influence on the result.

To achieve a parliament that is more representative, in which smaller parties can have an effective voice, and which is a real debating chamber rather than a rubber stamp for executive action, the demand of reformers has been for a more proportional voting system. Opponents of reform, however, point to Israel and its ultra-proportional system which can reduce government formation to back-room deals involving many minor parties, often giving disproportionate power to minority interests when it comes to forming ruling coalitions.

Israel's voting system makes most votes count in that most are cast for parties that gain representation in the Knesset. That, of course, is good but, in a society that is deeply divided by race, religion, ethnicity and attitudes to peace and war, elections using an excessively proportional system do not produce clear outcomes: who forms the government and the position of government on key issues is too often the result of post-election negotiations rather than the collective will of the electorate. In Israel the movement for electoral reform is at an earlier stage in its development, but a growing recognition that the present system does not serve the country well provides an opportunity for change.

The degree of proportionality is not, however, the only problem of Israeli politics. As with any 'closed list' system, voters can only vote for parties and not for candidates. Which candidates fill the seats won by their parties is a matter for the parties – not for the voters. Candidates placed at the bottom of lists may have no hope of selection, no matter how good or popular they might be, while candidates at the top of lists may almost be guaranteed seats, even if they lack popular support and are of questionable ability. As a result of MKs owing their positions to where they were placed on their party lists, they may feel more accountable to their party selectorates than to the voters and politicians can become even more detached from the people they are there to serve.

Aharon Nathan has proposed TR as a solution, or at least a partial solution, to the problems of democracy both in Britain and Israel. It would give Britain a parliament that better reflects the views of its electors but without abandoning the single-member constituencies on which its present system is based. It would move Israel away from the fractured politics produced by its extreme form of proportional representation, but without moving it to the unrepresentative form of politics from which Britain suffers. In the debate between proportional representation and first-past-the-post it seeks a middle road. It values the voter, seeking to make all votes effective and to ensure the accountability of politicians to those who elected them.

Total Representation (TR) is, like many great discoveries, amazingly simple. It involves a first-past-the-post election in single-member constituencies but then, rather than ignoring votes for unsuccessful candidates, these are totalled by party and further seats awarded to the parties on the basis of these totals. The 'party seats' won by a party are then filled by that party's candidates based on the number of votes they received individually in the constituency contests.

TR is therefore related to the 'Mixed Member Proportional' (MMP) family of electoral systems (in Britain MMP is used for Scottish Parliament and Welsh and London Assembly elections, and is referred to as AMS – the Additional Member System). These combine the election of members in local constituencies by first-past-the-post with the election of members from party lists on a regional basis in such as way as to improve the proportionality of the constituency elections. Generally this requires two votes – one for the constituency candidate and the other for a party list – but TR's ingenious use of 'unused' votes in the constituency contests avoids the need for a second vote.

However, if TR is to be regarded as more than just an interesting idea, we need to consider how it compares with other alternative voting systems that might be used in its place.

A first consideration must be the proportionality of representation. The arguments for, and against, proportionality run through this book because it is a book not just about the mechanics of an electoral system but about the nature of representative democracy. How important is it that parliament should reflect, and reflect as accurately as possible, the range of views within the electorate? Is there a choice to be made between elections that lead to representative parliaments and elections that produce effective governments? Advocates of PR argue that for governments to be strong they must have strong democratic mandates and not just enjoy the support of a minority of voters, that representative parliaments are needed to hold executives to account, and (with plenty supportive evidence) that coalition governments can be every bit as strong and effective as single-party governments. Opponents, however, argue that PR too often leads to elections decided by post-election bargaining rather than people's votes, and to weak governments which can be held to ransom by small parties which wield disproportional influence.

Too often the debate is polarised between those who see pure proportionality as an end in itself and those who see it as a recipe for confusion and compromises which subvert the decisions of the electorate. Aharon Nathan is too rooted in real politics to fall for either of these extremes. He seeks a middle way, recognising the need for a system that takes account of the views of as many voters as possible but rejecting forms of pure PR which can be an obstacle to the business of governance. His views, no doubt based on the Israeli experience, will not be shared by all readers of this book, but they are nevertheless challenging and cannot be dismissed without arguments that take account of that experience.

Nevertheless, TR should be regarded as a proportional system. Rather than accepting the crude outcomes of first-past-the-post, it seeks a fairer allocation of seats to parties and provides opportunities for smaller parties to gain representation. However, as with any proportional system, the degree of proportionality depends on the system's parameters. With TR, and indeed with other forms of MMP, proportionality depends largely on the ratio of party/regional to constituency seats: the more party/regional seats there are to compensate for any disproportionality in the constituency seats, the more proportional the system will be. A second factor is the size of the region, larger regions offering small parties a lower threshold for gaining representation.

Aharon Nathan proposes a small ratio for elections of national parliaments where there is a need for executives to have sufficient parliamentary support to govern, but not sufficient for them to be able to ride rough shod over parliamentary opposition. For other levels of government, such as the UK House of Lords and the European Parliament, the arguments for proportionality are greater and the ratio of 'Constituency Members' to 'Party Members' can be higher. Thus although TR may be a potentially proportional system, in practice it can be tailored to suit the needs of any particular election.

In terms of proportionality, TR probably is similar to other MMP systems: with the same ratio of regional to constituency seats and similar sized regions, we should expect similar degrees of proportionality (although further statistical work is needed to test this assumption). It is possible that TR gives a slight advantage to parties whose vote distribution allows them to do well in constituency contests as votes of losing candidates are not given equal value because of the lower number of regional seats, but whether this is or is not desirable is a matter of political judgement.

In terms of ease of voting, TR scores highly. There is, however, an argument that forms of MMP that require two votes offer voters greater choice - they can vote for their preferred constituency candidate, but separately can vote for the party they would like to see in government, even if that is not the party of their constituency choice. Here, however, we must differentiate between theory and practice. Evidence from Scotland and Wales suggests that voters do not necessarily know how to use their two MMP votes effectively. For example, many Labour voters in Glasgow have given both votes to Labour, although it is clear from any analysis of voting figures that Labour will win more than its share of seats in constituency contests in Glasgow and will not therefore be eligible for regional seats. There is also evidence that some voters have erroneously regarded their regional votes as second choices, thereby supporting parties they do not want to see in government. TR, which requires only one vote, might not offer the same sophisticated choice, but as a simpler system for the voter it avoids possible misunderstandings and mistakes.

In terms of making politicians accountable to their electorates, TR does not differ from other forms of MMP as far as constituency representatives are concerned, but may go some way towards overcoming the perceived problems in the lack of legitimacy of regional members in MMP. Where regional members are elected from party lists, there is a risk (as in Israeli elections) that because they owe their positions to their ranking by their parties in the lists, they are seen as not having the same legitimacy as constituency members, with a risk that they will be more accountable to their parties than to their electors. With TR, in which regional members must have been constituency candidates and have won sufficient votes as such, this danger may be at least reduced.

Both TR and other forms of MMP suffer from safe seats — constituencies in which it is quite clear that the candidate of one party or another will safely win. Where regional seats are allocated to candidates on the basis of their positions in party lists, there is little incentive for constituency candidates to campaign in situations in which they have no chance of success. Here TR may score. Even where candidates know they will not win in their constituencies, they will know that a good performance may gain them a regional seat. TR may therefore give all candidates more incentive to fight whatever their prospects as constituency members.

Many proponents of electoral reform will no doubt point to the things that TR would not achieve. Unlike the Single Transferable Vote system (STV), it does not offer preference voting (in which voters can rank candidates in order of preference); by using single-member constituencies it does not offer electors a choice of constituency members when they require a politician's service; and it creates two categories of elected members and the danger (as with other forms of MMP) that 'party members' will be seen as having second-class status. However, no electoral system can deliver everything that all reformers want – all systems have their strengths and weaknesses. Choosing a system involves compromises and discussion of what strengths are needed to achieve the political changes we want, and what weaknesses can be tolerated. Electoral reform is ultimately a political process: choices cannot be made in a vacuum but must take account of current political realities, and progress will depend on finding the reforms that are politically possible.

This book therefore demands the attention of politicians, policy-makers and all those concerned with democratic reform. It is clear that Aharon Nathan has given us a new alternative to be considered when electoral reform is on the agenda. TR has much to recommend it. Not only does it have an attractive simplicity and transparency, but in Britain it would be a logical extension of our voting system rather than a radical overthrow of what already exists while in Israel it could create a much needed change in the nature of the political system. For both Britain and Israel, and indeed for many other countries, a change to TR would be a pragmatic but important step, and this book will have served a purpose if it puts TR firmly on the agenda of those who want to see a better style of politics.

PART ONE

THE IDEA OF TOTAL REPRESENTATION

Aharon Nathan

Chapter 1
TOTAL REPRESENTATION – SYSTEM AND CONTEXT

The system

1.1 Total Representation (TR) is a new electoral system based on the premise that every single vote cast in an election has to end up with some representation in parliament, whether directly or indirectly.

1.2 It avoids the most serious defect of the constituency first-past-the-post system, under which votes cast for the successful candidate are represented in parliament, while all the rest of the votes i.e. those cast for the unsuccessful candidates are left unrepresented, though they may make up most of the votes of the total in some constituencies.

1.3 The proportional representation system (PR), on the other hand, does allow representation to all votes cast and gives them equal weight, but it encourages small political parties and splinter groups, resulting in weak coalition governments where factional rather than national interests take over. Its greatest deficiency, however, is the lack of a direct link between the members of the electorate and their individual representatives in parliament; unlike the single-member constituency system, it transfers this link to the political parties.

1.4 Total Representation (TR) offers a solution by combining the positive elements of both systems: i.e. the dominant element of representation in proportional representation and the direct link with the voter of the constituency first-past-the-post system.

1.5 In order to implement TR, parliaments would have two classes of MPs who would be equal in every way save for the manner by which they were elected. One class would be the Constituency MPs (CMPs) who would be elected by a simple majority on a constituency first-past-the-post basis, exactly as they are elected today in the UK. They would continue to fulfil their duties and obligations towards *all* their constituents, dealing with individual problems and grievances at regular meetings in the local MPs' offices (called *surgeries* in the UK) or addressing wider national issues in local public gatherings.

1.6 The other class, Party MPs (PMPs), would be elected by pooling all the votes cast for the unsuccessful candidates in all the constituencies and dividing them proportionally among all the parties which fielded candidates in the election. Each party would then award the PMP seats allocated to it by order of priority to its unsuccessful candidates in the constituencies according to the number of votes each scored. Once selected, the PMPs would concentrate on serving the party in parliament, initiating new policies and bringing coherence to its legislative programmes while waiting to compete in the next election.

1.7 The PMPs are selected as follows: before the election, each party would announce a list of all its constituency candidates. These national lists would be arranged with the party leader at the top, followed by its strongest and most prominent candidates, in order to appeal to the electorate as a party. Immediately after the election, once the constituency results were declared, all the successful candidates would drop off the national lists, which would then be re-arranged in accordance with the number of votes each unsuccessful candidate had scored in the constituency where he/she was competing. The re-arrangement should be made by each party before allocating its share of PMPs. This would provide an added incentive for the various candidates to fight for each vote in the constituencies, as it could be crucial in their being selected as PMPs by their parties if they failed to win first time around

1.8 For TR to succeed in its objective, the ratio between the number of Constituency MPs (CMPs) and Party MPs (PMPs) is crucial. I believe this ratio should vary between 80:20 and 70:30 in favour of the CMPs, depending on the circumstances of each country. In the UK I suggest 80:20; in Israel 70:30. This numerical ratio ensures the strength of the CMPs in parliament and consequently a high degree of government stability backed by the majority party in parliament. And, just as important, it keeps the direct bond between the individual CMPs, and encourages the PMPs to continue to keep in touch with their constituencies' lives throughout the life of a Parliament

1.9 The 20 to 30 per cent of PMPs also ensures the existence of a built-in opposition backed by representation, so that the voices of minority interests are heard speaking with authority on the floor of the parliament. It gives them power far beyond their minority status. Members of the majority (and therefore the government party) and members of the minority opposition draw their sovereign authority from the self-same voters in the constituencies. They both directly represent the people, i.e. the sovereign. This is a key difference between TR and the constituency first-past-the-post system. Under TR, each majority CMP is constantly on guard, competing either with a counterpart opposition PMP from the same constituency, or a potential future opposition rival candidate waiting to pounce in the next election in that same constituency. The so-called "safe seats" in the FPTP system are thus rendered less safe under TR.

1.10 This would be the case even if one party were theoretically to win all the constituency seats : under such a scenario, the majority party would secure 80% of the available spaces in parliaments, and would have spent all the votes it gained, but that would still leave 20% of the seats i.e. -- all the PMPs – for the opposition parties. This built-in opposition in the system lies at the heart of any democracy based on real representation, and should help to counter, to some extent, the 'tyranny of the majority' that John Stuart Mill warned against. However, the more the ratio is moved towards say 60:40, the more the system tilts towards PR with all its disadvantages.

1.11 It is important when talking about rights, freedoms and justice in an open society to bear in mind that all these concepts revolve around the idea of vibrant vocal social dissent or opposition of one kind or another, whose existence is essential and whose legitimacy has to be recognized and safeguarded as an official part of representative democracy and, thus, becomes heeded and respected by all sectors of society. And it is here that TR scores high. Its obvious merit is the balance it maintains in the results of elections between the winners and losers. This is an important innovative element. In this, it has the advantage over both major systems. Under constituency FPTP, the big parties dominate and suppress the voices of the smaller parties and pressure groups. Under PR, these small groups can keep a stranglehold on the big parties and, therefore, the government. The in-built balance in TR rectifies both faults to a great degree. The losers become the watch-dogs in the constituencies as well as in parliament, this preventing the majority MPs -- especially in *safe seats* – developing into an oligarchic establishment.

1.12 The concept of opposition and dissent in general, and political opposition in particular, is the kernel of an 'Open Society'. It is the door through which changes find their way to transform society. Its absence renders a society 'closed' and backward-looking. A political structure, therefore, should contain such a kernel, institutionalised as an integral part of that structure. This kernel must have the freedom to grow or give way to others within its wider social context. This is what the 'Open Society' is about. Social changes and the constant process of adaptation to new circumstances become "open-ended." And yet this does not mean automatically that the 'opposition' is there merely as a permanent obstacle to the way the majority of a community wants to govern. Permanent representation for the opposition must be - and traditionally has been, for instance, in the UK - at the heart of representative democracy in order to help it fulfil its function. Hence the concept of 'Her Majesty's Opposition', which means the Sovereign's Opposition in the UK Parliament. This phrase might look to outsiders as a quaint, contradictory expression of British eccentricity, but is in fact an essential ingredient of the UK's tolerant constitutional arrangement based on representation. Under this arrangement, the government of the country and the opposition both represent the Sovereign, the people. We should, therefore, not visualise the concepts of majority and minority as two inherently static, adversarial sections of the political structure. Rather, we should see them as parts of the same structural representation of the Sovereign, stimulating each other in a permanent ebb and flow of movement and change. And this is what TR facilitates.

The context

1.13 The strength of a democracy is not purely a function of its method of carrying out elections. However, close observation of two countries – Israel and the United Kingdom – over the past half-century has led me to the conclusion that such systems can make a substantial difference in persuading voters that it is worth being engaged with politics. In both countries, close to 40% of electors are not exercising their right to vote. Flawed or out-dated electoral models – even within a strong democratic framework – can lead to a feeling of frustration with politics, leading to voluntary self-disenfranchisement.

1.14 The United Kingdom is the classic example of a system which prizes stability and strong government above all else – and its Westminster, first-past-the-post model (FPTP) has many advantages. But FPTP tends to stifle change, discourages new political groupings, is bad at representing the views of minorities, and tends to leave them feeling outsiders. Israel lies at the other end of the spectrum: its pure form of proportional representation (PR) is, in theory, the fairest and most representative system in the world. But, in practice, Israeli politics has been bedevilled by instability, with minority parties able to hijack the agenda, bring down governments and distract attention from important national issues. Many people express exasperation at that but have come to accept that this is what has always been and you can't do anything about it. They have switched off.

1.15 I stubbornly sought a solution. My aim has been to find a way of fusing the best elements of FPTP and PR together into a relatively simple, mixed system that can provide stable government alongside fair representation. After considering the issue for many years, and having discussed and refined my ideas in consultation with political scientists and practitioners, I believe that the best way forward is Total Representation. In one sense, TR can be seen as a variant of STV – Single Transferable Vote – in that once a ballot is cast, it is preserved and given representation to whom it is intended. However, TR is simpler to operate and retains a large element of FPTP that brings with it a greater promise of stability than in PR.

1.16 I have already set out a basic blueprint for TR at the beginning of this chapter. The next three chapters explain how it works in detail, what its advantages are and a little about its theoretical origins. The rest of the book then considers concrete cases. In Part Two, I describe the strains in the British Westminster model, where rigidity has set in and interfered with the fluidity that has been inherent in its historical development – and I suggest ways in which TR could be used to rejuvenate British politics. In Part Three I turn my attention to Israel, highlighting the deficiencies in its electoral arrangements that have contributed to widespread public apathy about politics and depressingly low turnouts at elections. I trace a possible process of changeover from PR to TR, and use simulations to try to direct our minds to the outcomes that could arise from putting TR to work. Parts Four and Five of this book, written by my co-author, Professor Ivo Škrabalo, consider the case of Croatia, different from the others in its recent transition from totalitarianism to democracy. Prof Škrabalo looks at Croatia's recent electoral history, and opens the debate in that country to examine in what ways the introduction of TR could be of benefit there.

1.17 There is, of course, nothing unique about our quest to solve the problems created by inadequate electoral systems; and our proposed solutions draw to some extent on the work of others who have written around the topic. We have been travelling in the same direction. Some countries have already taken steps to try to resolve difficulties arising out of the interaction of political theories and specific situations. The model used for elections to the Scottish Parliament, the Additional Member System (AMS) which is another variant of STV, has many positive features – though it is still flawed, because of its two-ballot element which interferes with the simplicity of the idea of one, *Single* Transferrable Vote, as conceived by Thomas Hare and admired by John Stuart Mill.

1.18 In Israel, where the need for reform is urgent and greater, TR ideas are already under consideration: on 2nd April 2008, in the 17th Knesset, members of parliament from all three main parties tabled a Draft Law incorporating many elements of TR. The intervening election of a new Knesset (Israel's parliament) means that this draft law needs re-tabling. However, in my view, these proposals also need amendment – a point I come to in Part Three. And generally speaking, most of the electoral solutions canvassed in the world's democracies have been complex and the procedures cumbersome. If TR has two features that mark it out from other attempts at electoral reform, these are its simplicity and its transparency. Voters have traditionally wanted to vote for a known, preferably local, popular individual – somebody they can empathise and identify with politically. They do not want to be forced to undertake their own research or make complicated calculations when they go to the polling booth. We must always remember that individuals are *real*; parties are *virtual*.

1.19 TR aims to offer a solution which can be put into practice painlessly and without provoking controversy and upheaval. In the book, I offer some practical applications of TR – in general to the British House of Commons, but more specifically to the House of Lords, and to the Israeli parliament, the Knesset. In different ways, TR is flexible enough to give representation to the wishes of varied electorates. Recent debates in Britain have shown how much desire there is for reform both of the Commons and the Lords. Lord Strathclyde, the Leader of the Conservative Party in the Lords, wrote to me some years ago saying: "I think that in the 21st century the political members of a House of Parliament should be elected directly by the people." Shabby compromises involving the retention of a small rump of hereditary peers or, worse still, a totally or even partially appointed House of Lords, will not provide a satisfactory solution to the dilemma, but will rather reinforce the distaste ordinary people feel for politics. Recent scandals of MPs' expenses have led to similar demonstrations of disgust by members of the public, and a growing realisation that the two-party system – sustained by pure FPTP – is increasingly inadequate to represent the diverse views of a *modern* society. TR provides a possible resolution of this impasse, based on consensus rather than confrontation.

1.20 In October 2002 I sent an early draft of my ideas to Sir Michael Wheeler-Booth, then recently retired as Clerk to the (UK) Parliaments. He very kindly wrote back saying: "It seems to represent a new piece of thinking on a very complicated and difficult subject, and I very much hope you get it published and given publicity." He also commented on some aspects of the paper and advised me to simplify its presentation. Further, he suggested that I should send it to the Richard Commission in Wales and the Constitution Unit at University College, London. The Commission posted the paper on its website and I have received many comments from people who read my proposal there.

1.21 Professor Roger Scruton, who read the same draft, thought "the booklet idea is very interesting and obviously would be all the more effective on account of your experience in Israel." This encouragement led me to publish my proposals in a small book in May 2004 in order to focus on TR as a simple solution to a very significant electoral problem. Since then I have published several booklets and articles in Israel and learnt from the reactions to them how to temper my theoretical proposals with the more down-to-earth solutions propounded by the practitioners of politics. We theoreticians must learn from the reactions of the people on the ground. It is the patient, not the doctor, who knows what aches.

1.22 More recently, I have been greatly encouraged by the reaction of Dr. Ken Ritchie, the chief executive of Britain's Electoral Reform Society and Lewis Baston, its director of research, to my proposals. Although the ERS still recommends STV as their lead system, I am pleased that they have seen *merit in TR, have agreed to include it among the menu of options on their website and generously allowed this book to be published under the ERS banner.*

1.23 Over the past four years, I have also been fortunate to be able to join in debates on all these issues with many colleagues from all walks of life in Israel, and to offer tentative solutions. These circumstances provided me with new forums through which to expound and advocate the principles of TR. My meeting with Mr Isaac Nazarian, the founder and now the President of the Citizens' Empowerment Centre in Israel (CECI), provided me with this opportunity. He asked me to join the Board of Governors of CECI. At about the same time, the President of Israel graciously appointed me as a member of a Commission which was examining government and governance in Israel. After in-depth deliberations over two years, the Commission produced its final report, recommending in the main the principles of TR. What remained for me then to do was to join in lobbying the Knesset to accept the recommendations of the report and to modify them further, so as to adopt the principles of TR for the new electoral system in Israel. Part Three of this book details the different steps taken so far.

1.24 In conclusion I believe that TR is not only applicable to Israel or Britain. It is a system which provides a mix of stability and fairness that would be welcomed in many democracies around the world.

Chapter 2
APPLYING TOTAL REPRESENTATION IN DETAIL

Fixing the boundaries

2.1 To implement TR, the country would be divided into electoral constituencies, as is the case in the UK today. Candidates would be fielded within the constituencies as party nominees, whether local or national. Therefore all CMPs and PMPs would have started as candidates in the constituencies, whether they were sponsored by national parties or by independent local groups. With the constituencies playing such a central role in the TR system, wisdom and care have to be exercised in defining their borders.

2.2 The map of the constituencies is drawn up by a boundaries (or representation) commission, to be established by law and with a membership independent of parliament, consisting of senior members of an apolitical Judiciary, as well as established and recognised experts in statistics, demography and surveying. Its findings and decisions are still to be ultimately subject to the sanction of the Speaker of Parliament (in the UK Commons – or the equivalent presiding officer in other countries). However, any sensible Speaker will naturally exercise caution and refrain from party political interference in the working and decisions of the commission.

2.3 The country is divided from one end to the other into the required constituencies, based as closely as possible on similar estimated number of electors, not inhabitants. Owing to movement of populations and fluctuations in the number of electors, this division is reviewed and adjusted, if necessary, by the commission during the second year of the life of every third Parliament. General elections which occur within the first two years of that third Parliament shall follow the last boundaries division. All by-elections in mid-term likewise follow the last boundaries. There are many models of such commissions in countries as far apart as the UK and New Zealand.

2.4 Under TR, the neutral commission has to draw the boundaries of the constituencies on an equal consecutive territorial basis, cutting across and ignoring any ethnic or religious mix of the population. This is to avoid making decisions based on sectarian considerations that are always impossible to satisfy. TR is a self-adjusting, self-compensating system. It compensates the voters of the losing candidates in the constituencies by giving them a second chance to be represented by PMPs. So under TR, there should be no tolerance for gerrymandering: it is better that boundaries should be drawn "blindly", according to a universally applied principle. And it is important that each constituency should have (as nearly as possible) the same number of electors. In certain circumstances this principle of "blind" drawing of boundaries may need to be tweaked a little to address special considerations, but without departing from the principle of arbitrary spatial division based on single-member constituencies.

The Electoral Commission

2.5 An electoral commission is appointed by parliament to facilitate and monitor the orderly conduct of the election process. It should have the authority to determine and resolve any dispute arising between candidates. However, its authority can be superseded by appeal application to the courts of law. It is then that the electoral commission acts as an expert advisory body to the courts, especially in order to help them reach a quick resolution of disputes, in order to avoid obstructing the process of election.

2.6 The electoral commission should be given the power to determine the amount of money or monetary equivalent in total that each candidate can spend on the campaign – whether the money is paid or provided for directly or indirectly by the sponsoring party or group or by the state.

2.7 Either the candidate or the sponsor, be it a national or a local party, has to pay a fee and a deposit to the electoral commission. The deposit is returnable only to the successful constituency candidate. Apart from the deposit, each candidate needs, say, ten local sponsoring citizens (other than the candidate) who must provide certified proof of residence for at least two years within the constituency borders.

2.8 It is neither practical nor, indeed, desirable, to impose residential requirements on the candidate. MPs or candidates themselves may find it useful out of choice to become resident before or after their election, but such a requirement should not be a condition, as it would drive away able and talented people who have their roots and family commitments in other parts of the country.

2.9 In order to avoid the wastage of votes, rendering them unused and therefore unrepresented, each party list should declare before the date of the elections – if it so wishes, by notifying the electoral commission – its alliances with one other party list. This is done so that surplus votes can be transferred from one party to another in order to elect PMPs. Parties which do not enter such alliances before the election will be in more danger of losing their surplus votes, depending on the size of the surplus. Such an alliance is vital to single-candidate parties, who are the most vulnerable to this risk. Surplus votes are votes that failed to elect a candidate in a constituency and which are then aggregated with all other unsuccessful votes of the same party nationally, possibly enabling it to reach the required number of votes to elect a PMP.

2.10 Ballot papers bear the names of all the constituency candidates, listed in alphabetical order, with each candidate's name followed by the name of his/her party. Under TR, putting a cross besides one name is all a voter needs to do in order to exercise his/her right to vote, simultaneously, for a candidate and for his/her party. Of course, voting in the booth can also be carried out using an electronic voting machine, as is the case in many countries today. However, experience from the UK suggests that more "distant" forms of voting, such as postal and online voting, are subject to a great deal of abuse – every effort should be made to ensure that most people exercise their right to vote by actually going to a polling station.

2.11 TR, as outlined above, can be adapted and modified for any democracy, but is especially useful for emerging democracies, or old democracies with changed circumstances. By affirming the parliamentary route to democratic rule, TR asserts the primacy of the Legislature in the eyes of the public, over both the Judiciary and the Executive, and prevents tension and conflict developing between the three arms of the state – something which has come to the surface recently in many countries.

An Electoral Simulation

2.12 In order to describe graphically the working on the ground of TR, let us take, as a theoretical example, a country of five million inhabitants with an electorate of 3.2 million, and a Parliament consisting of 200 seats. Let us also assume that it was decided when TR was introduced that it should be done on the basis of an 80:20 ratio. So Parliament will have 160 Constituency MPs (CMPs) and 40 Party MPs (PMPs). The country then will be divided by the boundaries commission into 160 constituencies, each with an electorate of more or less 20,000 voters (3.2 million divided by 160 = 20,000).

Electing the CMPs – the successful candidates

2.13 A general election is held. Seventy-five per cent of the electorate – 2.4m people -- exercise their right to vote. Out of this 2.4m, 1.9m votes are cast for the 160 successful CMPs, each of whom beats the other candidates in his/her constituency by a simple majority. They are, therefore, the first to pass the post. All the votes that elected these 160 CMPs have gained their representation in Parliament – so these 1.9m ballots drop out of the total, leaving 0.5m votes to elect the 40 PMPs on a proportional basis.

Electing the PMPs

2.14 It is at this stage, once the total votes gained by each candidate in the constituencies are announced, that the parties rearrange their respective priority lists in accordance with the number of votes gained by each of their unsuccessful candidates. The only exception to this is the party leader: if he/she fails to secure a CMP seat, his/her name is kept secure at the top of the priority list in order to afford him the first PMP seat gained by his party.

2.15 The remaining votes – i.e. the aggregate of the votes that voted for the unsuccessful candidates, totalling 0.5m, (2.4m – 1.9m = 0.5m) – are to be distributed amongst the parties that fielded the unsuccessful candidates – to elect 40 PMPs. Therefore, 0.5m divided by 40 gives 12,500, which is the number of votes required to elect one PMP. Each party is allocated a number of PMP seats equal to the number of the multiple of 12,500 votes it secured. So a party whose unsuccessful constituency votes totalled 27,000 would win two PMP seats (2 x 12,500 equals 25,000). Of course, once this has happened, each party will be left with some fraction of 12,500 – i.e. a surplus of votes – which were not enough in each case to gain a PMP seat (in this case, 2,000 votes). At the same time, the allocation will leave a few PMP seats un-allocated: in our example, say, three seats. This is often referred to as the Hare Quota Check.

Dealing with the surplus votes

2.16 To explore how we deal with this surplus, let us assume that 37,500 votes are left over (12,500 x 3) in fractions amongst, say, seven parties, six of whom are pre-allied while one is not allied: A,B (allied); C, D (allied); E, F (allied); and G (un-allied). Each of them was left with the following number of votes: A9,000; B5,000; C4,000; D7,000; E5,000; F1,000; G6,500. All together there are 37,500 votes to be allocated to three PMP Seats.

2.17 The rules are that fractions of votes over and above the multiple of 12,500 votes are the surpluses which elect the shortfall of the 40 PMPs. Of two allied parties, the one with the higher surplus receives the votes of its allied party. The surplus of an un-allied party is lost unless it reaches the highest number amongst the new groupings of surpluses.

2.18 Let us see how the parties fare using the largest-remainder method. A and B together secured 14,000 surplus votes, so A is allocated one more PMP seat. Between these two parties, that leaves 1,500 wasted votes. Together, C and D secured 10,000 votes, so D is awarded one PMP seat. E and F secured 6,000 together, but they both lost because G on its own secured 7,500 – more than their combined strength – so G won the remaining PMP seat. If no party pre-allied itself with any other, then the three parties that scored the highest amongst the seven parties are allocated the three remaining PMP seats. All the calculations are done by simple arithmetic and understood by everyone without the need for formulas.

By-elections

2.19 In the case of the resignation or death of a CMP (Constituency MP), an ad hoc by-election is held to replace him/her. The successful candidate, i.e. the first to pass the post, wins the vacant CMP seat by a simple majority. The rest of the votes do not count in by-elections.

2.20 In the case of the death or resignation of a PMP (Party MP), he/she is replaced in the same way that is followed in PR systems today: i.e. by the next in line on the original general election list, as revised after the poll.

Electing the Party Leaders

2.21 TR suggests that party leaders should be elected using the smooth, transparent mechanism outlined below. This means that there is no need for primaries and all the resulting internal turmoil, as is the case today in many countries, especially Israel. This method also reduces the influence of money in politics – and eliminates a very common source of corruption. However, like other components of TR, it can be adapted to different situations and different traditions.

2.22 Any MP can stand in the leadership contest for any party in parliament if sponsored openly by a minimum of, say, 10% of the total MPs of that party in parliament. Challenging, outside the rules, the incumbent leader needs a higher percentage.

2.23 The supervision, counting and checking of the accuracy of votes can be entrusted to a panel of a number of elders in the party, or to a panel of independent arbiters of retired judges. In the case of complaint, say, by 5% of the party's MPs, the process of election can be appealed and scrutinised by the Electoral Commission, notwithstanding the fact that this is an internal party matter.

2.24 The people who cast votes in the leadership election are all the candidates who stood for that party in the previous general election – whether or not they were successful. This includes MPs (of both kinds) and non-MPs. But their votes do not carry equal weight; instead, each of them cast the actual number of votes that he/she won in the last election. If, for any reason, an unsuccessful candidate is no longer available to exercise this duty, the chairman of their local constituency party deputises in casting these votes.

2.25 At the end of this process, by this method, the party leader is elected by proxy, indirectly, by all those supporters who actually voted for the party at the last general election.

2.26 This method avoids conferring the right to vote for a leader partly or exclusively on the party's paid-up members. We have long since abandoned the idea of voting rights based on wealth. Paying a party subscription should not buy voting rights. It is reasonable to expect this right to belong to those who have actually chosen to vote for a party, even if this right can only be exercised by proxy, indirectly. An MP or an unsuccessful candidate who is asked to perform this duty is representing his or her supporters, exactly as they do when they vote on legislation in parliament. It would be only natural for there to be consultation with supporters in the constituencies before the leadership election. But this method avoids the possibility of bribery and corruption infiltrating the rank and file of the paid-up party membership by those who would be only too ready to pay for the purpose of acquiring votes on behalf of their preferred choice. This method can be adapted to elect party leaders in any p arliament under TR or indeed under any constituency electoral system – but not under the PR systems.

2.27 This method confers more legitimacy on the elected party leader than the existing systems, and minimises the temptation for unsuccessful leadership candidates to try to undermine the duly elected leader.

2.28 The author has been advocating this simple and transparent procedure for many years. Way back on 4th November 1980, *The Times* published his simplified version on its letters page. Its adoption could – in recent years – have spared political parties the embarrassment of ending up with their second or third choice as leader.

Chapter 3
THE ADVANTAGES OF TOTAL REPRESENTATION

3.1 The obvious merit of TR is the balance it maintains in the results of elections between the winners and losers. In this, it has the advantage over both the other major systems. In the constituency first-past-the-post system (FPTP), the big parties dominate and suppress the voices of the smaller parties and pressure groups. Under proportional representation (PR), these small groupings can keep a stranglehold on the big parties and, therefore, the government. The in-built balance in TR rectifies both faults to a great degree. The losers become the watchdog that prevents the winning parties from developing into an oligarchic establishment.

3.2 TR is a simple system – easy to understand and easy to implement. It avoids the complications of other hybrids that attempt to fuse the constituency and the proportional models together. Its purpose is to engage the entire electorate and enable parliament to represent all shades of opinion. It is hoped that its introduction and implementation will help restore the people's flagging faith in the democratic process.

3.3 TR does not go in for the complicated mathematical formulas that characterize PR systems based on Arithmetical Democracy. These started with Thomas Hare's commonsense STV (Single Transferable Vote), but were followed by D'Hondt and dozens of others with more complicated formulas. These are ways of expressing the broad principle of proportionality in a precisely specified manner. Nevertheless, today they pass over the heads of ordinary people, turning parliament and elections into a remote domain presided over by a new *clever* ruling establishment. TR attempts to bring simplicity back to the electoral process and to ensure the direct involvement of all the citizens in it.

3.4 TR encourages candidates to fight for every vote, even when they feel they may not have much chance of winning a particular seat. Such unsuccessful constituency candidates would be heartened by the knowledge that they might end up as PMPs (Party Members of Parliament) – if not in that same general election, then in a future one. So TR would encourage high-calibre candidates of one party to offer themselves even in constituencies where overwhelming support was enjoyed by another rival party, as is the case in *safe seats* in the UK, since all candidates are competing both for the positions of CMP and PMP. This system obviates the current practice of candidates offering to fight in "safe seats" of a rival party solely for the purpose of gaining experience and would induce their leadership to sponsor them in more hopeful constituencies.

3.5   Under TR, the centre of gravity of political life spreads throughout the whole country, with the constituency being the central area of competition. Those constituents who feel disappointed with the performance of their candidate in a general election will have four or five years during which to prepare his/her replacement in the following general election. With political activities diffused around different parts of the country, central political parties are forced to sustain their platforms by engaging local communities through their party constituency organisations. The bond between the constituency voters and their chosen candidates is kept alive and would probably survive even when a candidate failed to secure a CMP seat.

3.6   TR strengthens the link between the local candidate and the central party; it creates a mutual dependency between them. The central party needs to choose popular candidates, and the candidates need the backing of the central party – its manifesto, its leadership and its national media coverage – to display strength and influence vis-à-vis other competing candidates. The dynamic of mutual dependence between national political parties and their local branches minimises parties' reliance on costly and often corrupt primaries to choose candidates. It is false to assume that CMPs are there to represent only regional and not national interests. The practice of countries that have constituency systems does not support this assumption.

3.7   This division of labour between central and locally affiliated parties means that the central party becomes more cohesive and rooted in the country at large. So instead of, as at present in many countries, the party machine being preoccupied with internal jockeying, it concentrates on planning, guidance and reviewing policies. The roles of the leaderships of central and local parties become more defined. The duty of the local party is to capture the next Parliament. The role of the central party is to be a shadow government, an alternative. TR reverses the prevalent practice where in almost all countries today – except in federations like Germany and the USA – national leaders are chosen by central caucuses, who became a new establishment – indeed a new class of professional politicians. Under TR, national leaders can grow in the country, groom themselves amongst the people, and may then graduate and acquire national profiles.

3.8   The introduction of TR will result in the grouping of smaller parties and factions into bigger political groupings. By their nature and composition, such larger parties themselves become representative coalitions of interests and ideologies. So the curse of fragile and unstable government coalitions that plagues PR systems is moved away from parliament and into the political parties, where it causes less disruption to government.

3.9   Under TR, smaller parties or country-wide movements can easily gain a voice – but not a disproportionate one. Even if smaller parties' candidates are weak in every single constituency, their aggregate votes in the country can gain them one or more PMP seats. Such a movement – e.g. the Greens – can then fight its corner and strengthen its appeal inside the tent of the Legislature, rather than by campaigning and demonstrating outside in city squares.

3.10   TR abolishes blocking thresholds and renders them unnecessary. To start with, such blocking devices are undemocratic and – whether intentionally or not – deprive those votes of their right to representation. The purpose of the thresholds is to prevent the disintegration of parliament into small parties, which is bound to happen under the PR systems. But, to attain this goal, a very high percentage is needed, like, for example, 10% – as is the case in Turkey. Then the pressure builds up over the years and results in widespread disaffection amongst the public that may cause the system to implode. Even a smaller percentage of, say, 5%, as in Germany, forced the largest party in government there for decades to depend on, and therefore be dictated to, by the third or fourth-placed party. TR has a built-in blocking mechanism because, although smaller parties are allowed to have their voice heard through the proportional allocation of PMPs, the predominance of the CMPs means that such minority voices are not allowed to gain undue influence. It is to be borne in mind that a PMP needs at least three and often four or more times as many votes as a CMP to gain a seat.

3.11 Bringing all shades of opinion within the tent of parliament and allowing them unrestricted access to field candidates in the constituencies will blunt the edges of fundamentalist movements and draw politics away from the extremes and towards the centre. In order to increase their chances, candidates in the constituencies will naturally try to canvass all the voters in those localities and, therefore, inevitably – at least in order to gain a CMP seat – direct their appeal towards the centre ground.

3.12 One objection levelled against TR is that it gives different weighting to different votes and, therefore, creates two categories of MPs who are different in the way they were elected. This is a compromise that is there to ensure efficiency and stability in parliament and, therefore, in government. It keeps a balance between two often conflicting elements of any system: representation and stability. This is the reason why the ratio between CMPs and PMPs is to be adjusted according to the circumstances of each country. The idea of different weighting is not a novel one. Throughout the development of democracy, different representational weight has been given to different classes, religious leaders, property-owners or groups commanding big followings. John Stuart Mill himself, the champion and proponent of total, universal, egalitarian franchise, toyed with the idea of giving different weighting to the educated classes. But the element of weighting in TR is neutral and is not based on class, culture, ethnicity or ideology.

Chapter 4
THE THEORETICAL BACKGROUND TO T R

4.1 TR is based on a concept which lies at the heart of British democracy: representation. In England, democracy was founded on the famous cry: "no taxation without representation." This catchy slogan came to prominence in the American Revolution, when it was based on the fact that the House of Commons could tax the colonies without these colonies having any MP to representing at Westminster. However, the idea that the consent of the governed was required for taxation had a longer history in England. The principle that Parliament had to approve taxation was thought to be long-established and the summoning of such assemblies was often connected with the need to raise revenue. In our context here, it is significant to note that the slogan is: "no taxation without representation" – not "without voting" or "without referendum" – because the concept of representation preceded and gave rise to the franchise, the right to vote. In Britain, democracy evolved. It was not a copy of the Greek version of direct democracy. Nor did it attempt to put into practice theories based on imaginary social contracts in the way continental Europe did, beginning with Grotius and carried forward by Rousseau, whose ideas directly influenced the shaping of politics in Holland and France respectively. Their great counterparts in England – Hobbes, Locke, Hume and even John Stewart Mill – did not manage to have a similar direct impact on the practical politics of their respective times. Locke's ideas almost shaped the American political system but, although his political thinking permeated his native country, he could not claim the direct influence the continental European thinkers had. In England, the push for change came from the bottom up; it was never dictated from the top.

4.2 The English have always displayed pragmatism in the conduct of their public affairs. They have been guided less by political theory and more by expediency and continuous adjustment to new circumstances. That was how adequate representation became the root of the UK Westminster political system. Its essence is the right of citizens to choose representatives in a Parliament that will formulate policies and promulgate laws at least broadly acceptable to, and in line with, their needs and aspirations. In their enthusiasm for off-the-shelf, *instant* democracy, many developing nations – mesmerised by the concept of Arithmetical Democracy – have rushed into embracing electoral systems not compatible with their social circumstances or the stage of their political maturity. The disastrous results of this can be seen in abundance around the world, and they prompted Professor Roger Scruton to make the following succinct observation in his book "England – an Elegy":

> *'Nothing is better known about the English than the fact that they developed over the centuries a unique political system, and then planted it around the globe. Yet the nature of this system is widely misunderstood. The reason for this, I believe, is that the commentators have misidentified the fundamental principle on which the English constitution rested. Almost all popular historians and political analysts see the English system as an experiment in parliamentary democracy. In fact, however, the key notion was not democracy but representation, and it was as a means to represent the interest of the English people that we should understand the institutions of Parliament'*

4.3 The English Parliament, therefore, was historically an assembly of representatives of various regions and interests that came together and sought shared objectives in order to reach agreements based on compromise that could be imposed peacefully on a willing people. It was not designed to provide a tool which a majority could use to impose its will on a minority. Indeed, the opposite was true. This process of attempting to reach a consensual accommodation was helped over the ages by an underlying culture of fairness in the country at large, reflected by its representatives in Parliament. The concept of fairness and equity has always been, and remains even today, an overriding principle of British public life and as one of the pillars of its judicial system, i.e. the rule of law.

4.4 The contrast between the conceptualisation of democracy in Britain and continental Europe reflects not only different outlooks on society but, quite literally, two ways of thinking. Contrast the clear-cut assertive didactic of Jean-Jacques Rousseau's *Social Contract* with the tentative, reflective John Stuart Mill's *On Liberty*. The former proffers the diagnosis and the cure right from the start. The latter keeps the doubts, and sustains a pragmatic line throughout. One wonders whether this approach is embedded even in the structure of their respective languages. Or is it that the former is influenced by Greek culture and the latter by Rome? What concerns us here, however, is the effect these two approaches have had on subsequent political thinking and practice.

4.5   In the UK, the fusion of freedom of expression and the choice of representatives are at the heart of the cultural framework of representative democracy. The phrases "much might be said on both sides", or "he is entitled to his opinion" are often heard even today in the pubs and streets of Britain. These two basic ingredients – of representation and freedom of expression – are closely linked and create the fluidity that makes it possible to bring about peaceful political change in tune with constantly evolving social realities.

Justice and the Open Society

4.6   It is important when talking about rights, freedoms and justice to bear in mind that all these concepts revolve around the idea of vibrant, vocal social dissent or opposition of one kind or another, whose existence is essential, and whose legitimacy has to be recognized as an official part of representative democracy by all sectors of society.

4.7   The concept of opposition and dissent in general, and political opposition in particular, is the kernel of an "Open Society". It is the door through which changes find their way to transform nations. Its absence renders a society closed and backward-looking. A political structure should therefore contain such a kernel, institutionalised as an integral part of that structure. This kernel must have the freedom to grow or give way to others within its wider social context. This is what the "Open Society" is about. Social changes and the constant process of adaptation to new circumstances become "open-ended".

4.8 Therefore, permanent representation for the opposition must be - and traditionally has been, for instance, in the UK - at the heart of representative democracy. Hence the concept of "Her Majesty's Opposition" mentioned before. In this way, the government of the day and its opposition both draw their authority from the same sovereign, the people. So we should look at both as two parts of the same structural representation of the sovereign. And this is at the heart of the argument for TR.

4.9 The apex of the socio-political concept of fluidity and perpetual change was reflected in the work of Karl Popper, an Austrian Anglophile. When he talked about *The Open Society and its Enemies*, he had in mind an *open-ended society*. If changes are acceptable in the natural sciences, he argued, they should surely be even more so in the social sciences. Popper's dynamic approach caused many to declare the death of political ideologies and of Karl Marx's idea of attaining and sustaining the ideal stage of revolutionary class struggle.

4.10 And even when the American thinker, John Rawls, at a later date revived the debate and spoke of a theory (more truly, an ideology) of Justice, he insisted that freedom of expression, freedom of speech, should have priority and should come before the determination and administration of justice. And so he accepted that the last word must rest with the individuals who – in aggregate – make up society. This is another way of accepting open-ended social change driven by public opinion.

4.11 If this priority – of adjusting to change – is relegated to second place, it frustrates the actual attainment of justice, and can endanger it. Except in mythology, Justice is not carved in stone. It resides neither in Kant's imperatives nor in the United Nations Convention of Human Rights. John Stuart Mill, jealous as he was about the freedom of the individual, worked all his life to find a way of bringing together constantly colliding political forces: the freedom of the individual and the constraint of society made up of the total of the self-same individuals. Social malaise is caused by the fragmentation of society when new, emerging or grafted-on segments do not sit comfortably together and create an opposite centrifugal counter- force. TR helps in the resolution of that tension.

Arithmetical Democracy

4.12 The misunderstanding and confusion caused by the progressive decoupling of democracy from its historical roots of representation and equity has had a damaging influence on the practice of parliamentary democracy in many countries, especially those of the non-English tradition that have adopted the UK Westminster model. A simplistic definition of democracy based on arithmetical (and often on complicated and convoluted mathematical formulas) has become the foundation of their political systems. A fifty-one percent majority of votes cast, or of MPs elected, gives the stamp of legitimacy to many such regimes around the world, totally ignoring the important principle of catering for continuous and uninterrupted representation of the expressed interests of everyone – including the 49-per-cent minority – that the UK Westminster model started with.

4.13 The Westminster model in England itself has not escaped this decoupling. The pattern of representing groups and interests shifted in the twentieth century towards strict voting based on the numbers of individuals who made up the electorate. Representational Democracy descended into Arithmetical Democracy. This trend was helped by the rapid growth of the human rights movements and a growing acceptance of egalitarianism as the natural counterpart of these movements. That is why, in order to correct the resulting social and political strains, an electoral system is needed , like TR, that appropriates some power to the losers in elections, and not only to the winners.

4.14 In conclusion, the word "democracy", in connection with Parliaments, has become so much of a slogan that the time may have come to revert to talking more about "representation" To quote Professor Gideon Doron: from his essay in this book *"In Democracies, voting is not just about winning and losing. It is also about Representation"* Those researching this topic are well advised to internalise this wisdom. Representation is not about virtue or justice; it is rather about good policy – a policy which nips social conflicts in the bud and prevents them from being stoked.

PART TWO

ELECTORAL REFORM – THE UNITED KINGDOM

Aharon Nathan

Chapter 5
THE HOUSE OF COMMONS

Background

5.1 The first part of this book outlined a blueprint for TR – Total Representation – which fuses the electoral systems of constituency first-past-the-post (FPTP, as practised in the UK) with proportional representation (PR, as practised in Israel) to produce a balanced system that preserves the essence of each. The UK and Israel are examples of the extremes of each of these systems. Here, in Part Two, I look at the UK, first describing the strains in its main electoral model and highlighting its deficiencies. Then I show how, through the application of TR, the ties between the electorate and its representatives can be strengthened. I maintain that the principles of TR can be employed, adapted and adjusted to cope with the special circumstances that exist in Britain today.

5.2 TR retains enough of the English Westminster constituency model to make it widely understood and acceptable to the British public. It goes with the grain of British traditions, its main thrust being to add a dose (20%) of PR to the FPTP system, while strengthening the bond between an MP – as well as his/her rival competing candidate – and their shared constituents. I believe that TR is capable of revolutionising the way the British public feel about politics, but without creating a revolution.

5.3 In the short term, TR could also provide a welcome solution to the vexed question of what to do about the part-reformed House of Lords – something I look at in Chapter Six – but it also has the potential to restore the House of Commons to its proper role as the main political forum of the nation and the guardian of the people's interests against the encroaching powers of the Executive and the Judiciary.

5.4 In focusing this part of the book on the UK, I have avoided comparisons with other electoral systems. Such comparisons and evaluations must be left to the academic professionals who will hopefully be guided by the acid test of reality. I also try to be sparing in statistics and figures in order to concentrate on the wider possibilities of change that TR opens up. I am endeavouring, as one ordinary citizen, to address my fellow citizens, urging them to reassert their eroded rights to better representation in Parliament. There is no sophistry or sloganeering here, but a simple explanation of a better way of conducting elections, so that parliaments can represent all the people and restore their flagging faith in the democratic process.

Imbalanced representation in the House of Commons

5.5 Historically, the basis of democracy in England (and in the UK as a whole after 1707) was representation. This evolved rather than being formally instituted. Legislators were not concerned with models and blueprints. What guided them was expedience, not theory. They continued to find solutions to political problems as they appeared on the ground. Over the years, the English political system, with its core of representation, developed and evolved in a piecemeal fashion as needs arose or events dictated – a process helped by the absence of a rigid constitution. The system was underpinned and made possible by the acceptance of the Common Law in England, which fostered a sense of equity and fairness. This was anchored on past wisdom: the elastic concept of precedent.

5.6 During the course of the late 19th and early 20th centuries, the widening of the to include all citizens, irrespective of class or gender, brought pressure to bear on the British electoral arrangement by shifting its centre of gravity away from its original concept of representation – and towards the more appealing concept of voting for delegates by, for example, the working classes through their trade unions. Before this, members of Parliament – once elected

– were left to use their discretion and their judgment as to how best to represent their electors.

5.7 It was this increasing pressure from below, backed by class organisations and clubs at local level, that brought about the replacement of the Liberal Party by the Labour Party in a two-party system (with the Conservatives) in the first half of the 20th century, leaving the Liberals to languish in the doldrums for a long time. Their subsequent Lazarus-like recovery in the latter part of the century caused a progressive decoupling of democracy from its historical roots of representation, because the Liberals were able to gain a substantial share of the vote without gaining a corresponding number of seats in Parliament. There has been procrastination in dealing with the resulting new pressures on the FPTP two-party system, and this has caused – and is causing – strains and fissures in the UK's political structure.

5.8 The pull towards strict arithmetical representation and away from balancing the interests of groups and localities has been made worse by the theoretical arguments of those who advocate purer forms of PR as the preferred route to what they perceived to be a more democratic political framework. The advocates of unadulterated PR seem to overlook the essence of the constituency arrangement, which has evolved over the years: through MPs and Lords, it balances the interests of the people of the cities and the countryside vis-à-vis the central institutions of the state. This reliance on an arithmetical concept of election has given rise to more assertive behaviour by political parties.

5.9 In fact, the status of elected representatives has been gradually eroded by this evolving regime of central parties, to the point where – today – MPs and newly appointed Life Peers hardly relate to the regions or to the interests they purport to represent. Most of them have become party partisans. The centre of political activity has decamped from the constituency to the centre, to the "Westminster Village" that surrounds the Houses of Parliament. This trend has been aggravated by the deliberate break-up of local authorities and the gradual concentration of the media in London. This process, which has weakened the notion of representation, has been a major factor in the rise of Scottish and Welsh separatist movements, and added another dimension to the Irish issue. But, in England itself, the people have gradually become disconnected from their formal or official representatives. Change is needed, but has not taken place.

5.10 The mistrust that the growing disconnect between politicians and public has engendered has also resulted in a blurring of lines between the Legislature and the Executive. In the public perception, government and Parliament have merged. This has led to a clamour for referendums and for public inquiries presided over by independent judges. The practice of referendums is alien to the traditions of the UK. Political and constitutional issues are traditionally settled by Parliament as the proxy voice of the people. The new enthusiasm for the referendum tool encroaches on and subverts this. The seniority of the Legislature, where ultimate sovereignty should lie, is also being threatened by the elevation of the Judiciary to a dominant position in the public's perception, aided by a powerful human rights movement. Prescriptive politics is destabilising the political structure. This is not the way representative democracy, or indeed any form of democracy, should or was meant to work.

5.11 The push towards integration within the European Union, the recent inclusion in the UK of new ethnic and religious groups, and the emergence of an environmentalist movement, have all further aggravated the feeling of alienation. It has become imperative, therefore, to adjust the constitutional framework to the new underlying realities. The FPTP system, as it operates today, is not helping to address these trends. It is this element of the constituency system that needs repairing.

5.12 The pressure for change is being made more urgent by the breakdown of the balance of two parties alternating in government, as a result of the emergence of the Liberal Democrats as a credible third force in recent general elections. A popular third party may, paradoxically, precipitate unrepresentative landslide victories under FPTP. This happens because the emerging grouping naturally tries to gain votes from the second-ranking party in the constituencies, with the ultimate aim of taking its place. Tactical voting, with or without the overt encouragement of the dominant first party, will help propel it in that direction. In this case, the Liberal Democrats naturally try to appropriate votes from whoever is just ahead of them in the polls. This tendency became apparent in 1983, when the then SDP/Liberal Alliance caused Labour to suffer an even worse defeat than would otherwise have been the case. In 1997, it was the turn of the Conservatives to bear the brunt of attacks on two fronts, leaving the way open for a Labour landslide.

5.13 The Thatcher dominance in three Parliaments (1979, 1983 and 1987) and the more recent landslide victories of New Labour (in 1997 and 2001, followed by a more modest victory in 2005) can be examined in this light. In both cases, the beneficiaries, Margaret Thatcher and Tony Blair – intoxicated by their decisive victories – introduced far-reaching legislation, riding roughshod over the opposition, and even over internal dissent within their own parties. In pursuit of their strong personal convictions, what the people wanted became confused with what the people *should* want. The corridors of Parliament today see little of England's traditional bipartisanship or striving for consensus. Smaller parties fare even worse than the official opposition. This process is causing acute frustration to social and political groups, who feel unable to find expression and representation of their interests through parliament and the ballot box. To give vent to their frustration, they have resorted to Trafalgar Square and the streets. Demonstrations against Margaret Thatcher's poll tax and Tony Blair's university tuition fees – and, more acutely, his Iraq policy – were glaring examples of this (cited here by way of illustration, and not as an expression of opinion on the issues *per se*).

5.14 Demonstrating is of course a fundamental political right. But when it becomes the main channel for dissent, taking over the role of parliamentary cut and thrust, it threatens democracy. It is a sign of political malaise when the delicately balanced rights between the majority and the minority are disturbed. Perversely, it is then that the voices of a vocal minority outside parliament, seeking to exert its right to political expression, drown out the silent majority.

5.15 The growing pressure from the Liberal Democrats forced Labour at one stage to promise in its manifestos changes to the electoral system, with a view to incorporating an element of PR. Labour's subsequent failure to fulfil these promises has caused frustration in Lib Dem circles. In fact, instead of trying to remedy the underlying strains and stresses within the system as a whole, the Labour government broke up the system itself by establishing Scottish and Welsh legislatures. And, for good measure, in a surprise move, and without enough warning or a proper debate in the Commons, Tony Blair suddenly dismissed the majority of hereditary Conservative Peers and stuffed the House of Lords with a host of Labour appointees, in order to deprive the Conservative opposition of what was rightly perceived to be its previous in-built majority. So now, instead of one bi-cameral Parliament in London resting on one electoral system, we have ended up with four systems: one for the House of Commons; one for Northern Ireland; one for Scotland; and one for Wales. Besides that, we have a different system for elections to the European Parliament – and a House of Lords in limbo. In a separate chapter, we will examine how the new Scottish electoral system is working, compared with TR.

5.16 For the time being, the lack of resolution of the underlying strains resulting from the above constitutional issues is causing disquiet amongst the British electorate as a whole. The following table and analysis of the results of the 2001 general election in the UK illustrate the problems discussed above and the causes of the current malaise. These figures were put together for an earlier publication soon after the results were declared. More recent elections have not changed the general picture.

TABLE 1: GENERAL ELECTION RESULTS 2001
(Electorate 44,403,327)

	Votes as % of electorate	Successful votes	% of votes cast	Seats in the Commons	Unsuccessful (wasted) votes	% of wasted votes
Labour	24.188	10,740,344	40.76	413	2,490,934	19.19
Conservative	18.824	8,358,382	31.72	166	4,803,560	37.00
Lib Dem	10.842	4,814,341	18.27	52	3,752,721	28.91
Subtotal	53.854	23,913,067	90.75	631	11,047,215	85.10
SNP	1.046	464,305	1.76	5	398,494	3.08
UKIP	0.899	399,043	1.51	0	399,043	3.07
UUP	0.488	216,839	0.82	6	106,470	0.82
Plaid Cymru	0.441	195,892	0.74	4	143,168	1.10
DUP	0.41	181,999	0.69	5	93,730	0.72
Sinn Fein	0.397	176,063	0.67	4	85,912	0.66
SDLP	0.382	169,873	0.64	3	100,415	0.77
Green	0.375	166,477	0.63	0	166,477	1.28
Kidderminster	0.064	28,487	0.11	1	0	0.00
Others	0.993	440,853	1.67	0	440,853	3.40
Grand Total	59.349	26,352,898	100.00	659	12,981,777	100.00

Analysis and comment on the above figures

◆ The total votes cast represent 59.35% of the electorate – the lowest percentage since 1918.
The apathy of the electorate is fuelled by its inability to influence party politics between general elections. Local issues rise to the surface only when they become (or the media turn them into) matters of adversarial party conflict or emotive anecdotal events. The electorate perceives politics to be dominated by remote party politicians knocking each other about in the "Westminster Village". General elections do not excite the public either; and by-elections, local and European elections seem to excite them even less, attracting lower voter turnout.

- Out of 26,352,898 votes cast, 12,981,777 were cast for unsuccessful candidates. These secured no representation in the House of Commons. Indeed, they were wasted and disenfranchised.

  Especially in constituencies where one party historically predominates (i.e. in safe seats), electors feel less incentive to go out and cast a useless vote; they become virtually disenfranchised. Surely they would feel differently if every ballot ended up with some representation?

- Labour won the 2001 general election with the support of only 24% of the electorate (which refers to all eligible electors including those who did not cast a ballot), winning 413 seats in Parliament, while the Conservatives and Liberal Democrats together won the support of 30% of the electorate, yet ended up with only 218 seats.

  Given such figures and percentages, one would hope that the winning party would pursue consensus politics by reaching out to the 76% of the electorate who did not vote for them. In fact, the opposite seemed to be the case.

- The same picture is also reflected in the actual votes cast. Labour gained 40.76% of the total votes (10,740,344) and secured 413 seats. The Conservatives and Liberal Democrats together gained 49.99% of the total votes (13,172,723) but together secured only 218 seats.

  Here again, instead of the forty-one-per-cent minority government reaching out to the opposition parties, who represented 59% of the voters, in search of accommodation and bipartisanship, we find ideological and adversarial politics fanned by the black-and-white presentation of events in the media.

- The two Unionist parties (UUP and DUP), concentrated in localised constituencies, together won 1.51% of the votes (408,836 votes) and together gained 11 seats in Parliament. The UK Independence Party (UKIP) which is spread around all constituencies, on the other hand, won exactly the same percentage of votes – 1.51% – (399,043 votes) but secured no representation at all in Parliament.

- Similarly, the SDLP won 0.64% of the votes, gaining four

seats, while the Green Party won 0.63% of the total votes cast at the election, ending up with no seats at all and therefore no representation in Parliament.

In both these cases, voters for UKIP and the Greens are justified in feeling disenfranchised. It might therefore be understandable if they felt that referendums and demonstrations were the only alternatives left to them. It is not unreasonable to expect that these two parties, for example, might have attracted far more votes had electors believed they could win representation in parliament.

◆ The Scottish National Party (SNP) polled not many more votes than UKIP (1.76% as opposed to 1.51%) yet won five seats while UKIP won none.

5.17 In summary, the current electoral system in the UK leaves 13 million voters unrepresented in Parliament. The main thrust of this part of the book is to find a simple method of giving these citizens representation. It cannot be fair or tenable that the representatives of 24% of the electorate (or 40% of the actual votes cast) rule the country virtually unopposed for the duration of a whole Parliament. John Stuart Mill must be turning in an unquiet grave recalling his warning of the tyranny of the majority, especially as it is a sham majority.

5.18 One answer to this absurd situation, as advocated by some Liberal Democrats, is a complete change to proportional representation (PR). But if they insist on this, they will keep treading water – and Labour and the Conservatives will stick to their guns that they do not want to change the FPTP system. It would be better if the Lib Dems adopted a policy of inching slowly forward. Politics is the art of the possible, and it *would* be possible to campaign for a partial solution; they could lead this and carry other interest groups with them on a narrow, well-defined path without needing to go hand in hand with these other groups on wider issues. They should seek an alliance with, say, the Green Party and UKIP (UK Independence Party) in a marriage of convenience – a coalition of the willing. The fact that they are close to the Greens on some policy issues but – in the main – utterly at odds with UKIP would not affect this. This is not without precedent. Some very prominent Conservative leaders campaigned on the same side as Labour in the 1975 referendum on whether or not to stay in the European Common Market.

5.19 But the call for a change to full PR is not undesirable simply on the grounds that it is unlikely to happen. PR – even when modified – is far from being a fairer system. In some ways it is even more unfair, because it leads to weak, unstable governments in which small, minority parties have a disproportionate say. We have witnessed such systems in other countries, notably, but not exclusively, in Israel, where PR makes a mockery of democracy: small political parties or factions exert far more power than their numbers warrant.

5.20 One does not even have to look at Israel, where the small religious parties have formed part of every government since 1948, to find examples of the minority tail wagging the majority dog. In Germany for example, both major government parties – CDU and SPD – have had to water down the manifesto policies on which they were elected to accommodate the demands of their minority coalition partners, the FDP and the Greens. When this is done in politically mature societies, it can be positive and beneficial in the sense that it may drag sharply divergent big parties into the centre ground. However, these mixed systems usually end up struggling to adjust to new circumstances by raising their electoral blocking thresholds, as in Israel, or creating overhang seats, as in Germany.

5.21 However, even when full PR is not on the table, it has still proved difficult to achieve a consensus on reforming the electoral system for the House of Commons. In 1997, the then Labour prime minister, Tony Blair, asked the late Lord Jenkins to come up with a solution to the issue. But the proposals which emerged – known as "AV Plus" and based on some change to the electoral system – were clearly going to be ignored, not least because you could hardly find any ordinary citizen who could explain their convoluted calculations. Clearly, this was inspired by purely academic, theoretical thinking. I, for one, maintain that a more modest modification of the existing, pure constituency FPTP system might have been easier to swallow for the vested interests of the two big parties, and paved the way for further modifications in the future. Public debate and preoccupation with such modest change could have deflated the balloons of the Scottish and Welsh drive towards independence.

5.22 The quiet shelving of the Jenkins Report showed how difficult it is to introduce root-and-branch change in the UK. This is an electoral tradition whose Parliament is steeped in history and culture and rests on complex constitutional institutions that have evolved over many centuries. When confronted with the necessity of change, the majority of the British people balk and prefer to opt for a cautious, gradual, tentative and pragmatic approach.

5.23 For all these reasons, a combination of PR and FPTP systems would go a long way towards resolving the above problems and might prove to be more appealing to the vast majority of the population – provided that the new system is simple, easy to understand and operate, and can be adopted without upheaval. The TR system proposed and described in the first part of this book could constitute such a combination.

Grafting TR onto the present House of Commons – two solutions

5.24 For TR to succeed in its objective, the ratio between the number of Constituency MPs (CMPs) and Party MPs (PMPs) is crucial. I believe that in the UK this ratio should be around 80:20 in favour of the CMPs. This ensures the strength of the CMPs in Parliament and consequently a degree of governmental stability, backed by the majority party. And, just as important, it keeps the direct bond between individual MPs and their constituencies. The 20% of PMPs on the other hand, ensure the existence of a built-in opposition backed by representation, so that the voices of minority interests are heard speaking with the authority of the sovereign on the floor of Parliament.

5.25 As explained in Part One of this book, this would be the case even if one party were theoretically to win all the constituencies: the majority party would secure 80% of the seats, but that would still leave 20% for the opposition parties. Once this is safeguarded, it is important not to move the ratio too much in favour of the PMPs. If it reaches, say, 60:40, the system tilts towards PR and destabilises the government of the day. **5.26** One party might gain particularly from a switch to TR. Even today, many Liberal Democrats cherish the idea that they could hold the balance of power in a future parliament. But under the current system – on past analysis – the possibility of such an outcome is so remote that it has started to become frayed at the edges. And even if they combined with the Irish and the Nationalists, it is unlikely that Lib Dems could maintain a permanent alliance which would hold that balance. TR, on the other hand, could make their hopes in this regard more realistic.

5.27 But although a switch to full TR would probably be the best solution for the House of Commons, one has to be realistic. The political environment in the UK is such that it is unlikely that either of the two big political parties or public opinion will rush to adopt radical changes, desirable though that would be. Even though full TR retains a large element of FPTP, it may still be seen by some to be too revolutionary.

5.28 However, the desire to rectify the anomalies of the present system is strong amongst the active and vocal elements of the electorate. Therefore, another, more step-by-step solution – once publicised and understood – might galvanise enough support to prompt the House of Commons to debate and adopt it. I believe we are at a good juncture for exactly this first step. Unless something is done to address the legitimate demand for better representation by the Liberal Democrats and other smaller parties, political strife will spill out into the urban squares of the cities.

5.29 This is partly because, sooner or later, the present government headed by Gordon Brown – a UK MP representing a Scottish constituency in the House of Commons – or a future government has to face what in the UK is called the "West Lothian Question". This question was first raised by another Scottish MP, Tam Dalyell, in the 1970s, when he was the MP for the Scottish constituency of West

Lothian – hence the name. He pointed out that in post-devolution Scotland, English-constituency MPs would not be able to vote on matters devolved to Scotland, but Scottish-constituency MPs would be able to vote on these matters for England. The Conservative Party has already spoken out against the idea that Scottish Labour MPs be allowed to vote on a policy that does not affect Scottish constituents. They said that it would be "unfair" if Scottish MPs were allowed to vote on such a proposal. However, the Labour government – because of its own vested interests – flatly refused to reduce the number of Scottish MPs at Westminster when it set up the Scottish parliament. And although this issue was subsequently resolved somehow, the public perception that the English always have to give concessions to "minorities" is growing and needs to be addressed.

5.30 Similar situations, although not identical, arise with regard to Wales and Northern Ireland. When the Labour government tried, following devolution to Scotland and Wales, to introduce devolution to the English regions to give a semblance of equal treatment, they could not arouse any interest in the matter. The English regions lost their appetite for separate identities because the power of local governments and town hall prestige had been transferred to, and would remain with, the central government.

5.31 For all the above anomalies, interim solutions could be found to avoid internal conflict. For example, the government – through the Boundaries Commission – could legislate to reduce the number of the constituencies in the three devolved territories (Scotland, Wales and Northern Ireland) which would, of course, automatically increase the size of their constituencies and therefore their MPs in Westminster. At the same time, they could add, say, 100 new parliamentary PMP seats, using the principles of TR, to be distributed proportionally, in order to represent the unsuccessful votes, which have hitherto been thrown away and ignored. This change is less radical than the one outlined above because many of the existing CMP seats would remain as they are today, with the PMP seats simply constituting an *addition* to Parliament. Much inter-party haggling and bargaining would still have to be performed in order to arrive at an agreement on such an essentially constitutional matter, but the opportunity could present itself if this element of PR were included to satisfy the Lib Dems' cry for fair representation and to give space both to the Greens and UKIP.

5.32 To illustrate this injection of an element of PR into the electoral system through the use of TR, let us suppose that 100 PMP seats in the House of Commons are added to the existing seats without decreasing their number. Let us then superimpose this addition on the results of the 2001 General Election to examine what would be its impact on Parliament. The outcome can immediately be seen, even without adjusting the size of the non-English constituencies. The 100 PMP seats thus created are to be distributed along TR principles to the various parties: i.e using the votes cast for the unsuccessful candidates in proportion to their contribution to the actual results. This simple exercise demonstrates how easy it is to end up with a more balanced, reformed House of Commons without creating a drama. The Liberal Democrats end up with better representation. But, more importantly, UKIP and the Green Party, who command reasonably large followings in the country, gain their justified representation in Parliament.

5.33 The following adjusted table of the results shows how simple it is to achieve at least an interim reform. This is an illustration rather than a recommended model. However, an actual adjustment is not difficult to achieve. Boundaries need to be redrawn anyway following the devolution of power to Scotland, Wales and Northern Ireland, and a small reduction in the total number is overdue to make the House of Commons less unwieldy. And if the House of Lords is reformed along lines guided by the principles of TR, we could end up with an up-to-date, supervising Legislature overseeing the other two arms of the state, rather being slowly chipped away at by them.

TABLE 2: GENERAL ELECTION RESULTS 2001 PLUS 100 PMPS ADDED TO THESE RESULTS
(Electorate 44,403,327)

	Votes as % of electorate	Successful votes	% of votes cast	Seats in the Commons	Unsuccessful (wasted) votes	% of wasted votes	PMP seats allocated	Grand Total
Labour	24.188	10,740,344	40.76	413	2,490,934	19.19	19	432
Conservative	18.824	8,358,382	31.72	166	4,803,560	37.00	37	203
Lib Dem	10.842	4,814,341	18.27	52	3,752,721	28.91	29	81
Subtotal	53.854	23,913,067	90.75	631	11,047,215	85.10	85	716
SNP	1.046	464,305	1.76	5	398,494	3.08	3	8
UKIP	0.899	399,043	1.51	0	399,043	3.07	3	3
UUP	0.488	216,839	0.82	6	106,470	0.82	1	7
Plaid Cymru	0.441	195,892	0.74	4	143,168	1.10	1	5
DUP	0.41	181,999	0.69	5	93,730	0.72	1	6
Sinn Fein	0.397	176,063	0.67	4	85,912	0.66	1	5
SDLP	0.382	169,873	0.64	3	100,415	0.77	1	4
Green	0.375	166,477	0.63	0	166,477	1.28	1	1
Kidderminster	0.064	28,487	0.11	1	0	0.00	0	1
Others	0.993	440,853	1.67	0	440,853	3.40	3	3
Grand Total	59.349	26,352,898	100.00	659	12,981,777	100.00	100	759

Boundaries – and a simulation of TR on the basis of the 2005 election results

(I am indebted to Mr Lewis Baston, director of research at the ERS, for the valuable and practical suggestions he made in the following section.)

5.34 The nature of TR is that it is an adjustable system. As long as one is sticking to its principles, it does not rule out amendments either because of the specific circumstances of the country where it is being applied, or because it is felt to be better to inch forward in stages. Rigidity is not helpful in the *art of the possible*. Therefore, even if the option chosen were to be a switch to full TR, the "equalisation" of boundaries need not necessarily be done on quite the strict basis outlined in Chapter Two. It could be argued that in the UK context, frequent changes of constituency areas disrupt the traditional relationship between MP and a defined geographical constituency. Every two, or even three, Parliaments might be sufficient, and there is more leeway and tolerance for variation around the average size in compensated systems like TR.

5.35 As things stand in the UK at the moment, boundary determination is a complex question of administrative, social and physical geography. The Commissions are required to have regard to community identity, continuity with past boundaries, compactness and, most importantly, getting within an acceptable range of electorate (5-10% or so either side) of the ideal size. In the UK context, it might make sense to build on all this rather than insist on strict arbitrary divisions, even if that were to dilute TR – and it mig ht keep gerrymandering simply as a threat to be watched.

5.36 This flexibility on the issue of boundaries also applies to the allocation of the proportional top-up PMP seats. The basic idea of TR is that these extra seats should be distributed on a nationwide basis (in other words, by looking at the total number of "unsuccessful" votes a party received throughout the whole country). However, Mr Lewis Baston has kindly run simulations of TR for this edition on the basis of the 2005 General Election using three different sets of boundaries, although keeping the allocation formula (largest remainder) the same. The first allocates (as in the original TR concept) the additional members on a UK-wide level; the second uses the 12 regional units within the UK (i.e. Northern Ireland, Wales, Scotland and the nine regions of England), and the third uses the county areas as the basis for distributing seats. In England these would be the counties; in Wales they would be the five Assembly regions; in Scotland approximations of the eight Parliament regions; and Northern Ireland would be treated as a whole unit. This involves slightly larger units on average than t he areas proposed in the Jenkins report for its top-up members.

5.37 Under the simulation, there would have been 792 seats overall, based on 646 constituency MPs and 146 party top-up MPs.

A majority in the Commons would have therefore required 397 MPs, leaving Labour just short of an overall majority under all these alternative bases of calculation. The principal differences are that the UK-wide version gives more compensatory seats to the smaller parties; in the version using small units these would tend to go to the larger opposition parties (Lib Dem and Conservative).

5.38 A whole-nation tier of top-up members would certainly make sense for a relatively small country with a unitary state, but might possibly come under strain in a large country with asymmetric devolution like the UK. The regional basis could be a possible compromise. Another option might be to treat England as a single unit, which would give an overall result not far off the UK-wide model (the Labour and Conservative additions would be exactly the same, while the Lib Dems would have 49 seats rather than 48, and UKIP 6 rather than 7). Smaller units than the UK as a whole would be a relatively fair concession to national, regional and local feeling without compromising the principles or model results of TR.

5.39 It is to be emphasised here that all these calculations – with their larger number of MPs than is the case today – are for illustration only, and that the time has come for a smaller and more manageable House of Commons. The ratio of CMPs to PMPs recommended under TR is 80:20. Therefore, out of a total of 600 MPs, the breakdown would be 480:120; out of a total of 500 MPs it would be 400:100 – and so on.

TABLE 3

	FPTP seats	UK-wide allocation		Allocation by 12 regions		Allocation by county units	
		Added	Total	Added	Total	Added	Total
Labour	355	30	385	29	384	28	383
Conservative	198	44	242	45	243	48	246
Liberal Democrat	62	48	110	50	112	57	119
UKIP	0	7	7	7	7	2	2
SNP	6	3	9	4	10	4	10
Green	0	3	3	2	2	0	0
Democratic Unionist	9	1	10	1	10	1	10
BNP	0	2	2	2	2	1	1
Plaid Cymru	3	2	5	2	5	0	3
Sinn Fein	5	1	6	1	6	1	6
Ulster Unionist Party	1	1	2	2	3	2	3
SDLP	3	1	4	1	4	1	4
Respect/ SSP	1	1	2	0	1	1	2
Veritas	0	1	1	0	0	0	0
Alliance P NI	0	1	1	0	0	0	0
Independent	2	0	2	0	2	0	2
Speaker	1	0	1	0	1	0	1

Chapter 6
APPLYING TR TO A REFORMED HOUSE OF LORDS

Background

6.1 A wholly-elected House of Lords is an idea that is becoming widely accepted. It is overdue, imminent and very much on the political agenda. Its arrival is only a matter of time. A case can therefore already be made, at this stage of the debate, for the adoption of TR as its electoral system. Introducing TR here could prove to be very successful, and could – if efforts to reform the House of Commons are unsuccessful – make up for the deficiency of the FPTP electoral method in the lower House, without creating a political upheaval.

6.2 In an earlier book, I suggested a partial reform of the Lords based on using the discarded votes cast for the unsuccessful candidates for the House of Commons. I have realised since then that this was a mistake. It is difficult enough to introduce changes in one House. To tinker with both at the same time would appear to many to be a folly. Moreover, it is not credible to build the new House of Lords, wholly or partially, on unsuccessful Commons votes. So I have changed my mind. Theory has always to bow to reality. Instead of a hybrid solution, what is called for is a wholly-elected House of Lords.

6.3 A new electoral system is needed for this new second chamber, dispensing with Hereditary Peers, Life Peers and Appointed Peers – and restoring in the process the long-lost link between the Lords and their original roots in the country. TR is ideal for this purpose.

6.4 The problem arises that a wholly-elected House of Lords based on TR would be seen as more representative and more democratic than an unreformed Commons – and rightly so. The new situation would become even more apparent to the public if the

House of Commons were left resting entirely on (mostly) minority votes in its constituencies as a result of the simple majority rule. The primacy of the Commons over the Lords might be challenged, precipitating – on the face of it – a constitutional crisis. But as things stand today, the approval of TR for the Lords could only be effected through legislation in the House of Commons. In fact, the latter holds all the cards. The new Act of Reform would need to fully define the powers and functions of the reformed House of Lords. First, it would have to confirm its status as a secondary revising chamber by reciting within the new Act the old 1911 Parliament Acts – as amended in 1949. These Acts limit the Lords' legislative function to revising and not opposing the will of the House of Commons – thus asserting the primacy of the latter. Limiting any delay in revising legislation to no more than one year at the most would guarantee the supremacy of the Commons. On the other hand, the complaints of those MPs who today often castigate the Lords as "unelected" would be silenced once and for all. Mutual respect would be restored.

6.5 The grafting of practising judges into the new, reformed House of Lords is vital. The Montesquieu principle of separation of powers is not meant to render the three arms of the state parallel. The present constitutional arrangement in Parliament is precious. The Executive is enmeshed within the House of Commons and up until now, the House of Lords has had an important judicial function. However, the new Supreme Court (which starts work in October 2009) is intended to supplant or preclude the link between these two arms of the state, since its newly-appointed judges (i.e. those who are not already Law Lords) will not be members of the House of Lords. But in my view, a reformed second chamber *should* include within its ranks some members of the Judiciary with real Bench experience, so that the direct and constant link of the sovereign people to all these three arms of the state is preserved.

6.6 The link could, for example, be maintained in the following way: the new Supreme Court would delegate a number of judges from the practising Judiciary to sit ex-officio in the Lords for a certain limited period – say six years – during which they would participate in deliberations but would not be allowed to vote. After these six years, they would be rotated and replaced by others.

6.7 Along the same lines, the Queen, the Sovereign, could at her pleasure appoint, say, some religious dignitaries from amongst leaders of the different religions to sit in the new House for periods of six years, after which they would be rotated. These religious figures would have the right to take part in debates, but not to vote. This arrangement could neatly solve the problem of how to replace the Bishops and the Law Lords, giving an added gravitas to the new second chamber.

6.8 The solution proposed here is essential, given the background in Britain of a steady loss of social cohesion and uniformity, both because of social and ideological trends from within, and as a result of an influx of immigrants from without. This problem is faced by many other countries and societies. Norms of behaviour, guided hitherto by religion and age-old social customs, are giving way by necessity to the guidance of the rule of law, bringing to the surface the questions: which law, whose law? Luckily, while other countries are engaged in asserting rigid principles of human rights, importing them wholesale into their legal framework, the UK is superbly suited – one might say blessed – by a lack of rigidity in this respect. This, of course, is because of its lack of a written constitution and the flexibility of English law – underpinned by the elastic use of the concepts of equity and precedent. The new Supreme Court should preserve its right to rule against or criticise the EU courts' judgements, thereby throwing any such rulings back into the melting pot of Parliament to be looked at.

6.9 The process of implementing TR as the solution to the constitutional limbo that Tony Blair has created and bequeathed to his successor may smooth the path of reformers. The dilemma facing the reform camp is what to do with the present Life Peers and the remnants of the Hereditary Peers, whose vested interests militate against a speedy solution? The answer is simple. The political parties who choose, delegate, or appoint their candidates to the newly-created regions to elect the new members of the House of Lords can give priority to those deserving sitting Peers of their different parties. By choosing them to run for election to the new House, they will in fact be given two chances each: to succeed in their regions as Regional Lords, or to accede to the position of Party Lords within the party lists. Even if they fail to capture regional seats, their efforts will be rewarded if they succeed in scoring highly in the regions to propel themselves to the top of their party lists. Their chances of acceding to the posts of Party Lords will depend as much on their own canvassing efforts as on the support of their parties.

6.10 Some commentators say that we need appointed Lords to ensure the presence of experts. This is a spurious argument. Government and select committees of both Houses can and do always draw on expert advice from outside. Parliaments are there to represent democratically the ordinary citizen, not to create oligarchies and establishments that distance further the representatives from the represented.

Implementation

6.11 The new House of Lords will have 300 members. Two hundred members are to be Regional Lords (RL) and 100 Party Lords (PL). Both categories (RLs and PLs) are elected in accordance with the TR system, as detailed in Part One of this book. For this purpose, the country is demarcated in a geographically successive manner, being sliced into 200 regions by the Boundaries Commission without regard to the make-up of the population. The only consideration is to ensure that the number of electors (not inhabitants) in each region is as similar as is possible and practical.

6.12 The ratio of 200 to 100 corresponds to a percentage of 66:33. The reason why we have swung the pendulum downwards, below the ratio of 70:30, is that in this situation a bigger dose of representation (i.e. of PR) is needed to counterbalance the excess rigidity of the House of Commons' electoral method of first-past-the-post.

6.13 Elections take place every six years for half of the House of Lords. Unlike in the House of Commons, this period is fixed and the House of Lords cannot dissolve itself. A by-election for a Regional Lord is initiated and moved by the House Committee within two months of the death or resignation of a Regional Lord. In the event of the death or resignation of a Party Lord, the next in line on the party list accedes automatically.

6.14 One way of easing the transition from the present House of Lords into a wholly elected chamber is to start by electing just half its members – to be followed in six years' time by the other half. The next question that springs to mind is: which half to start with? The best solution is to follow the precedent of the reduction of the Hereditary Peers. The present House of Lords can reduce its members to 150 by electing from among themselves the 150 Lords who will stay behind. These can serve their remaining six years to ensure continuity and help to induct their 150 new, elected counterparts into the superb traditions of the House. Those who stay behind are designated as 100 Regional Lords and 50 Party Lords. So although 200 regions have been created, elections take place in only 100 of them, leaving the other 100 to be represented by the remaining ex-appointed Lords. These will terminate their service six years later, when elections take place for their replacements.

6.15 Members of the House of Lords are to be paid salaries. These are revised from time to time and fixed by a committee in the House of Commons, presided over by the Clerk of the Parliaments, to ensure neutrality and adequate consultation between the two Houses.

6.16 A minimum age requirement – say 40 years – would add gravitas and experience to the House. The service of a member of the House of Lords is limited to the lower of three periods and retirement at 70. This is to avoid inertia and renew its vitality. The modern composition of the House of Commons is made up of young people who look at their membership of Parliament as a career. They have become professional MPs. But membership of

Parliament should not be a profession. It is the recent evolution of this practice that has contributed to the chasm between citizens and their representative MPs, who look at their membership as a job for life. It is only the enterprising amongst them who move on and use their positions as launching-pads to go forward into other, more remunerative or more rewarding careers, in business, journalism or academia. To avoid creating a similar situation in the Lords, fixing the minimum age at 40 would attract individuals with experience, a number of whom would have already made their mark or their fortune, and so would be able to devote the mature years of their lives to public service rather than building up their careers.

6.17 The biggest problem arising in implementing TR for the Lords is in drawing the boundaries. This task of course will be entrusted to the existing Boundaries Commission or a new commission. In either case, instructions would have to be issued by its chairman, who is the Speaker of the House of Commons. Since these would be new boundaries, delineated on a clean slate, it would be advisable to add the Clerk of the Parliaments and the chairman of the Electoral Commission to the membership of the Boundaries Commission.

6.18 Unlike the existing boundaries, the new ones for the Lords need to be drawn in a geographically successive sequence from north to south, ignoring national, ethnic or any other local considerations, to avoid as far as possible the curse of gerrymandering. The danger of the impact of gerrymandering is reduced anyway to a minimum under TR because it is a compensatory system. Moreover, unlike with the boundaries for the House of Commons, where it is important for the local MP to have regular meetings with the electors of his/her community, the strict and continuous contact of the Regional Lord is optional and discretionary. His/her contact with the region is more a matter of gauging the political temperature of that region and using this contact to contribute to the deliberations of the House. He/she is not meant to set up a "surgery" similar to that of an MP. The deliberate differentiation of the ages of members, the timing of elections, and the boundaries between the two Houses of Parliament, will result in them complementing, rather than coinciding with or duplicating, each other. This in itself will add to the value of the Lords as a revising chamber.

6.19 Any prediction or simulation of the results of the elections to the House of Lords under such a system is valueless. However, it is safe to assume that it will never mirror the composition of the House of Commons. To start with, TR is a balanced system and its results can never mirror the results of FPTP. Secondly, the timing of elections to the two Houses is very unlikely to coincide. Thirdly, even if the election of one half coincides with the Commons, the other half will not. Moreover, the shapes and sizes of the regions are bigger and cannot overlap with the constituencies of the Commons. Add to all this the age and maturity of the new Lords, which will make them less dependent on their parties and less inclined to be easily led by party whips. All that will give them more independence in their contributions, which will add tremendously to the value of their revising function. The debates in the Lords will command respect and attention by the House of Commons and the public at large.

Chapter 7
APPLYING TR TO THE SCOTTISH PARLIAMENT

7.1 The electoral system used in the general elections for the devolved Scottish Parliament is a version of the Additional Member System (AMS). AMS is intended to reflect the voting preferences of the electorate in a more representative manner than the Westminster model, retaining the best features of FPTP – direct though limited accountability – while introducing proportionality between parties through party list regional voting. So Scottish electors each have two votes: one to elect 73 Constituency Members of Parliament, using FPTP; and another vote to elect 56 Regional Members, using PR. Broadly speaking, the percentage of votes obtained by the parties in the list vote (for Regional Members) determines their overall number of representatives; these party lists are used to top up the FPTP seats to the required number.

7.2 So if a party has won two seats in the constituencies but its results in the Regional vote gives it a proportion equivalent to five seats, the first three candidates on its list are selected in addition, and it ends up with five MSPs (Members of the Scottish Parliament). Here lies the first defect of AMS as compared with TR. The first two seats are elected directly by *real* individual constituency electors. The other three are selected indirectly by *virtual* impersonal parties. Under TR all MPs must be elected directly by constituency votes in order to find their way to parliament..

7.3 And yet on the face of it, AMS seems to be the system which comes nearest to fulfilling the principles of TR. The two systems have common features: the mix of FPTP with PR; and the idea of electing two categories of MPs who are equal in every respect save for the method of their election. These are steps on the right path, and by putting AMS into practice, Scotland has made it easier for its electors and those elsewhere in Britain to understand TR.

7.4 However apart from the above, AMS has several other flaws. Its topping-up method, which involves complex calculations using the D'Hondt method, is not straightforward and is hardly understood by the mass of electors. It may appear to them as not transparent, and as belonging to the domain of the political and academic establishments. Whereas under TR the topping-up element represents a small but significant adjustment, that of AMS is so dominant that the direct link between the electors and the specific constituency MP is overshadowed.

7.5 Another aspect of AMS that needs to be discussed is its use of two ballots rather than one. On the one hand – on the positive side – because Scotland is a small part of the Union (the UK), AMS can be seen as fulfilling an important role in deciding the direction of politics as the reflection of a special social framework. At the most recent (2007) election, Scottish voters appeared to want a nationalist alternative (the Scottish National Party or SNP) to a Labour-led executive, but without necessarily embracing the SNP's desire for full Scottish independence and the break-up of the Union with the rest of the UK. It can be argued that by splitting their ballots between different parties, Scottish voters got more or less what they wanted: a change in government, but a Parliament with a strong Unionist majority that would resist moves to independence. In that sense, the AMS experiment in Scotland shows the power of STV and its variants, including both TR and AMS.

7.6 However, in my view, giving voters two ballots is potentially dangerous and destabilising. My reason for saying this is that it tends to make people think in two different directions – and the system can become a playground for machination and manipulation by professional politicians and their public relations advisers. Nowhere was this danger more evident than in the Israeli elections of the 1990s (as explained fully in Part Three). In 1992, the Israeli parliament (the Knesset) enacted a Basic (constitutional) Law to use two ballots: one to elect the prime minister directly, the other the parties in parliament. The aim was to stabilise the government by cutting small pressure groups/parties out of the job of choosing the prime minister by a vote in parliament, where they could use their support to bargain for advantages from the coalition government. But the result of the 1992 reform was the exact opposite. The two ballots were used like this: one to elect the prime minister; the other to elect the small parties/pressure groups – which destabilised parliament and the government even further. After three unsuccessful attempts, the law had to be abandoned.

7.7 The stock answer to the problem of the use of two ballots is that the purpose of AMS, and indeed the purpose of Single Transferable Vote (STV), is to give the voter a second chance to use his/her ballot if that voter fails to elect their first-choice candidate. TR solves this problem neatly. Why should a voter give his/her second choice to another party or indeed to another candidate? Under TR, the vote for the preferred candidate stays with the same candidate – or at least with that candidate's party (and hence the voter's party) albeit with a different weighting. The result under TR is that if the candidate of choice does not succeed as a CMP, he/she might still succeed as a PMP – or at least the vote stays within the "family" i.e. within the same preferred party. This is more logical and more plausible, because the vote stays consistent. TR is simpler and more transparent, sacrificing a little of the fairness of pure PR in favour of achieving the stability that FPTP provides. In simple terms, TR leans towards FPTP, while AMS gives more weight to the PR element of the system. Hence AMS is often referred to as a form of PR.

7.8 There is another point worthy of note. Under the single-ballot TR, every vote is equal to every other, whether this is one for a big party or a small faction or for that matter for a single-member independent. Under the two-ballot system of AMS, the vote for the successful constituency candidate counts, while all the other votes in that constituency are thrown away – just as in FPTP. In fairness, this is compensated for to a degree by the convoluted, modified D'Hondt formula. The question is: why use this complicated method when very similar results, and I say better, are obtained by the straightforward TR?

7.9 The following table details the breakdown of votes in both categories (Constituency and Regional) in the 2007 General Election for the Scottish Parliament. A close examination of the results shows why the system is likely to become unviable. It is important to bear in mind when reading it that the calculations of the Regional seats are not based on simple straightforward conversion of percentages into seats to determine the resulting number of Regional representatives for each party. The calculation simply determines the topping-up requirements. That is why, for example, you find that almost equal percentages of votes of 29.1 and 31.0 for Labour and the Scottish National Party result in them winning 9 and 26 Regional seats respectively. The idea is to compensate the latter for its lack of success in the constituencies. TR, on the other hand, does not need all these convoluted calculations. It simply compensates automatically by giving different weights to the votes for the unsuccessful candidates in the same constituencies, making topping up and regional voting unnecessary.

SCOTTISH ELECTION 2007
Share of Constituency and Regional votes by Party

	No of Seats	Share of Seats	Constitu-ency Votes	Seats	Regional List Votes	Seats	Total Votes
Scottish Labour	46	35.7%	648,374	32.1%	37	595,415	29.1%	9	1,243,789
Scottish National Party	47	36.4%	664,227	32.9%	21	633,611	31.0%	26	1,297,838
Scottish Liberal Democrats	16	12.4%	326,232	16.2%	11	230,651	11.3%	5	556,883
Scottish Conservative & Unionists	17	13.2%	334,743	16.6%	4	284,035	13.9%	13	618,778
Scottish Green Party	2	1.6%	2,971	0.1%	0	82,577	4.0%	2	85,548
Scottish Socialist Party	0	0.0%	525	0.0%	0	13,096	0.6%	0	13,621
Solidarity	0	0.0%	0	0.0%	0	31,096	1.5%	0	31,096
Scottish Senior Citizens Unity Party	0	0.0%	1,702	0.1%	0	39,038	1.9%	0	40,740
Margo MacDonald	1	0.8%	0	0.0%	0	19,256	0.9%	1	19,256
Totals:	129	100.1%	1,978,774	98.0%	73	1,928,775	94.2%	56	3,907,549

7.10 Before the recent (2007) Scottish General Election, it was expected by the UK government that Labour, which was thought to be the most supported party, would win a majority. In fact, the desire of both the Labour government in London and the Labour Party in Scotland was to frustrate the efforts of the Scottish National Party to promote its platform of independence, and to show through the outcome of the election that the nationalists were in the minority and that Scotland did not want to break away. But close scrutiny of the above table shows how AMS, the Additional Member System, subverted the results, and how a determined nationalist party, riding on a strong, emotional platform of independence, managed to overtake among the electorate the hitherto-more-supported Labour Party's objective of staying within the Union. The results of the Constituency votes compared with those for the Regional List votes already show the manipulation of the votes between the two ballots. Eventually AMS will break down for the same reason that it broke down in Israel. Sooner or later the voters will split their votes in order to push forward the fortunes of sectional interests of minority parties – that is, unless the Scottish nationalists succeed in seceding from the Union. But that will be a different ball game.

7.11 To examine the results meaningfully, one needs to compare the results of each participant party, and especially the way its voters split their votes in different directions. This comparison is especially significant when one sees that this split occurred in a big way among those who cast their constituency ballots for the Liberal Democrats and the Conservatives and others – but not among those who voted for the two big warring blocks: Labour and the SNP. The final results show the power of emotional, negative protest rather than rational opposition. A basis like this is bound to cause the system to fail sooner or later, sending the authorities back to the drawing board. A detailed examination of the next table, below, reveals how – over three general elections – the Scottish Nationalists inched their way to the top. Their dip in the middle served to spur the voters of the other parties on to support them through the Regional votes to attain their objective of independence.

7.12 All this occurred also, of course, because the Scottish National Party was better led and more organised at campaigning in 2007 than in 2003, and the demand for a non-Labour government was greater. In 2003, a large number of smaller parties, notably the Greens and the SSP, were elected, mostly from the list part of the ballot. It was in that election that the difference between constituency and list voting was more apparent and most significant, while in 1999 and 2007 there was less of a gap between the two.

SCOTTISH PARLIAMENT with 73 Constituency Seats and 56 Regional Seats – Summary of Seats by party

	Constituency MSPs			Regional List MSPs			Total MSPs Elected		
	1999	2003	2007	1999	2003	2007	1999	2003	2007
Scottish Labour	53	46	37	3	4	9	56	50	46
Scottish National Party	7	9	21	28	18	26	35	27	47
Scottish Liberal Democrats	12	13	11	5	4	5	17	17	16
Scottish Conservative & Unionists	0	3	4	18	15	13	18	18	17
Scottish Green Party	0	0	0	1	7	2	1	7	2
Scottish Socialist Party	0	0	0	1	6	0	1	6	0
Solidarity	0	0	0	0	0	0	0	0	0
MSP for Falkirk West	1	1	0	0	0	0	1	1	0
Save Stobhill Hospital Party	-	1	0	-	0	0	-	1	0
Scottish Senior Citizens Unity Party	-	0	0	-	1	0	-	1	0
Margo MacDonald	-	0	0	-	1	1	-	1	1
Total	73	73	73	56	56	56	129	129	129

7.13 The AMS method is further complicated by its use of multi-member regions in order to elect the extra members who are to top us and compensate for the election of the Constituency Members. Under TR, these seats would be distributed according to how a party performed across the whole country. Under AMS, the extra MSPs are known as Regional Members precisely because their seats are allocated on a region-by-region basis.

7.14 There is a reason for this – and like most things, it is a mix of principle and political calculation. The principled arguments are three-fold. One is that an all-Scotland list tier would lower the threshold for election to a very low level (unless an artificial threshold was imposed) and allow all sorts of minor parties in. Second, is that people perceive representation as being local, and the regional lists are a compromise, maintaining some element of localism. Without regions, the parties' lists would be very long, and the elected members would be allowed to become very detached from the concerns of the electorate because they would not be answerable to anything other than a centrally controlled party body. Third, following on from this, is that if a party is well represented in one part of what is a large country geographically, this does not necessarily help its supporters in its weaker areas much and neither does having a national tier. For instance, Labour in the Highlands has significant support but does not often win seats, and the sense of a Labour representative from the Highlands (on the list) is worth something. But there is also an element of political calculation. The regional aspect of the Scottish AMS model was designed to tilt the system slightly in Labour's favour. Because Labour is dominant in Glasgow, Central Scotland and to a lesser extent in West of Scotland, the party tends to get more MSPs here in the constituency section than is proportional. If the extra seats are allocated within regions, the compensation does not spill over and reduce the party's representation in its stronger regions.

7.15 However, I believe that this way of allocating the extra, top-up seats is mistaken and unnecessary. After all, the local element of the system and the link to a Constituency MSP is already satisfied by the single-member constituencies. The proportional element could be better and more accurately served by treating Scotland as one whole region to maximise the utilisation of each vote? Under TR, even the PMPs have links with the constituencies where they contested the election, because they will tend to have been the strongest runners-up across the country as a whole, and thus already have bonds which involve them with the life of that community.

7.16 Another weakness of AMS is the ratio that the scheme employs between Constituency and Regional MPs in Scotland. In TR, the ratio between the CMPs and the PMPs should fluctuate between 80:20 (for more stability) and, say, 70:30 (where strong representation is required). All this depends on the particular circumstances of the country. In the British House of Commons, 80:20 is recommended in order to preserve the stability which exists and needs to be maintained. In the Knesset in Israel, on the other hand, a 70:30 ratio is more appropriate in order to cater for an electorate made up of disparate orientations that have become used to wider representation over the course of 60 years. A ratio of less than 70:30 is, under certain circumstances, needed to allow more representation where stability is assured, as is for example recommended in Chapter Six for the new House of Lords, since stability is guaranteed in the House of Commons. It is argued that part of the founding principles of Scottish devolution is that a reasonably proportional system is needed. However, a modified approach should not be seen as breaching this understanding.

7.17 The ratio most recently employed in Scotland was 73 Constituency seats to 56 Regional. This equates to a percentage ratio of 57 to 43. A few arithmetical simulations show that the system will sooner or later descend into proportional representation (PR), with all its disadvantages. Maybe this is the reason why AMS is often described as a form of PR. A more adequate ratio for Scotland can, for example, be created by halving the number of Regions under AMS to 28, which will result in a ratio of 73 to 28 – this is the same TR percentage ratio of 70:30 recommended for Israel. By simply halving the results of the 2007 Regional Election to reflect this amendment, the results will be tilted in favour of the constituency votes – and increased stability will be achieved. The following table shows what the make-up of the Scottish Parliament would have been after each of the last three elections if such a reduction of Regional seats had been carried out under AMS. For the sake of illustration, some fractions were rounded up, others down. The rounding is not material in the context of this illustration. Moreover, it is important to remember that the arbitrary halving of the numbers of the Regional seats is distorted here because the topping-up method may give different results. It is useful, nevertheless, to bear this rough illustration in mind.

SCOTTISH PARLIAMENT with 73 Constituency Seats and 28 (instead of 56) Regional Seats Summary of Seats by party									
	Constituency MSPs			Regional List MSPs			Total MSPs Elected		
	1999	2003	2007	1999	2003	2007	1999	2003	2007
Scottish Labour	53	46	37	1.5	2	4.5	54	48	41
Scottish National Party	7	9	21	14	9	13	21	18	34
Scottish Liberal Democrats	12	13	11	2.5	2	2.5	15	15	14
Scottish Conservative & Unionists	0	3	4	9	7.5	6.5	9	10	11
Scottish Green Party	0	0	0	0.5	3.5	1	1	4	1
Scottish Socialist Party	0	0	0	0.5	3	0	0	3	0
Solidarity	0	0	0	0	0	0	0	0	0
MSP for Falkirk West	1	1	0	0	0	0	1	1	0
Save Stobhill Hospital Party	-	1	0	-	0	0	-	1	0
Scottish Senior Citizens Unity Party	-	0	0	-	0.5	0	-	0	0
Margo MacDonald	-	0	0	-	0.5	0.5	-	1	0
Total	73	73	73	28	28	28	101	101	101

7.18 But it would, of course, be simpler and more stable to change completely over to TR (in place of AMS) and confine the election only within the present 73 constituencies. Or, better still, in order to avoid future constitutional wrangling, simply to divide each of the 73 constituencies into two, dispensing with the Regional seats altogether and increasing the number of Constituency seats to 146 to widen the field for representation and – as importantly – to induce the existing parties to swallow the change. It also eases the work of the Boundaries Commission. By differentiating the constituencies of the UK House of Commons from those of the Scottish Parliament, it makes it easier to enlarge the former and reduce their current number. It is argued that the three constituencies of Orkney, Shetland and the Western Isles – with their low populations – need to be allowed a smaller number of electors than the rest because of community distinctiveness and geographical remoteness. But this interferes with the deliberate splicing of TR and could be the thin end of the wedge that would destroy TR and bring back the danger of gerrymandering. Notwithstanding all this, TR is meant to be an adjustable system and not a rigid ideology of electoral processes. Each country can modify TR to suit its special circumstances but without departing too far from its principles.

7.19 Taking the results of 2007 and applying TR in a simulation based on the 73 current constituencies, we end up with the results in the following table which are much closer and clearly more in line of what was anticipated before the 2007 election. A change to 146 seats will of course not be identical but will most probably be similar to the results of this simulation, more or less doubling the strength of each party; it might also let other, smaller parties secure some representation to keep them inside the tent of the Scottish Parliament.

APPLICATION OF TR TO THE SCOTTISH PARLIAMENTARY ELECTION 2007

Constituency Votes by Major Party			L	S	D	C
Region	Constituency		Lab	SNP	Lib Dem	Con
South of Scotland	Ayr	C	8,713	7,952	1,741	12,619
South of Scotland	Galloway and Upper Nithsdale	C	4,935	10,054	1,631	13,387
South of Scotland	Roxburgh and Berwickshire	C	2,108	4,127	8,571	10,556
Lothian	Edinburgh Pentlands	C	8,402	8,234	4,814	12,927
Successful votes						49,489
Unsuccessful votes			24,158	30,367	16,757	

Region	Constituency		Lab	SNP	Lib Dem	Con
Highlands and Islands	Caithness, Sutherland and Easter Ross	D	3,152	6,658	8,981	2,586
Highlands and Islands	Orkney	D	1,134	1,637	4,113	1,632
Highlands and Islands	Ross, Skye and Inverness West	D	4,789	10,015	13,501	3,122
Highlands and Islands	Shetland	D	670	1,622	6,531	972
Lothian	Edinburgh West	D	5,343	7,791	13,677	7,361
Lothian	Edinburgh South	D	9,469	6,117	11,398	5,589
Mid Scotland and Fife	Dunfermline West	D	9,476	7,296	9,952	2,363
Mid Scotland and Fife	North East Fife	D	2,557	6,735	13,307	8,291
North East Scotland	Aberdeen South	D	5,499	8,111	10,843	5,432
North East Scotland	West Aberdeenshire and Kincardine	D	2,761	9,144	14,314	8,604
South of Scotland	Tweeddale, Ettrick and Lauderdale	D	4,019	10,058	10,656	5,594
Successful votes					117,273	
Unsuccessful votes			48,869	75,184		51,546

Constituency Votes by Major Party			L	S	D	C
Region	Constituency		Lab	SNP	Lib Dem	Con
Central Scotland	Airdrie and Shotts	L	11,907	10,461	1,452	2,370
Central Scotland	Coatbridge and Chryston	L	11,860	7,350	1,519	2,305
Central Scotland	Cumbernauld and Kilsyth	L	12,672	10,593	1,670	1,447
Central Scotland	East Kilbride	L	15,334	13,362	3,092	4,115
Central Scotland	Falkirk East	L	13,184	11,312	2,136	3,701
Central Scotland	Hamilton North and Bellshill	L	12,334	7,469	1,726	2,835
Central Scotland	Hamilton South	L	10,280	6,628	1,610	2,929
Central Scotland	Motherwell and Wishaw	L	12,574	6,636	1,570	1,990
Glasgow	Glasgow Anniesland	L	10,483	6,177	2,325	3,154
Glasgow	Glasgow Baillieston	L	9,141	5,207	1,060	1,276
Glasgow	Glasgow Cathcart	L	8,476	6,287	1,659	2,324
Glasgow	Glasgow Kelvin	L	7,875	6,668	2,843	1,943
Glasgow	Glasgow Maryhill	L	7,955	5,645	1,936	1,028
Glasgow	Glasgow Pollok	L	10,456	6,063	1,437	1,460
Glasgow	Glasgow Rutherglen	L	10,237	5,857	5,516	2,094
Glasgow	Glasgow Shettleston	L	7,574	4,693	1,182	946
Glasgow	Glasgow Springburn	L	10,024	4,929	1,108	1,067
Lothian	Edinburgh Central	L	9,155	7,496	7,962	4,783
Lothian	Edinburgh North and Leith	L	11,020	8,044	8,576	4,045
Lothian	Linlithgow	L	12,715	11,565	2,232	3,125
Lothian	Midlothian	L	10,671	8,969	2,704	2,269
Mid Scotland and Fife	Dunfermline East	L	10,995	7,002	2,853	3,718
Mid Scotland and Fife	Kirkcaldy	L	10,627	8,005	3,361	2,202

TOTAL REPRESENTATION

Constituency Votes by Major Party			L Lab	S SNP	D Lib Dem	C Con
Region	Constituency					
North East Scotland	Aberdeen Central	L	7,232	6,850	4,693	2,345
South of Scotland	Carrick, Cumnock and Doon Valley	L	14,350	10,364	1,409	6,729
South of Scotland	Clydesdale	L	13,835	10,942	2,951	5,604
South of Scotland	Cunninghame South	L	10,270	8,102	1,977	3,073
South of Scotland	Dumfries	L	13,707	6,306	2,538	10,868
South of Scotland	East Lothian	L	12,219	9,771	6,249	6,232
West of Scotland	Clydebank and Milngavie	L	11,617	8,438	3,166	3,544
West of Scotland	Dumbarton	L	11,635	10,024	3,385	4,701
West of Scotland	Eastwood	L	15,077	7,972	3,603	14,186
West of Scotland	Greenock and Inverclyde	L	10,035	7,011	3,893	2,166
West of Scotland	Paisley North	L	12,111	6,998	1,570	1,721
West of Scotland	Paisley South	L	12,123	7,893	3,434	2,077
West of Scotland	Strathkelvin and Bearsden	L	11,396	8,008	4,658	5,178
West of Scotland	West Renfrewshire	L	10,467	8,167	2,206	8,289
Successful votes			**413,623**			
Unsuccessful votes				**293,264**	**107,261**	**133,839**

Constituency Votes by Major Party			L	S	D	C
Region	Constituency		Lab	SNP	Lib Dem	Con
Central Scotland	Falkirk West	S	11,292	12,068	2,538	2,887
Central Scotland	Kilmarnock and Loudoun	S	12,955	14,297	2,056	4,127
Glasgow	Glasgow Govan	S	8,266	9,010	1,891	1,680
Highlands and Islands	Argyll and Bute	S	4,148	9,944	9,129	5,571
Highlands and Islands	Inverness East, Nairn and Lochaber	S	7,559	16,443	10,972	4,635
Highlands and Islands	Moray	S	4,580	15,045	3,528	7,121
Highlands and Islands	Western Isles	S	5,667	6,354	852	752
Lothian	Edinburgh East and Musselburgh	S	9,827	11,209	5,473	3,458
Lothian	Livingston	S	12,289	13,159	2,158	2,804
Mid Scotland and Fife	Central Fife	S	10,754	11,920	2,288	2,003
Mid Scotland and Fife	North Tayside	S	3,243	18,281	3,175	10,697
Mid Scotland and Fife	Ochil	S	11,657	12,147	3,465	4,284
Mid Scotland and Fife	Perth	S	4,513	13,751	4,767	11,256
Mid Scotland and Fife	Stirling	S	9,827	10,447	3,693	8,081
North East Scotland	Aberdeen North	S	7,657	11,406	3,836	1,992
North East Scotland	Angus	S	5,032	15,686	3,799	7,443
North East Scotland	Banff and Buchan	S	3,136	16,031	2,617	5,501
North East Scotland	Dundee East	S	8,790	13,314	1,789	2,976
North East Scotland	Dundee West	S	9,009	10,955	2,517	1,787
North East Scotland	Gordon	S	2,276	14,650	12,588	5,348
West of Scotland	Cunning-hame North	S	9,247	9,295	1,810	5,466
Successful votes				265,412		
Unsuccessful votes			161,724		84,941	99,869

TOTAL REPRESENTATION

Constituency Votes by Major Party			L	S	D	C	
Region	Constituency		Lab	SNP	Lib Dem	Con	
Total constituency successful votes:			413,623	265,412	117,273	49,489	
Total constituency unsuccessful (ie. wasted) votes:			234,751	398,815	208,959	285,254	1,127,779
Total unsuccessful votes divided by 56 (number of regions for allocation to party lists)							20,139
Number of seats to be allocated to unsuccessful votes			12	20	10	14	
Therefore total seats:							
			37	21	11	4	73
Party list seats (Unsuccessful votes)			12	20	10	14	56
Grand Total:			**49**	**41**	**21**	**18**	**129**
Actual results:			46	47	16	17	126
Excluding Greens (2) and Margo MacDonald (1)							3
							129
Plus/Minus to actual results			+3	-6	+5	+1	

Note

The above is a simulation of the results of the Scottish Parliamentary election 2007 using the Total Representation system, "TR". Only constituency votes are used in order to restrict voting to one-ballot one-vote, thereby avoiding duplicating votes with two ballots: one constituency and the other regional.

First-past-the-post is used to allocate 73 seats and pure proportional representation is used to allocate the other 56 seats proportionally amongst the parties.

Chapter 8
THE UK, THE EUROPEAN PARLIAMENT AND ITS ELECTORAL SYSTEM

8.1   The project of European integration, as conceived originally by France and Germany, has been an attempt to foster harmony and avoid future wars in a continent scarred by historical conflict. But there has always been tension between this ideal and the view of other countries – such as the UK – which see the EU more as an alliance of independent states and are wary of intrusions that threaten their national way of life. Unfortunately the creation of the European Parliament (EP) has done little or nothing to resolve these tensions. In this chapter, I look at the problems with the EP, both as it relates to the UK and more generally to the rest of the European Community. I conclude by showing how the application of TR to elections to the EP could be employed to further the aim of bringing more coherence to its various parts.

8.2   It is not a revelation to say that the EP is dysfunctional, and since its creation has contributed more than any other European Union (EU) institution to its disrepute in the eyes of the English public. I say the English and not the British, because the EP has provided a platform for the Scots, the Irish and to a lesser degree to the Welsh to assert their desire for a separate identity from the English, while retaining their inclusion in Europe. In that respect it has also given a platform to the Green Party and, paradoxically, also to the anti-EU UK Independence Party (UKIP) to propagate their messages – an opportunity denied them under the political structure of the UK. In this way, the European Parliament has partly made up for the lack of adequate representation that is the main weakness of the UK's political structure.

8.3   But EP members – more than those of any other institution – are identified with extravagance and abuse of office, even though their expenses system was reformed in 2008 and is now reasonably transparent. But why, in the age of cheap flights and TGV trains, should the EP still need two centres: one in Brussels plus one in Strasbourg merely to serve the French national ego and French coffers? There is plenty of corruption associated with this cost. And yet despite the occasional flurry in the British media, it hardly elicits any reaction from the country as a whole, because the EP is so isolated from its electors. Without this link of the people to their representatives, the European Parliament is perceived to be a lofty and remote debating society.

8.4   To add to this unusual situation, legislation passed by the EP is subject to ratification by the UK Parliament. This adds to the uncertain and uneasy relationship between the two bodies. So resolutions by the EP, or for that matter by other institutions of the EU, are continually being questioned on the floor of the House of Commons. This happens even when EP Acts and EU directives are anchored on legislation previously ratified by the UK Parliament. The Convention of Human Rights itself does not escape this challenge. Westminster's scrutiny and understanding of European law and directives continues to be paltry.

8.5   The root of all these problems lies in the way the EU was set up. The Council of Ministers and other EU institutions, including its Parliament, were thought out first and imposed from the top down. This of course is typical of the way politics is conducted on the European continent, in contra-distinction to the way it evolved historically in England and later on in the UK as a whole. In continental Europe, it is the ideal that is sought, without enough attention being paid to the practical and the consensual, which is more valued in Britain. Consequently it was natural that the UK, having governed itself over the centuries without the need for a constitution, would suspect and resist proposals for a European Constitution. These clashes and the fact that the English have not embraced Europe wholeheartedly stem from this difference of approach. For many English people, the beginning of the European Common Market had overtones of the first stage of Bismarck's "Zollverein", which led in the 19th century to a federated and intensely nationalistic Germany.

8.6 Successive UK governments, especially in the latter half of the last century, have become more and more aware both of the shortcomings of the first-past-the-post system (FPTP) and the appeal of proportional representation (PR) as an alternative to or a cure for these shortcomings. Unfortunately, all the reforms offered and the experiments conducted in the UK have proved to be patching-up operations rather than root-and-branch solutions. Examples of these patching-up operations are the voting system in Northern Ireland, and devolution in Scotland and Wales. None contains the flexibility of constant self–adjustment automatically to evolving situations that TR could have provided. The negative aspects of these experiments have become even more apparent lately. In Northern Ireland, the separation of Catholic and Protestant populations – by way of managing social conflict – has become institutionalised and rigid, and will only perpetuate divisions along religious lines (a la Lebanon). In Scotland and Wales, these experiments have encouraged those who want separation from the UK, leaving the English electorate passive and alienated – turnout at recent elections has sunk to only sixty per cent.

8.7 So when it comes to the obvious clash of two sovereign authorities – the UK Parliament and the European Parliament – this has led some politicians and British representatives in the EU to seek in the new duality a compromise that would make up for the weakness of the FPTP system at home. They thought that a solution could be found by the two parliaments – the Westminster and the European – complementing each other, with the first based on FPTP and the second on PR. Such a scheme could have worked to the advantage of the UK. It could have provided the gradualism – so ingrained in the English character – that was needed for the country to experiment with PR at the margins, and not to plunge into drastic upheavals. Unfortunately, the use of multi-member constituencies in the electoral system for the EP has defeated the whole purpose of the combination. While the Westminster Parliament continues to lack full representation of every voter, the European Parliament lacks the constant link and accountability to the electorate in its multiple-member UK constituencies. The inadequacy of the voting system for the EP can easily be tested by asking people from all walks of life in England: who is their MEP (Member of the European Parliament)? Hardly anyone offers the correct answer. And even if they know who he/she is, how can they tell which individual MEP in their multi-member area is to be held individually answerable – and punishable in a subsequent election – in the way that he/she would be under the single-MP constituency regime?

8.8 A plausible response to this new situation would be to suggest treating the whole of the UK as one constituency for the purpose of EP elections, and applying a pure PR system. In this way, accountability would move from individual MPs to political parties. But this solution raises many difficulties. It would encourage even more the rise of extremist groups within the UK contingent in the EP. A better solution would be the use of TR based on single-member constituencies. This would limit the tendency toward extremism, and if handled gently by the UK, could bring about the integration of Europe – slowly – instead of using the big bang of a European Constitution imposed on all countries from above.

8.9 One possible argument against TR for the European Parliament is that the constituencies would become too big for any MEP to manage. This argument shows the misunderstanding of the duties of an MEP or for that matter any MP. It all arises out of the ambivalent concept of MPs' "surgeries", which in the UK have recently descended into the roles of citizens' advisory bureaus. But this function of a *surgery* should be limited to dealing with individual grievances only in as much as they represent a wider problem. The most important role of an MEP or an MP for that matter is to gauge the political temperature in their constituency in order to learn how to use their vote and exert pressure to represent that geographical area. In this way, policies are formulated or changed to reflect general trends, rather than responding to individual problems.

8.10 One can add to this the fact that many of the electorate of the small countries that have recently joined the EU from Eastern Europe feel that they are being forced to take on a new yoke of domination, having just shaken off their previous yoke in favour of national patriotism and an identity that they are now free and keen to display. They have not yet fully realised and grasped that 19th century nationalism is giving way to globalised ideologies and aspirations. The big, dominant countries of the EU – the UK, Germany and France – have to work harder to eradicate the Eastern European trauma of having been conquered first by German national socialism, and subsequently by the hegemony of Soviet Russian communism. The EU has to opt for gradualism. And while a constitution can only be imposed rigidly from above, TR works gradually from the bottom up. If such a gradual approach is adopted, it will propel the EP to become the senior arm of the EU and could over a period bring about the cohesion of the motley, disjointed parts that the EU has become. A real, representative EP will provide the glue that joins these pieces of the mosaic together. TR, through its application, can do just that, gently and gradually.

8.11 Under the current EP system – of PR in multi-member constituencies – there is no constant link between electors in a constituency and their MEP. Under TR, in contrast, members of a local constituency party would be able to nominate their candidate (whether or not he was a native citizen of that country), just as they do in the current Westminster system. But the current lack of a real bond between MEPs and electors means that Britain is able to persist in a stance which, wittingly or not, is sabotaging the very process of the future integration of Europe. It provides, in other words, an opportunity for the UK government to pay lip service to the idea of Europe, while actually remaining outside it. Germany and France, the backbone of an integrated Europe, have not been unaware of this manoeuvring but have been unable to overcome it; instead, they have tried to use palliatives, including referendums. But this has exploded in their faces – twice: first when France itself voted against the proposed Constitution devised by its own Giscard d'Estaing; and more recently when a minuscule number of Irish voters pierced the balloon of an alternative Treaty to replace that Constitution.

8.12 A referendum is an appealing and populist concept. Politicians often use it as a means to get out of difficult dilemmas. So in the UK too, politicians conveniently ask: why modify the electoral system? When big and controversial issues surface, they argue, we should resort to referendums and consult the entire population directly. The answer is that there is no tradition of referendums in Britain, unlike for example in Switzerland, where the idea is embedded in every citizen's political instinct. There, generations of people have grown up with them, because local communal issues are settled in this way. So when it comes to big, federal issues, Swiss people understand them, practise them and respect their results. It is different in the UK. Unless voting in referendums is made compulsory, or the outcome is made conditional on a high percentage vote (say 80%), referendums will fare no better than any other elections, where apathy is nowadays the rule. Even then, of course, the result of any referendum has to be ratified by the national parliament. What if it does not get ratified – and what therefore is the use of it? Why not go directly to parliament instead of the roundabout way of a referendum? The truth is that referendums in Britain are being promoted by the strident, dissenting minority, which could result in distorting the will of the majority. Even worse, in other contexts they can be a harmful tool in the hands of a government which tries to use them to stifle dissent by submitting issues to a referendum when it suits their purpose. So why not rely on home-grown representative democracy, and let parliament decide political issues? This is the way Britain has been used to conducting politics over centuries of parliamentary democracy.

8.13 In conclusion, referendums are no solution, certainly not for the UK. The late Clement Freud, the grandson of Sigmund Freud, and a former Liberal Party MP, recalled (in a BBC television interview with David Frost) that his English constituents did not understand why they were being asked to vote in a referendum on whether to stay in the European Common Market. After all, he said they told him, *"we voted for you to vote for us"*. Nothing sums up what representative democracy is all about better than this succinct sentence.

8.14 The theme that runs throughout the pages of this book is that TR is a concept and not a mathematical formula. It is adaptable and adjustable to the different circumstances of countries and communities. TR translates the express will of all the people into real practical, representative democracy. Adopting it for elections to the EP will also serve in time to integrate the populations of Europe and override narrow national sentiments. Every systemic institutional change in a social community impacts and causes changes in turn on other institutions in the same community. And systemic changes in the political structure of a community have more power than others because they directly affect the lives of every member of that community. I believe that applying TR in the way I have described in this book to all members of the EU in a uniform fashion will eventually help Europe in its aim and direction towards integration – without the need for a divisive Constitution.

Application of TR to the European Parliament

8.15 In today's world of globalisation and globalised ideologies, the social and political integration of the countries of the EU is bound to occur sooner or later. The UK cannot afford to stand aside. It will not be possible for it in the long run to exclude itself either from the Euro or from an integrated political structure. If the UK takes the lead and pioneers the use of TR for the EP, this will hasten its adoption everywhere, as it will come from the mother country of representative democracy. To do that it may need a special "dispensation" to use the UK as an experiment that will ultimately help the EU to democratise itself.

8.16 So how is TR to be applied in the context of the new Europe? When dealing with this application, we have to bear in mind that the different countries of the EU vary in the size of their populations between the smallest – Luxembourg – and the biggest – Germany. Notwithstanding this, the essence of applying TR to Europe in all its diversity is similar to the way that I have applied it to political structures as diverse in size of population and patterns of culture as the UK and Israel. Small modifications have to be introduced to avoid pitfalls in this respect in its application in Europe. After all, TR will have to be superimposed on national legislatures that are elected under a variety of systems as diametrically different as those of Holland and the UK.

8.17 The first and second chapters of this book dealt with the application of TR in general. Only a few minor modifications are needed to apply the same procedure to elections for the European Parliament, eventually in uniformity across all EU members. These modifications are needed because we are dealing here with culturally diverse populations living across national borders, inside which they follow different ideological concepts and political structures. We may need a generation or two for these populations to converge – as indeed they are slowly doing. Applying TR will help the process of convergence. But notwithstanding these modifications, two essential ingredients of TR have to be preserved. These are that all candidates and therefore future EP members have to start as constituency candidates, and that in any variations in the ratio between Constituency and Party members, the preponderance has to be of the former.

8.18 The usual ratio recommended in TR between Constituency and Party members of 80:20 to 70:0 has to be lowered further to 66:33. This is in line with that for a second-tier Legislature, as indeed the EP is (the ratio recommended for the British House of Lords is similar). So, in the case of Luxembourg, its 6 EP seats have to be divided 4:2 (Constituency : Party), and in the case of the UK it will be 48:24. An upwards adjustment in favour of Party MEPs should be employed where a clear-cut division is not possible. For instance, in the case of 7 seats, it remains still 5:2, but 11 seats is 7:4 and so on.

8.19 The present allocation of seats in the EP will have to continue until a fuller integration of the EU countries takes place. It is then that all constituencies will have electorates of an approximately similar number, thus enabling the whole of the EC to be treated as one country. Until then, the present formula adopted for the allocation of seats between the countries is adequate and reasonable. As convergence is achieved, so the size of the electorate across the countries can be adjusted.

PART THREE

ELECTORAL REFORM IN ISRAEL

Aharon Nathan

COMMENTARY
by Professor GIDEON DORON,
President of Israel's Political Science

In democracies, voting is not just about winning or losing. It is also about representation.

William Poundstone, the author of several popular science books published in 2008 another cutting-edge study: "Gaming the Vote: Why Elections Aren't Fair (and What We Can Do About It)".[1] Mr. Aharon Nathan, whose spirit and wisdom affects every page of this book, provides a precise answer to Poundstone's question: A new electoral scheme that makes the outcomes of elections more reasonable and hence, reflective and fair. Nathan offers a clever idea: a certain way of mixing the outcomes of both regional and national elections so that they will more accurately reflect voters' preferences. The resulting mix provides a sensible solution to two of democracy's main problems: ineffective governance and partial representation.

I began studying the intrinsic rational-choice oriented attributes of STV (Single transferrable Vote) in 1977. In several articles I have shown that STV is inconsistent and may even not be representative.[2] These are quite dramatic conclusions. They mean that in STV, this very interesting voting scheme, it is possible, amongst other things, for a voter to make an IRV (instant-runoff voting) candidate lose by ranking him higher.[3] Almost 30 years later, when I first heard about Nathan's voting scheme, I remembered the remarks John Stuart Mill made about another great invention of his times. That invention was accredited to Thomas Hare, the creator of STV. Indeed, Mill, in what should undoubtedly be considered his seminal work, "Considerations on Representative Government" (1862), expressed his opinion that Hare's system was "one of the greatest improvements in the theory and practice of voting methods".[4] I think no less of Nathan's invention.

What preconditions are required to make one of us produce meaningful creative ideas is still a mystery for us. Mr. Hare had a simple new idea. He proposed that instead of people actually going to vote twice or more until a decisive winner is obtained (as they do, for example, in the French presidential election where the scheme is called TSMR - Two Stage Majority Rule), under STV they are asked to express their preference order only once in relation to several candidates (first place, second place etc.) whose names appear on the ballot. Thus they save extra trips to the polling station. If their first placed candidate is not elected, their vote is not wasted: their second and even lower-placed choices are used to elect other candidates until all the winners are declared. Since then this voting scheme has been used in Ireland, Australia, Malta and some other places - but not in England.[5]

Very much like Mr. Hare, Mr. Nathan - a devoted liberal – has also presumably been driven by the need to solve a practical problem. Indeed, the origin of the specific problem is British. There, the plurality rule (the so-called "first-past-the-post") used in the context of single-member-district voting scheme, often produces extremely unfair consequences. It is well known that the British system tends to under-represent third parties when seats are allocated for the House of Commons. More specifically, the Liberal party continuously obtains fewer seats than indicated by its share of the popular votes.

Let us see how this works:

Suppose that the electoral competition is conducted in only two voting districts, where three parties are competing in each. Let us say that Party A represents Labour voters; Party B represents the Conservatives; and C the Liberals. For simplicity, let us also assume that in each district there are only 100 voters who are asked to cast votes for one of the three parties. In the first district, these 100 people voted as follows: A=51; B=0 and C=49. Party A was awarded the district's seat because it obtained an absolute majority of the votes. In the second district the outcomes were as follows: A=0; B=51 and C=49. In this district party B obtained the district's seat. Thus, while A and B got one seat each in parliament, C – the party that received almost as many votes as both A and B together – obtained no seats.

If you are a Liberal, if you aspire to fair play, or alternatively, if you believe that democratic voting schemes should reflect as accurately as possible people's preferences – then the above results should be very disturbing to you. So what can you do? How can you fix the problem so that the gap between voters' revealed preferences and the actual allocation of seats will be as small as possible?

The 19th century non-liberal approach to such issues had been to use "proportionality" as the prime criterion for a fair distribution of seats. (The term "liberal" is used here in its ideological sense to denote that "individuals" are the focus of society in counter-distinction to concentration on groups, classes, sectors etc.)

Let us see how this works:

Let us assume that in one voting district 100 voters are asked to cast their votes for one of eight competing candidates. The tally of their votes showed the following: A=20; B=19; C=12; D=10; E=10; F=10; G=10; and H=9. Under the plurality system (used in Great Britain and the United States) Candidate A would be declared the winner even if he/she only represents 20% of the voting body. Under this rule, it is possible that 80% of the voters in the district could be against "their" representative. By contrast, under PR (proportional representation), if the agreed-upon rule is that the first three who obtained the most votes will be elected, then candidates A, B and C – who between them hold 51% of the votes (that is, an absolute majority) – will be sent to Parliament. However, one can see that A received almost twice as many votes as C, but was rewarded, like C, with only one seat. Subsequently, various PR methods have calculated "the proportionality" differently, and indeed some are designed so as to award two seats to A and none to C. We can also see that under the PR used in multi-member districts, the outcomes will lead, most often, to coalition agreements[6].

The probability that the coalition to be formed will consist of the three winners – A, B and C – depends to a large degree, among other things, on the ideological location of these three parties. If for example, the three are located close to each other on a one-dimensional spectrum that extends, say, from Left to Right,[7] or if the three parties share a similar policy orientation[8], then not only does the likelihood of a coalition forming increase, but its chances of political survival improve dramatically.

But what if there are 15 parties in the parliament whose leaders know that in order to survive politically, they must differentiate themselves from other parties? In such a case, each member of the coalition may pull in his/her own direction, making maintenance and hence governance an extremely difficult task. This is the situation in Israel, where the country consists of one electoral zone that sends 120 members to the Knesset, and where at least 30 party lists are competing in each general election – and between 10 to 15 parties obtain representation.

David Ben Gurion, Israel's first prime minister and indeed, next to Theodore Herzel, the one who should be accredited with the title of the founding father of modern Israel, well understood the above problem. He understood how a fragmented political system could develop high tension between representation and governance, making the latter unable to meet its tasks. He therefore suggested, in the early 1950s, that the country move to a new system – a regional scheme consisting of 120 single-member voting districts, just like in England. He believed that this scheme would produce a two-party system that enables governance.

Even though Ben Gurion was considered a powerful politician and an effective prime minister, he could not command a majority among Knesset members that were willing to support his regional election idea and transform it into a law. The reasons being that:

A. most Knesset members live in both the Tel Aviv and Jerusalem areas;
B. the political base of most players is in the party;
C. and as individuals, they are not very attractive to the voters.

Hence, by supporting a regional bill they might, come the next election, find themselves out of the Knesset.

Several "regional" ideas have surfaced on the public agenda over the years. Nathan's Total Representation idea towers amongst them: it is simple, clever and politically feasible.

Let us see how Nathan's idea works:

Instead of having the entire country divided into 120 equal-in-size voting zones, under Nathan's system the country is divided into only 90 single-member districts. The rest of the seats are obtained by using PR over the remaining 30 seats. But where do those votes used to allocate the 30 remaining seats come from?

This question reflects the essence of Nathan's idea: the votes for the "extra" 30 seats come from voters whose most preferred candidate has not reached first place in the regions. As a result, "second place" candidates, and for that matter all those votes not cast for winners, are pulled into one account, tabulated and distributed. This provides a "second chance" for small parties to be represented. Moreover, it encourages accountability in the sense of having voters directly oversee the quality of the performance of their representatives. Indeed, this is an improvement over the current practice of having the Israeli voters choose a fixed list of names they hardly know from a "party list". Indeed, Nathan's scheme brings representatives closer to the voters. Finally, because of the "compensation" provided to non-winners, the chances of this system being politically feasible increase (i.e. being able to overcome the natural resistance of Knesset members to new ideas or policies).

Several simulations were conducted to find out what could have been the results if old election results had been tabulated in accordance with Nathan's scheme. Findings showed that under the "new" system, the three large Israeli parties of 2006 (Labor, Likud and Kadima) improve upon their sizes in the respective elections, while the small parties continue to stay alive and are represented. Hence, both democratic functions – representation and improved chances of stable governance – are obtained by the proposed voting scheme.

NOTES

1 See: Published in New York by Hill and Wang.
2 Doron, Gideon and Richard Kronick. 1977. "Single Transferable Vote: An Example of a Perverse Social choice Function." *American Journal of Political Science* 21:303-311. See Also, Doron, Gideon. 1979."The

Hare Voting System is Inconsistent," Political Studies, Vol. 2, No. 2, November,283-286. and Doron, Gideon. 1979. Is the Hare Voting Scheme Representative?" Journal of Politics, Vol. 41, July, 918-923

3 See Petrie, A.J. 1981. "Consistent and Inconsistent Voting System: Thoughts Prompted by Doron and Lakeman." *Political Studies*. 29.4: 622-625.

4 See: Published in New York by H. Holt. 1980.

5 Lakeman, Enid. 1974. *How Democracies Vote*. London: Faber and Faber.

6 See Rae, Douglas. 1971. *The political consequences of Electoral Laws*. New Haven: Yale University Press.

7 See Axelrod, Robert. 1970. *Conflict of Interest*. Chicago: Markham.

8 See de Swan, Abraham. 1973. *Coalition Politics and cabinet Formation*. Amsterdam: Elsevier.

Chapter 9
THE CRISIS OF DEMOCRACY IN ISRAEL

9.1 In the last commentary, Professor Doron explained the advantages of TR over other electoral systems, and its application to the specific circumstances of Israel. In this chapter, I give a general overview of the crisis that has been developing steadily in that country's democracy as a direct result of its system of pure proportional representation, which is ill-suited to resolving its festering problems. In the remaining chapters of Part Three, I look briefly at previous attempts to reform Israel's electoral regime (from the 1950s onwards), and at the work of the President's Commission on this subject, of which I myself was an active member from 2005 to 2007, and which ended up accepting the main components of TR. I then consider the Draft Law resulting from its recommendations which was tabled in the Knesset in April 2008 and suggest ways in which it could be improved to provide Israel with the most effective way of carrying out elections to suit its specific circumstances. I conclude with some simulations, analysis and opinions of the most recent elections of 2003, 2006 and 2009 to try to delineate future patterns of voting intentions.

9.2 Israeli society is tribally and ethnically divided, because it is made up of a multiplicity of groups of Jewish immigrants grafted on to a sizeable Arab minority. Far from giving space to every strand of society, PR has created a majority that disregards minorities – Jewish and Arab alike. What happened in the Knesset (parliament) was that the "tribal" Jewish groups gradually organised themselves into factions on a communal or religious basis, and used their leverage to extract benefits for their groupings. The Arab Muslim parties/factions – in stark contrast to the Arab Druze community - then isolated themselves and were unable to use the leverage of their numbers to gain influence in a political arena that was wide open to them. This led to frustration among their electors, who began to develop resentment against the state. The Druze, who integrated themselves into the big parties, have done better in taking advantage of this open door to represent – in fact to over-represent – their community.

9.3 Putting aside these special circumstances for a moment, Israel also faces the same crisis in the governance of its polity as other democracies throughout the world. These nations are being forced to examine their electoral systems because of the discontent and disconnect between citizens and their representatives. The search for new, better electoral systems has even reached the mother of parliaments in the UK. As we have already seen, changes have been introduced to accommodate the Scottish Parliament and the European Parliament. New or modified systems have also been introduced in countries as far apart as Eastern Europe and New Zealand. Broadly speaking, both major groups of systems – i.e. PR and constituency FPTP – are under pressure as a result of the many similar factors that I highlighted in Part One. This disconnect between the people and their representatives is widening. I believe no amount of education of citizens or preaching to politicians can drastically change this. Only **institutionalised, systemic reforms** can produce changes in the attitudes of the citizenry by engaging them in such a way that they feel that their votes and their individual participation in the electoral process count and endure thereafter.

9.4 To return specifically to the Israeli situation: on the face of it, under PR, all citizens' votes theoretically count. However, the manipulative behaviour of the centralised and remote political parties robs ordinary voters – especially in the peripheries and among minorities – of political participation and influence over these parties. This makes them feel frustrated and helpless; hence the need to find remedies.

9.5 However, instead of concentrating on core systemic changes, some political scientists in Israel are exhorting political leaders to correct their behaviour and adhere to higher standards of morality and professional ethics. The celebrated Professor Yeheskiel Dror's (Hebrew University) "Letter to A Jewish Zionist Leader" is a notable example. It is wise and laudable. But so too were the exhortations of Plato on the qualities of the Ruler. Unfortunately, we are living in a Machiavellian world where fear, not love, is the engine and the tool of leaders. Morality and fair behaviour are cultural attributes that grow gradually, gaining acceptance by societies as they develop towards uniformity and cohesion. Unfortunately, the opposite is happening. We find countries all over the world suffering from divisions and fissures in their societies. And nowhere are these centrifugal forces more evident than in Israel.

9.6 As an idealist in my younger days, I found myself in absolute agreement with the sentiments of Professor Dror's letter. But having left the protective warmth of academia and stepped out into the real world of power, greed and living for the day, I found myself amongst people poor in spirit and weak in the flesh. That is why I concluded that the only way to get better leaders is by instituting systems that compel them to be good for their own selfish interests, while devising strict enduring systemic supervision over them.

9.7 You cannot dictate moral or ethical behaviour to people or politicians, but you *can* legislate for it – and then only if you back it by sanctions. In a democracy, the voter is the only effective brake on corrupt rulers. This is the essence of Karl Popper's *The Open Society and its Enemies*. When published in 1945, this book was hailed as the last word in defending the concept of freedom of the individual and the definition of liberal democracy, because its main theme was the elasticity to change – hence "Open", i.e. "open-ended". The shackles of religious rigidity and philosophical imperatives are replaced by Popper's alternative of an automatic engine of continuing change to preserve the ideals and the cohesion of society.

9.8 The scourge of fanatical religious movements that use terror and emotion rather than reason and debate to propagate their views and coerce others to follow their lead has also created problems inside the legal frameworks of many countries. The human rights of individual fanatics are precariously balanced against the existential rights of society. The human rights movements grew against the social and political background of the 19th and early 20th centuries in the West. John Stewart Mill was trying to balance the freedom of the individual against the growing power of society. To some people today, it looks as if the pendulum has swung too far in favour of the individual and the time has come to redress that by adjusting this pendulum back to the centre to restore balance.

9.9 In Israel, while putting the instability of government at the centre of the argument, people tend to overlook what is happening to the third arm of the state, the Judiciary. The emancipation of our "Jewish Tribes" from the Diaspora brought about a breakdown in traditional Jewish values and sharpened the divide between the religious and the secular. With the growing weakness of the Legislature (the Knesset or parliament) and the incessant preoccupation of the Executive with pressing security issues of life and death, it has been left to the Judiciary to determine and implement normative constitutional and moral issues, while forgetting that they are essentially there to apply the law, not to make it; in other words, to judge the decisions of the first, sovereign arm of the state – the direct representative of the people – on these matters. It is not fair to blame the Supreme Court judges when a spineless Knesset forces them to legislate from the bench. In the eyes of large sections of society in Israel, these judges are making, not applying, the law.

9.10 Moreover, unfortunately, instead of drawing on centuries of Jewish traditions, where legal justice and social justice converged into the Talmudic concepts of *Tsedek* and *Tsedaka* (Justice and Equity), judges in Israel have adopted the modern mantras of human rights as defined and dictated, not by the present circumstances and the past traditions of the people that any parliament should always follow, but by the philosophical reasoning of judges who take their lead from the United Nations and from continental Europe. The Common Law practice inherited from the British Mandate is not alien to Israel's own Talmudic procedures. Recently, there has been a lively debate in the Anglo-Saxon world about how to find an accommodation with the overpowering Convention on Human Rights that comes from continental Europe. Where does Israel stand vis-à-vis all this? Instead of aligning itself with the legal base rooted in its inherited English Common Law, we find its judges giving a new interpretations of a Basic Law on human rights of the early 1990s, which is being transformed in the hands of the Supreme Court into "the Constitution." Here, the amorphous concept of "Dignity" has taken precedence over wider interpretations of truth, equity and justice rooted in Talmudic and Common Law precedents.

9.11 And when the lives of innocent people are set against the rights of individuals who seem hell-bent on destroying them, human rights is fast becoming in the eyes of sections of the citizenry a pernicious "new religion" not to be questioned, leaving many ordinary Israelis numbed and confused. The conclusion, therefore, is that reform is needed here as well as in the other two arms of the state. And the only arm that has the power to reform them is the Knesset, as the repository of the sovereignty of the nation. **But to start doing that, it needs first to reform itself.**

9.12 Problems in Israel echo what is happening in the old, established democracies. They are more acute in Israel because of the special, precarious coexistence with its Arab neighbours and its own Arab minority, which makes up 20% of its population. Israel's very existence is in danger because of outside pressures and internal divisions. It cannot afford the luxury that other nations enjoy of letting events create and shape their own solutions. It has to be more proactive. Ordinary citizens feel helpless at what they perceive to be an unholy alliance of academia, the political establishment and a social elite who are intent on preserving the status quo. It was this background that in 2005 prompted the President of Israel to establish a public commission to resolve this acute problem, which is set out in the next few chapters.

9.13 Israel's democracy is not new, even if its practice is only 60 years old. Most of its citizens came either from the West, where they experienced open, direct democracy, or from the East, where they themselves practised communal democracy centred on the synagogues and institutions they established, independent of the polities of their host countries. The myth – inadvertently fostered by publicists and some academics – that Oriental Jews have no understanding of democracy has gradually created oligarchic walls behind which the European/Ashkenazi Jews remain mainly in charge of the political establishment. Until recently immigrants from the East despaired at being unable to pierce these barriers; they sought prominence in the fields of finance, services and industry. They succeeded – and the more successful of them cast aside their ambitions of political responsibility, leaving the field wide open to community religious leaders to assume political leadership among their peoples. Hence the increasing power of religious parties supported by Oriental Jews. Under the pure PR system, these parties, in alliance with traditional Western Jewish ultra-orthodox factions, have become pivotal in holding the balance of political power and dictating the formation of coalition governments.

9.14   And while the old political establishment of the 1950s -- reinforced by an increasing supply of ex-army generals – is ageing, the second tier of mainly Oriental and some Russian Jews, is coming of age to fight for its rightful place in the national arena. Messrs Katsav, the Shetreets, Amir Perets and Silvan Shalom are obvious examples of new national leaders emerging from Oriental communities, and Sharanski and Avigdor Lieberman from the Russian one. Israel should delight in and celebrate this trend, as it will consolidate, cement and give cohesion to a revitalised Jewish society. Systemic tools are needed to speed up this process, while at the same time finding a place and rationale for the Arab minorities to integrate into it. The TR system can propel and sustain this process, building political leadership from the grass roots, from the bottom up.

9.15   In seeking a medicine for the general malaise that is enveloping and frustrating the Israeli public, the old leaders are looking at political realities from a different angle and trying to remedy the problem from the opposite direction – i.e. from the top down. They are more concerned with the stability of the government than the cohesion of the Legislature. The Knesset is disunited and fragmented into many factions: ideological, theological, ethnic – and individuals who display downright egotistical self-interest. It seems to escape party leaders that the reason they have unstable governments is because they have a fragmented Knesset, where all factions claim divine right, not least amongst them the secular.

9.16 Recent opinion polls have pointed to a desire among Israelis for a strong leader. In the simplistic nature of opinion polling, the public cannot be specific about which leader they want for which policies. The reason for this confusion is that the public has not been able to focus on clear policies or ideologies from the big parties, because in their struggle to survive in coalitions, these have tended to converge and water down their convictions to accommodate each other. As a result, the leaders of the main three parties – Sharon, Shimon Peres, Ehud Barak and Netanyahu – are lumped together in the public mind without distinction as a political establishment that is only interested in power and is therefore jointly responsible for the prevailing malaise. The government and the Knesset are certainly perceived by the public to be one entity. So even unity coalitions have not been functioning properly, because there has been an absence of real alternatives in the shape of realistic oppositions that hold the government relentlessly to account. As a result, the public is confused, looking in vain for an elusive alternative, a strong leader, a Ben Gurion, an executive president. This is the reason for the popularity of the presidential image of Sharon and his Kadima Party, which was a patching together of old politicians from the left and the right.

9.17 However, the TR system is designed to produce a genuine, effective, stable opposition to a stable government. In this way, with a leader in the Knesset marshalling a strong opposition, the public can distinguish alternative policies, an alternative government and an alternative leader through parliamentary debates rather than through the sensationalist media. Democracy is not only about the power of the majority, but also about the freedom of legitimate minority dissent.

9.18 Therefore, those who now advocate a change to a presidential system are looking to cure only the secondary infection of the illness. It is the instability inherent in the structure of the Knesset that is causing the instability of the government and depriving the nation of a real opposition, underpinning a real democracy. Israel has therefore to give priority to electoral reform and then see whether it still needs to follow it with presidential government. Moreover, changing to such a system would involve the repeal and replacement of the two existing constitutional Basic Laws of the President and the Government. This is a tall order, which amounts to dismantling the state and rebuilding it anew. Why is such a sledgehammer needed when the same objective might be achieved by a tuning screwdriver provided by TR? Moreover, a strong Knesset born of TR will be needed even more under a presidential executive, should this be favoured and established. TR is not an alternative to such a system; rather it is – both in academic theoretical terms and against the background of Israel's political realities – a prerequisite for initiating it and setting it up. In other words, the TR horse is needed to pull the presidential cart. Let us put the horse in front of the cart and see if it is needed at all.

9.19 In conclusion, the crisis of democracy in Israel can be addressed by specific, straightforward solutions. Such solutions have to be **systemic structural ones at the heart of which is TR**. Any general exhortation to higher standards in public life will fall on the deaf ears of politicians with vested interests and only increase the confusion and disillusion of ordinary citizens. Apart from the problems of the security of state borders and the country's vulnerability to radicalised Muslims inside Israel, ordinary citizens are in fact engaged by the normal necessities of their daily lives. It is unrealistic to expect these people to find the solutions we are looking for themselves. If they want a strong leader, it is because they need one to allow them to get on with their lives. If we encourage our citizens towards mass protests or civil disobedience of any magnitude, as some writers advocate in order to put pressure on the present national leadership, we will not be able to contain them and will inevitably end up with some form of civil strife or even violence. Solutions have to be initiated, not decided, from above, and the President's Commission has taken an active role in helping the political leadership by offering them clearly defined, practical and workable solutions.

9.20 Professor Gideon Doron, echoing J.S. Mill's comment on Thomas Hare's STV model, has described TR as a breakthrough in the theory and practice of representative democracy. Political scientists will readily see the powerful argument of TR as reflecting voters' preferences. Moreover, its application to the special situation of Israel will contribute to solving the four major problems of the country, which are: 1) creating a personal bond between the elector and the elected; 2) fusing the Jewish tribal communities into a national entity; 3) integrating the Arab minorities into the body politic; and 4) helping to subordinate sectional to national interests, thus drawing politics towards the centre, and away from extremism, whether Jewish or Arab.

Chapter 10
THE KNESSET: ATTEMPTS AT REFORM FROM THE 1950s ONWARDS

10.1 In this chapter, I highlight more specifically the deficiencies in Israel's electoral arrangements that have contributed to widespread public apathy about politics and depressingly low turnouts at elections. I do this by sketching the history of previous attempts at reform from the 1950s up until the present day. I then give recommendations as to how the major parties and other supporters of reform should go about the process of achieving a better electoral system. Simulations follow in a later chapter in order to direct our attention to the outcomes that are anticipated to flow from putting TR to work.

10.2 As explained in Chapter Nine, the political system in Israel is at odds with the present realities not only of its political life, but also of its social and cultural life. The desire to create cohesion and reconciliation among the tribal and ethnic elements of its population is impeded by the pure PR system that sustains and entrenches them. When conceived and introduced, it fitted the pre-state Jewish political framework of the time. That was an era when leaders thought that PR would reconcile and unite the different social and cultural segments of countries. Holland in 1917 was a case in point, when PR was designed to bring together socialist seculars with Catholics, Lutherans and Calvinists. There, the underlying consensus was built on a constitutional monarchy. In the case of the future Jewish state, it was built on the Zionist dream. But this PR system is now utterly out of date. Everybody says so, but for a variety of reasons, and mainly because of vested interests, reform is pushed aside. The delay is, however, becoming manifestly harmful to the future stability of the country and to the ability of its government to function. Most important of all, it paralyses every effort or initiative to bring about peace with the Palestinians. To achieve peace, a strong and stable government is needed, backed by a stable majority in the Knesset – and not resting on fluid coalitions of small, self-serving, factional parties within it. The root of the problem lies in PR, which breeds small parties based on narrow, sectional interests that tend to hijack the political agenda – causing major national issues to be pushed aside.

10.3 There have been previous attempts at reform. In the 1950s, Ben-Gurion, the father of the Israeli state and its first prime minister, tried to change the system. Although he had some eminent young supporters (Moshe Dayan, Shimon Peres, Yitzhak Navon and others) he was defeated by his party's old guard and he failed. Once his idea was rejected, it was very difficult to revive its fortunes. Notable amongst leaders who tried much later to introduce a regional system was Mr Gad Yaacobi, a senior member of the Labour Party. His reform attempts in the 1980s might have succeeded had they not collided by the interest of the then-prime minister, Yitzhak Shamir, who was far more anxious to preserve his coalition.

10.4 Then there was talk of changing over to a sweeping presidential system – but this failed to gather enough support. So a novel and rather clumsy scheme was devised to bestow presidential power on the prime minister through the back door. The passage of this controversial reform was spurred by a three-month-long government crisis in the spring of 1990, during which Israelis looked on in horror as MKs (Members of the Knesset, the parliament) indulged in an unseemly public display of floor-crossing and bargaining, with political parties and individual MKs scrambling for place, preferment and political advantage. In 1992, the pressure of public opinion led to a change in the Basic (constitutional) Law. From then on, a separate election for prime minister would be held in addition to the ballot for the Knesset. In some countries with a presidential system, this division of the sovereign authority of the people works: in France, for example, or in the USA. But the Israeli prime minister – although popularly elected – would still depend on a parliamentary vote of confidence. This was the seed of the idea's destruction, because a clash was created between two sovereign authorities: directly elected prime minister and directly elected Knesset.

10.5 The new system was applied three times -- in the 1996 and 1999 general elections and in the February 2001 by-election in which Ariel Sharon defeated Ehud Barak of Labour – after which it became clear that this particular reform would not work, and the law was repealed. In the general election for the 16th Knesset in 2003, the country reverted to its old system of pure proportional representation. Instead of separate ballots for prime minister and political party, voters were again given only one ballot for political party – and the leader of the party that was able to put together a majority coalition in the Knesset (not necessarily the biggest party) was to become the prime minister. The upshot was that Israel was back to a PR system which was clearly harmful to the objective of forming a government capable of taking decisive measures at home and of speaking with a powerful voice abroad.

10.6 It is important to study this episode in detail because it exposes the disjointed nature of the debate among Israeli academics and politicians on the subject of electoral reform. This debate often focuses on the problem of the stability of government in isolation, without regard to its interaction with the specific social and cultural environment of the country. This interaction needs to be understood, along with a consideration of how people are actually represented. It is surprising that the eminent professors involved in the initiation and formulation of this law on direct election of the prime minister were unable to foresee the consequences of its application. TR, simple as it is, takes care of the balance between stability and representation. Applying it also obviates the need for electoral thresholds as a means of achieving stability, and – more importantly – renders the use of corrupt pre-election party primaries redundant.

10.7 In the last three decades, the Knesset has been dominated by two major ideological groupings, respectively to the left and right of centre. Until recently at least, one could say that the left-wing was represented by Labour, and the right-wing by Likud. They were very evenly matched. Recently, splinter groups from each have broken away to form the Kadima Party – but this was essentially another right-of-centre grouping owing to the preponderance of ex-

Likud members. It was more a New Likud than a new party. Sharon and then Olmert tried to strengthen within Kadima the influence of balancing left-of-centre elements. But it was only Tsipi Livni in the last election of 2009 who was able to project Kadima as a separate, third big party by attracting secular and feminist votes. It then veered so much to the left that it crossed the centre to become a New Left Party. Only time will tell whether the powerful right-wing faction within Kadima will succeed in pushing it back to its roots, choose to secede and start a separate faction, or simply rejoin Likud. This would leave Kadima to replace the Labour Party or to be absorbed in it.

10.8 So that will take Israeli politics back to where it was before: with two parties Labour (or Kadima) on the left and Likud on the right. These two groupings will continue to alternate in power, forming precarious minority governments, gathering around them shifting coalitions of small minority parties whose support they need to hang on to office. As they continue to splinter, they will become too weak to last the full four-year terms of parliament, as has indeed been the case for two generations.

10.9 Even putting the national imperative to one side, it is still in the interests of both of these groupings to introduce changes to the electoral system which would strengthen their presence. Moving over to TR might guarantee them continued existence as alternative parties of government, representing two wider ideological movements. They still have just about enough power to pilot the successful introduction of this system through the Knesset on their own. The combined strength of Kadima, Labour and Likud in the last Knesset of 2006 amounted to 60 out of 120 seats. In the present Knesset of 2009 that figure is 68. If TR is adopted, it could preserve and improve their respective positions, as the new electoral regime would eventually force many of the small factional groupings to align themselves with one major party or another. However, the medium-sized parties with full national programmes could still continue to exist and garner strength, hoping to join a government, especially as TR does not altogether eliminate the possibility of coalition governments, but only minimises the likelihood of one occurring.

10.10 Therefore, the movement towards the proposed TR electoral system in Israel must be accompanied by a joint campaign by the two groupings (in other words, the three big parties) to explain to the supporters of the smaller parties or political factions – and of course to the country at large – that the new system is democratic and fair, and, above all, continues to guarantee representation to all sections of the citizenry. They must also explain that the door is still open for medium-sized parties or movements to grow into major parties in the future by having their voices clearly and continuously heard through representation in the Knesset – which the new system allows. And last but by no means least, in the way it is constructed the new system must meet the specific challenge of a population made up of disparate Jewish religious and cultural factions living together with a sizeable Arab minority. It should seek to integrate the Arab and the ultra-orthodox, religious Jewish voters into the body politic of the country through interdependence of Arabs on Jewish votes to a degree in certain constituencies – and vice-versa. Through its operation, TR helps to subordinate sectional interests to national interests, and it draws politics towards the centre, away from extremism.

10.11 The main political groups must also take the trouble to demolish an unhelpful idea which is particularly strong in Israel: that the will of the voters has to be translated absolutely and proportionately into seats. This, of course, is the principle behind PR and its derivatives. This principle has become so powerful that even when a hybrid method of election is attempted, mathematical calculations and formulas are to circumvent this and ensure that the final result in number of seats somehow corresponds or comes near enough to the proportionality of PR. (The top-up mechanism in AMS in Scotland is a good example of this). But theoreticians and political scientists forget that it is these convoluted formulas that put voters off: they fail to understand them and feel baffled and alienated. The disconnect between politicians and people in some democracies is no doubt at least partly the result of this problem. And for all its lofty representational ambition, Israel's pure PR system is actually leaving about 40% of the electorate unrepresented, since roughly that proportion of people are not even bothering to vote.

10.12 Over the last five years, I have been fortunate to join debates about all these issues with many colleagues from different walks of life in Israel – and to offer tentative solutions. These circumstances have provided me with a platform to expound and advocate the principles of TR. My meeting with Mr Isaac Nazarian, the founder and now the President of the Citizens' Empowerment Centre in Israel (CECI), provided me with this opportunity. He asked me to join the Board of Governors of CECI. At about the same time, the President of Israel graciously appointed me member of a Commission which was examining government and governance in Israel. These two appointments gave me the forum and the platform to spread the principles of TR in Israel. Early on, I was also most fortunate to meet Professor Gideon Doron, the president of Israel's Political Science Association and one-time strategic advisor to Prime Minister Yitzhak Rabin. Professor Doron immediately understood and embraced the principles of TR. His support and guidance were invaluable in opening doors for me and added weight to my contribution to the President's Commission. After in-depth deliberations over some two years, the Commission produced its final report, recommending most of the principles of TR: i.e to use one vote per person to elect a parliament made up of regional members and party members. What then remained for the supporters of TR was to lobby the Knesset to accept the recommendations of the report and to modify them further by adopting the system's third principle: the use of single-member, rather than multi-member constituencies. In 2008, a Draft Law, a "White Paper", along these lines was tabled in the Knesset by senior MKs (Members of Knesset) representing the three major parties: Kadima, Likud and Labour. But the sudden dissolution of the Knesset and the new elections of 2009 threw this Draft Law out by default, thus forcing us once again to lobby for its re-tabling in the new Knesset.

10.13 Therefore, the best way to describe the circumstances that may at last lead Israel to change its electoral system is to tell the story of the President's Commission, and to analyse the Draft Law subsequently tabled in the Knesset, while also pointing out its shortcomings in the hope that these will be corrected before it is re-tabled again. It will be interesting for countries who are engaged in reassessing their electoral systems, especially the young democracies of Eastern Europe, to study in more detail than the scope of this book allows the development and conclusion of this story. Israel may yet prove to be a good laboratory and a testing ground for innovations in systems of government.

Chapter 11

THE PRESIDENT OF ISRAEL'S COMMISSION FOR EXAMINING THE STRUCTURE OF GOVERNMENT AND GOVERNANCE IN ISRAEL (2005-2007)

11.1 On February 17th 2003, at the opening session of the 16th Knesset, the President of Israel, Mr. Moshe Katsav, stated: "I call for the establishment of a Public National Commission consisting of public figures and experts that will discuss and recommend reforms concerning the structure of government." In this chapter, I will try to give a bird's eye view of the deliberations of this Commission and its final report. The deliberations covered almost every aspect of debates about electoral systems and related fields of governance. The rec ords of the minutes and submissions have been preserved and could be invaluable for future students of this subject.

11.2 The Citizens' Empowerment Centre in Israel (CECI), spearheaded the formation of this Commission, and on September 25th 2005, the President's Commission for Examining the Government and Governance of Israel was established under the chairmanship of Professor Menachem Megidor, president of the Hebrew University of Jerusalem. Upon delivering its mandate, President Moshe Katsav said:

- *"I request that you analyse carefully the Israeli government structure, to examine the suitability of every alternative to the Israeli reality and the needs of the country, and to try to create a proposal that will assure increased power, stability, and effectiveness. I intend to submit these proposals to the Knesset and the cabinet."* The President went on to say: *"Israeli democracy has, in my view, succeeded through the years to withstand the test of time, despite the many upheavals...the mounting elitism of the power structure can undermine the strength of the democracy more than security threats...*

- *Power instability can cause more extensive damage to the strength of the democracy. Despite it having withstood the trials of time, I think that power instability also prevents governments from properly fulfilling their tasks. If a recently elected government is immediately threatened by further elections, it is unable to fulfil its task properly...*

- *I am concerned with the decline of the status of the Knesset -- precisely because I appreciate that it is primary among power structures, and a sovereign authority. For that reason I am much concerned with and regret its negative public image.*

- *I am also concerned with the fact that the Executive authority has almost unlimited power over the Legislative branch. It is able to do whatever it wishes with the Knesset, while the Knesset, the Legislative branch, has developed an intolerant dependency on the Judicial branch. They apply for court rulings for every little thing, while such decisions should have been reached in the Knesset itself without this insufferable dependency.*

- *I know there has been a lot of talk about changing the electoral system, and I have my opinion on the subject, though I will not voice it here. This issue must be examined versus the consideration and the consequences of such change. The national and state interests must be weighed. The question when, if at all, the cultural, sectional and regional interests may be preferred over the national interests must be answered.*

- *I beseech you to analyse carefully the Israeli government structure to examine the suitability of every alternative to the Israeli reality and the needs of the country, to try and create a proposal that will assure increased power stability and effectiveness, and to propose a structure that would ensure meeting the challenges which confront the state of Israel in our generation.*

- *I intend to submit these proposals to the Knesset and the cabinet and for public discussion, and I hope that the Commission's recommendations will gain the widest possible acceptance"*

11.3 I have quoted the President's statement at length, as it authoritatively encapsulated the weaknesses of Israel's political structure that the Commission was given the task of grappling with. After months of deliberations, its final report was handed to the President on 1st January 2007; he in turn presented it – as he had promised – to the Speaker of the Knesset and the prime minister.

In the aftermath of the Second Lebanon War of 2006, its findings, conclusions and recommendations were becoming more urgent and relevant.

11.4 To carry weight with the public, such a report had to take a clear-cut and unified approach on the issue of how to bring about an effective and representative Knesset and a stable government. Structural recommendations based on changes to the electoral system and changes in the Knesset and government needed to be presented in a clear, straightforward package for the public to judge them. I offered the Commission my submission for the electoral reform part of the package. I stressed that I believed that no reform would endure and no system would be accepted by the electorate in Israel unless it was anchored and based on "Single Vote, Single Ballot, Single Constituency". Explaining the case for TR to the members of the Commission, I put it to them that it was simply the same Westminster system which had been functioning successfully for hundreds of years in its native Britain – but modified and adapted to the social and political needs of Israel. Its adoption by the Knesset would avoid forays into new, untested grounds which had given rise to the debacle of the direct election of the prime minister.

11.5 Unfortunately, instead of sticking to the guidance of its mandate for clear recommendations, the Commission cast its net so wide that it lost focus in the process. Much time was wasted on reviving the debate about a presidential versus a parliamentary system, especially amongst the academic members. This was largely caused by the way the sub-committees were divided. Instead of there being just one committee discussing electoral reform, responsibility for this basic issue was spread between three sub-committees. This was bound to result in divergent views that Commission Chairman Professor Megidor, a clear-thinking physicist, found hard to reconcile.

11.6 Whatever its value to students of political science and government, this long and hard-fought debate seemed to me to be irrelevant and unnecessary in the context of the Commission's terms of reference. In the heat of the battle raging between the sub-committees, the protagonists forgot a fact that they should have understood: the two examples *par excellence* of the presidential and parliamentary systems – the USA and the UK respectively – both draw on the same theoretical background of John Locke, Montesquieu etc. The essence of both systems is representation of the people, and a government that is subject to checks and balances.

11.7 The Commission was also sidetracked into trying to find a system that would produce a strong leader, which is what they believed – rightly – the public was clamouring for. But why did they ignore the fact that the powers of the British prime minister actually exceed those of the US President? Israel's prime minister only lacks power because he/she lacks solid parliamentary backing. Professor Doron, despite his passion for a presidential system for Israel, was aware of the sterility of concentrating on the label rather than the content. In collaboration together we suggested a solution based on a strengthened parliamentary system which would in turn be based on the internal reform of the parties. Party cohesion would be consolidated, thus giving more stability to the Knesset and the government. I believe that, irrespective of the recommendations of the Commission, this Doron/Nathan solution (see Chapter Twelve below) will be the one that both the public and the Knesset will eventually go for – but only after reform of the electoral system.

11.8 Another way in which the Commission became sidetracked was in debates on how to reach recommendations that would satisfy and be acceptable to politicians. This was further complicated by some members fighting for their own narrow political affiliation, instead of grappling with the whole spectrum of party political platforms. This was, of course, the wrong approach to the issues, because suddenly we found ourselves seeing things from the point of view of a 3,000-strong political establishment, rather than minding the interests of 3,000,000 electors. It is, after all, these last who will ultimately push for and force the Knesset to legislate for an electoral system that guarantees direct elections of individual members of the Knesset who can be directly held accountable to their constituents. And it was this element of accountability that the President stressed most in his brief.

11.9 From my perspective as a member of the Commission, I had to contend with yet another tug-of-war on electoral reform, between academic advocates who favoured proportional representation at all costs, and others who pushed for the regional or constituency principle. And the compositional mix of the membership did not help us converge. The blunt, black-and-white views of army ex-generals and the legalistic argumentation of ex-senior judges clashed with the "on-the-one-hand-and-on-the-other" style of the 33 senior professors who were members of the Commission. And all this debate was often conducted in a very theoretical fashion – with less emphasis on what was suitable for the specific conditions of Israel's society and its population mix.

11.10 In the end, the central message dawned on my colleagues in the Commission that in choosing an electoral system, we should not only aim for the best in theory, but also aim for what was most suitable to answer the basic problems facing Israel today. These problems are: a fragmented Knesset; unstable coalitions; a failure to draw our Jewish tribes together; and, above all, a failure to integrate our minorities – Arabs and extreme orthodox Jews – into the mainstream of our political and social life. We have to contend with the combination of all four problems when reforming the PR system that has sharpened and sustained the divisions in the country. A structural systemic change in Israel can only endure if it takes account of all these problems together.

11.11 The main purpose of the President's Commission was to find an alternative to proportional representation. My presentation of TR as an alternative provoked many reactions in the Commission, some positive and supportive, others negative and hostile. Zeev Segal, a notable professor of law at Tel Aviv University, told the Commission that TR represented new thinking because it took care of the losers, which was its innovative approach. Thus he hit on of the essence of the concept of compensation in TR: i.e allowing the voices of voters who did not manage to win seats for their candidates still to be represented in the final outcome of the election (albeit with lesser weight) – thus bringing all voters by proxy inside the sovereign tent of parliament.

11.12 Prof Doron, on the centre-left, Mr Yoash Tsidon Chatto, on the centre-right, and Mr Jamal Majadle, a member of the Commission who provided the Israeli Arab perspective, never wavered in their support for TR and kept its caravan on the road throughout. On the other hand, Professor Naomi Chazan, the chairman of a sub-committee, led many members of the Commission in fighting tooth-and-nail for preserving the status quo of pure PR. Belonging to the Meretz Party, a splinter Labour group in the Knesset, it was obvious that her narrow interest in its independent survival took precedence over her better academic judgement. In the end, she lost the battle of ideas and – together with a few of her supporters in the Commission – refused to sign the final report.

11.13 Professor Kaniel of the Hebrew University sought a solution in some mathematical formula based on the modified D'Hondt formula. He could not be convinced that none of the Commission members, let alone the general public, could fathom its intricacies. Professor Brichta of Haifa University, on the other hand, produced a challenging but clear and readable alternative to TR. He claimed that TR did not accurately translate the results of the elections into seats in the Knesset. He said that Israel was a sectarian and divided society and the new system needed to reflect this pluralism. He further assumed that a reform that took the representation of small parties out of the Knesset could not recruit their present MKs to support TR and would therefore be doomed – or if it succeeded, it would drive them underground, on to the streets and squares outside. But where does Professor Brichta's point lead him? He could not see that he was in fact negating the very purpose of setting up the Commission. The main purpose of the President's Commission was to find an alternative to PR, not to find new tools to confirm its validity. Moreover, instead of healing the division in search of unity, his proposals sought to perpetuate them. With the final report leaning to a great degree to the principles of TR, Professor Brichta too ended up refusing to sign it.

11.14 It was obvious that Professor Megidor, the Commission chairman, was torn between the two camps of the TR and PR systems. Shimon Shetreet, Professor of Law and a brilliant biblical scholar, mild in manner and conciliatory in tone, recommended a compromise composite recommendation. Fatigue set in, and the chairman of the Commission, in his final report on electoral reform, accepted the compromise, which is basically a modified version of TR, but opting for multi-member instead of single-member constituencies. Thus he confirmed the main principle of TR: i.e. to elect the candidate and his/her party with one vote, using one ballot paper. Together with the majority of other members, I signed with alacrity, knowing full well that the next stage – sooner rather than later – would be to fight to change the multi-member constituencies to single-member ones.

11.15 It is incredible that it escaped those who helped the chairman to write his conclusions that they missed the central requirement of the President's brief and the Commission's own self-imposed guidelines: i.e. to embody the principle of accountability of the MK to his/her constituents. This is what the chairman stated in his preamble to his report:

The Commission examined several voting systems within the framework of the following principles:

- *The need to boost the accountability of elected representatives to voters.*

- *The need to foster stability by encouraging the formation of larger political blocs.*

- *The need to maintain a reasonable level of representation, especially for minority groups.*

11.16 Indeed, Professor Gideon Doron asked, in a penetrating commentary published by the Citizens' Empowerment Centre in Israel (CECI) in the wake of the publication of the Final Report: who in a multi-member constituency (as recommended by the Report) is accountable to his/her constituents in order to hold him/her accountable and therefore punishable in the next election? The answer to this question challenged those members of the Knesset who set out to implement the Commission's recommendation. Senior MKs representing the three biggest parties – Kadima,

Labour and Likud – tabled a Draft Law in the Knesset on 2ⁿᵈ April 2008. It replaced multi-member constituencies with single-member ones, and thus incorporated all the principles of TR. The next chapter is an attempt to correct the deficiencies of this Draft which chose a ratio of CMPs to PMPs of 60:60, instead of the 90:30 ratio recommended by TR.

11.17 The following is the official summary of the Final Report that the tabled draft law adopted in parts:

The System of Knesset Elections
The Commission believes that the system of Knesset elections should be changed to encourage the formation of large political blocs and greater accountability to constituents; i.e., giving greater weight to personalities in the electoral process. At the same time, the Commission believes a reasonable degree of representation must be maintained.

To counterbalance these two requirements, the Commission recommends the following changes:

1 *Half the number of MKs (i.e. 60) will be elected from national lists, the current practice.*

2 *The other 60 MKs will be elected from 17 constituencies as per the (Ministry of the Interior) breakdown into districts and sub-districts; the number of representatives per constituency will vary according to voter population (practical terms, this means two to five representatives per constituency...)*

3 *To encourage party consolidation, voters will vote in a single ballot for both regional representatives and a national list (In other words, voters will not be able to split their ballots).*

4 *To correct somewhat the distortions of proportional representation resulting from regional divisions, there will be a compensatory mechanism to transfer party votes "lost" in regional elections to that party's national list in order to strengthen it. (The proposed mechanism is described in detail in the full report below).*

5 *To some extent, voters will be able to determine the composition of the national and/or regional list/s by preferential votes (the*

mechanism of which is elaborated in the full report).

The election threshold will be raised to 2.5% of the valid ballots in national elections or to party victory in at least three separate constituencies in regional elections.

Chapter 12

THE ELECTORAL DRAFT LAW (2008-9)

12.1 Following on from the Final Report of the President's Commission, and after much deliberation and lobbying, on 2nd April 2008 senior MKs from the three big parties in the 17th Knesset tabled a Draft Law which embodied the main principles of TR – with some modifications.

12.2 These four MKs were: Professor Menachem Ben-Sasson (Kadima), chairman of the Law and Constitution Committee; Mr Gideon Saar (Likud), chairman of the Likud Party in the Knesset; Mr Ophir Pines Paz, an ex-minister and the chairman of the Home Affairs Committee; and Mr Eitan Cabel, another ex-minister and chairman of the Labour Party in the Knesset (both Labour). Together, these three parties had 60 out of the 120 members of the Knesset. To pass a law on electoral reform, the votes of 61 MKs are needed. So these three parties needed the support of all their own members – by no means a foregone conclusion – and also the support of at least one other party.

12.3 However, since writing the above, the 17th Knesset has been dissolved and a new, 18th Knesset elected. It is hoped that the Draft Law will be revived and re-tabled as required by law. The four senior MKs mentioned above have retained influential positions: Mr Gideon Saar, who was number two in Netanyahu's Likud election campaign, is now Minister of Education; Professor Menachem Ben-Sasson replaced Professor Megidor as the new president of the Hebrew University; Messrs Ophir Pines and Cabel retained their positions as senior and influential MKs but refused to join their leader, Ehud Barak, in Netanyahu's new coalition. However, all four of them enjoy prominence and popularity with the public. It is within the combined power of their three parties to table and pass as law their old Draft Law in the new Knesset. Together, their three parties now have 68 MKs. While further developments are pending, it is interesting to continue to examine and suggest modifications to the Draft.

12.4 The most important existing improvement in the Draft is the rejection of multi-member constituencies in favour of single-member ones. This is an advance on the President's Final Report and a leap forward for TR. Otherwise, the Draft Law follows the Final Report in offering a 60:60 mix of constituency CMKs and party PMKs. In this and a few other details it has deviated from the basic principles of TR. The following is a summary of these deviations. I will analyse them one by one, looking at the rationale behind them and at how to overcome them in order to confer the full benefits of TR on the new law.

Suggested Changes to the Draft Law

Ratio of 60:60 Constituency:
Party Membership of the Knesset

12.5 In this, the Draft Law follows the President's Report. On the face of it, it looks symmetrical and reasonable. The real motive behind this, however, is rather different – although of course it is not plainly expressed. Today, Israeli candidates and the order of their appearances in the lists for the general election are mostly determined by the leadership and the central organs of each party. They are in fact appointed by them and not elected. And even where primaries *are* held by some parties, these are mostly manipulated and corrupt, and lead to the choosing of candidates who are beholden to the leadership and unrepresentative of the supporters of those parties in the country at large. It is natural that MKs who have been selected in this way (and who are the same people that will have to vote for the Draft Law on its journey towards ratification) are afraid that most of them will lose their seats under a new election regime. In fact, their declared support for any change towards regional and therefore accountable seats in the Knesset is derived not from goodwill or sound judgement, but because of pressure from the public. So these MKs hope that the 60 Regional CMK seats will be a sop to satisfy public demand for regional reform, while giving enough space through the other 60 Party seats for most of them to manoeuvre their way back into the exclusive club that the Knesset provides them with.

12.6 There is another compelling reason why the present MKs want to preserve at least 60 Party seats to safeguard their immediate future survival. The majority of them reside in Tel Aviv and its surrounding areas. Their natural fear is, of course, that regional candidates from outside this orbit will push them out and slim down their chances of being chosen, particularly if a 90:30 ratio is used. The Draft Law feeds these fears because it stipulates that candidates need to be resident in their constituencies. But this condition is not necessary and may in fact cause many able potential candidates to shy away from putting their names forward and start disrupting their home life even before their possible, but not certain, election. And although some candidates – once elected – may choose to move to their new constituencies or to acquire secondary accommodation there to gain local popularity, this should not be a pre-election condition. Moreover, keeping this condition will – psychologically – create two types of MKs: one local, complete with certified residency, and the other national, which of course is not the intention behind the division of 60:60 or 90:30. Dropping this onerous condition will help allay the fears of the current MKs – and help solve the problem of fixing the ratio between the two.

Counting the Votes

12.7 Although it is not completely clear from the Draft Law, the assumption is that votes for the candidates and their parties are counted only once, in the first instance to choose the CMKs. Once the CMKs are elected by the votes of the majorities in each constituency, all the *remaining votes* only are aggregated and distributed amongst the parties for choosing their PMKs. Any idea, as some have suggested or the Draft may perhaps have hinted at, of using the votes again in their entirety to choose the PMKs would be tantamount to counting the CMK votes twice. In the case of Israel, such double utilisation of votes would give a huge advantage to the Arab and ultra-orthodox religious Jews, because of their concentration in some localities. These minority parties would be given two bites of the cherry: once to elect their CMKs and then using these votes again, together with what remains, to give them PMK seats. Once this idea is excluded, we are left with the simple TR method of sharing and dividing the same votes between the CMKs and the PMKs.

Order of Priority in Party Lists

12.8 Another pitfall that the Draft needs to rectify is the order of priority of party lists. The most efficient and fair method is that offered by TR. Before the general election, it is natural that each party wants to display its star candidates to attract votes through the canvassing process. Therefore, it needs to put their names at the top of its list to show the public who their prominent and eminent future MKs will be. However, once the results of the general election are declared for each constituency, and therefore each successful CMK is declared and named, TR suggests that the original list of each party be re-shuffled and rearranged in accordance with the number of votes each candidate has scored. This re-arrangement of priorities could be made by each party before their share of PMKs is allocated. This would provide an incentive for the various candidates to fight for each vote during the election, as it could be crucial in their being prioritised as PMKs for their parties. It also dispenses with the need for pre-election primaries. However, although this procedure is desirable and I would prefer it to be embodied in the electoral law, I also accept that it could be left to each party to decide for itself how to proceed in this case.

12.9 Another thing that could help the existing MKs to swallow the change to 90:30 is to increase the number of Knesset seats available. The Knesset's present membership of 120 has remained static for 60 years despite a sevenfold increase in the Israeli population. With many MKs continuing in their positions for decades without being replaced, the membership has become stale, and this has contributed to the image of the Knesset as an ancient, exclusive club, closed to and remote from ordinary citizens.

Increasing the membership to 160 would facilitate dividing them into a ratio of 120:40 or even 100:60, instead of the proposed 90:30. This move would also make the proposed law more palatable for the present MKs, as it would increase their chances of survival under the new regime. The change to a similar system in New Zealand in 1996 was accompanied by a large increase in the number of MPs. Linking this sweetening measure to the bitter prospect of some incumbent MKs losing their seats in the changeover to TR might help in pushing the new electoral law in the Knesset. The appeal of introducing the regional representation of TR would also make this increase more acceptable to a public that has recently grown dismissive and sceptical of anything connected with the Knesset.

To Secure the Party Leader

12.10 The order of priority of each party's candidates list would be declared beforehand, putting the party leader at the top in a reserved slot to ensure his/her place in the Knesset, whatever happens. The reason for this is that in an FPTP system, the opposition will throw all its weight behind its candidate in the constituency of the leader of its rival party, in order to defeat him/her and embarrass his/her party. The reserved top spot for the leader also helps avoid upsets and confusion in the aftermath of a general election if the leader fails to win his/her constituency seat which – though unlikely – is of course, possible. Some parties may likewise want to secure the places of their secretary or chairman, and their election operation officer, as these would need to devote their whole time to serving the party during the election period and might not be able to attend adequately to canvassing in their respective constituencies. But again, this issue is the business of each party and may not necessarily need to be stipulated by the electoral law.

12.11 Once the Draft Law has taken care of all the above points, the exact ratio of CMKs to PMKs becomes less crucial, and although a ratio of 90:30 is the optimum, a slightly higher proportion of PMKs might be more suitable for Israel's population make-up. However, a ratio of 60:60 will definitely gives the PMKs too much power, and will not serve the purpose of the desired electoral reform, as it will

Blocking Threshold

12.12 What is left is the electoral blocking electoral threshold. The Draft suggests that each party has to gain at least 2% of the total votes and to win at least one CMK seat before qualifying to enter the Knesset. These conditions are added to what is inherent in every electoral system. They are, in fact, grossly unfair measures that affect minorities, as they deny representation to their small parties and groups. It amounts to blocking their way to obtaining support amongst the electorate and is tantamount to disenfranchising them. Such a blatant blocking mechanism increases resentment, and nourishes extremism and conflict. And, anyway, even a 10% threshold – as used in Turkey – did not prevent the religious party from getting a majority in the end and forming a government. Of course, having said all that, we should remember that every electoral system has an inherent blocking mechanism – and so has TR. Under a regime of 90:30, in order to gain one Knesset PMK seat, a party needs $1/30^{th}$ of the total votes left for allocation to PMKs. This is 4% of these "unsuccessful" votes, and is actually an even higher percentage of the total votes. The way TR is constructed, as explained in Part One of this book, is to obviate the necessity of both post-election blocking thresholds and pre-election primaries.

12.13 Whether the renewed Draft Law will proceed and overcome all the stages of legislation to become the new electoral law is an open question – it cannot be taken for granted. But the genie is out of the bottle, and it is too big to be squeezed back in. Regional election is in the air in Israel and in the public domain. Any political party aspiring to lead in Israel will ignore its call at its peril. Some form of regional/constituency system will have to be introduced, primarily to ensure direct accountability of individual MKs to their voters. This, after all, was the prime reason cited by the President's Commission. There is no compelling reason why full TR should not be chosen as the model for this fundamental change, in order to repair the fractured political structure of Israel and to strengthen the Knesset – it could ultimately help in turn to solve many of the internal and international problems of the country.

Supplementary Measures and Regulations

12.14 The weakness of the political structure in Israel is not entirely due to proportional representation. Holland is another country with PR, and yet its system functions properly, and has been functioning for centuries, without causing the kind of instability that Israel suffers from. The reason for this difference is that Israel's population lacks the social cohesion and the long tradition of parliamentary democracy that underpins Dutch politics. The make-up of the Knesset reflects the national religious and cultural divisions of what Haim Ramon, the former deputy prime minister, has described as Israel's tribalism. And although TR can help enormously in bringing about cohesion and integration, it alone cannot bridge these wide social divisions overnight.

12.15 Therefore, to ensure stable government and efficient governance, the introduction of any new electoral system needs to be supplemented by structural changes and regulations relating to the internal workings of the Knesset and the government. The most important of these changes centres on the cohesion of political factions in the Knesset, and the tenure of the prime minister and the manner of his/her appointment and dismissal. Only such supporting regulations can ensure that the Knesset completes its term and that the government will therefore last the full four years. These changes can be incorporated into the electoral law or instituted internally by the Knesset and the political parties. The following are few of these regulations: some are essential; others are optional.

Political Parties in the Knesset

12.16 Under TR, MKs are allocated seats in the Knesset as members of parties. It is logical therefore to register their allegiances to these parties in the new Knesset. As candidates in the general election, most of them would anyway have declared their link or loyalty to one party or the other who sponsored them as its candidates in the regions – and remember that under TR all candidates have to stand in the constituencies. In general, these allegiances need not be 100% binding on them as MKs. Not being delegates, but representatives of their voters, they should have the right to change their views and their votes in the Knesset according to changed circumstances and their conscience. However, for MKs whose party forms part of the government, the situation is different. Some measure is needed to avoid the specifically Israeli phenomenon of the slow disintegration of the government during the Knesset term, and to prevent changing party allegiances (in Israel called *Kalanterism*; in Britain it is referred to as taking the Party Whip.) So, I propose that every MK whose party forms part of the government is deemed to have declared allegiance to his party at the time of the vote of confidence in the new government of which that party forms part. At that stage, each MK has the choice of whether to cast his/her vote in favour of forming that government, or to withhold it and still retain his/her seat. Thereafter all party MKs who voted for joining the coalition must exercise collective responsibility within their party in supporting their party in the Knesset. Therefore, except for free votes declared by their parties (e.g. on grounds of conscience), MKs who vote against their government (i.e. the government he/she voted willingly for initially) should be deemed to have resigned and would be replaced by the next in line on the party list or through a by-election. In Israel, this needs to be embodied in the parties' respective constitutions, and together with other regulations specifically on the financing of parties, may need to be anchored in state laws. The logic of this measure is obvious. As a Party/List MK (PMK), his/her position is derived from the party which gave him a seat on its priority list. Therefore if he is voting against the party, it is logical that he should surrender back to the party his position by resigning. If he is an MK representing a Constituency (CMK), then naturally he should resign because he represented himself to his constituents in the general elections as a member of that party and pledged his allegiance by voting it into government. By revoking his pledge, which was given freely when the government was formed, he should resign and offer himself, if he so wishes, for re-election in a by-election as an independent candidate. This is both decent and logical, but it needs apply only to the party or parties of the coalition and not to all MKs. Apart from being logical, this proposal may also restore both discipline within the Knesset and collective responsibility within the government. Today both are precarious in what looks like a free-for-all regime.

Appointment of the Prime Minister

12.17 At present, the business of forming a government after a general election is too long and tortuous. The initial first step of the President is superfluous. Once the results of the general election are announced, the party leader with the highest number of MKs should automatically try to form a government. He/she should immediately set out along broad lines his party's or his coalition's programme, and proceed to ask for a vote of confirmation in the Knesset. If he fails to present his government within, say, three weeks, only then should the President intervene and start a procedure to ask another acceptable MK to form a government. Under the new TR system, with a ratio of 90:30, the emerging first party after the general election is bound to have the support of close to half the Knesset. If not, it is still unlikely to need the partnership of more than one other party to form a stable coalition.

12.18 The confirmation of the prime minister-designate and his government requires a majority of 61 MKs out of 120: i.e. an overall – not a simple – majority (in other words, 51% of the Knesset, ignoring abstentions or absentees). His dismissal can be effected by the same majority – but only on a specific motion of no confidence in the government, to be tabled with adequate prior notice and not suddenly sprung on the parliament. Such a vote should signal the start of a procedure for the dissolution of the Knesset and the declaration of a new general election. The constructive dismissal of the prime minster, as is sometimes suggested, is problematic and creates instability in the system. There are good reasons why, for example in the UK, it is the prime minister who chooses the time of dissolution of parliament during its term. That is one of the reasons why the UK premier is more powerful throughout his term – right up until the last day – than the US President, who in the last months of his predetermined time in office is regarded as a lame duck.

12.19 The PM should appoint an MK to be deputy PM. This appointment also needs a parliamentary vote of 61 MKs. The same majority is required for a replacement should the PM decide to replace him/her. Thus, with this backing of parliamentary authority, the deputy can accede without an upheaval to the position of the prime minister in the case of the latter's death or incapacitation.

12.20 A constructive vote of no confidence is not practical, and indeed is not necessary under the above proposition, simply because those MKs who had supported the government will have to resign once they voted against it. This avoids electing a government and immediately afterwards exposing it to the danger of collapsing. This has become unacceptable to the public in Israel.

Appointment of Ministers

1. The PM should appoint all ministers and their deputies and should have the power to dismiss and replace them. MKs thus appointed need confirmation by 61 votes, *en bloc* initially when the government is voted in, or individually if appointed later on. Only ministers appointed by the PM from outside the Knesset should be subject, in addition, to a Knesset committee hearing followed by confirmation by 61 MKs.

2. The PM is to be free by law to appoint **no more** than half of the ministers and deputy ministers from outside the Knesset. They can be dismissed and replaced by him as above. This is designed to bring into the government professionals with experience. In some countries this professionalism is provided by the corps of the civil service. Unless outside ministers are restricted to no more than half the government, we will be creating a presidential system through the back door.

3. Each ministry must have either the minister or his/her deputy as an MK. In cases where a minister is appointed from outside the Knesset and has no deputy, an MK is appointed by the minister, with the approval of the prime minister, as Knesset liaison secretary to represent and answer for the ministry in the Knesset. This ensures

the supremacy of parliament without compromising the authority of the PM or the ministers.

4. All the above keeps a balance between the Knesset and the government and renders irrelevant the very unusual "Norwegian Law" advocated by some in Israel whereby an appointed minister has to resign his seat in parliament and is replaced by a deputy, who in turn has to vacate the position once the minister leaves the ministerial post and returns to parliament. The Norwegian arrangement is peculiar to Norway and is part of a much wider political and cultural environment specific to that country or other similar countries.

5. Many people ask how the party leaders are elected under the TR system, especially when primaries seem to lose their importance. This question is dealt with in Part One of this book. Basically, each party leader, apart from the prime minister, is elected or re-elected in the middle of the Knesset term by those **candidates** who stood for the party at the last election (not by the party's current MKs, a group which will naturally not include all the candidates). To elect the new leader, all these candidates cast the actual votes they individually obtained at the preceding general election – these are added together to selecting their leader. These votes are those of the real supporters of the party at the last election, and not the votes of paid-up members who often are recruited for this purpose. The selection becomes clean, with no corrupt practices. The procedures for re-electing party leaders should be declared in mid-term, but if no candidate challenges the incumbent, the re-election is dispensed with, as the incumbent is automatically reconfirmed.

6. The prime minister need not submit himself for re-selection, because he won his mandate by coming top – ahead of the other leaders – and thus fulfilled his role and his party's manifesto. He is therefore entitled to continue in his role as leader of his party. This exception also adds to the stability of the government, and is normal in other progressive democracies.

ANALYSIS OF FUTURE VOTING TRENDS

13.1 Dr Fany Yuval of Ben Gurion University has conducted rigorous simulations showing how the introduction of the TR system as described here, if applied, would have changed the composition of the 16th, 17th and 18th Knessets elected in 2003, 2006 and 2009 respectively, leading to the creation of larger groupings, while safeguarding the right to representation of minorities, especially Arabs and ultra-orthodox Jews. Her findings are given below in 13 tables, using various different possible scenarios and groupings of the members of these Knessets. The simulations were based on the actual votes cast at these elections, and were conducted according to well-known and accepted academic standards.

13.2 The essence of TR is that the person who votes in a single constituency, is – with his single ballot – taking advantage of two voting systems at the same time. He is giving his first preference to one individual as his choice for MK under the constituency first-past-the-post system. But he is also stating that if his vote does not succeed in counting towards his choice of MK, he wants that vote not to be wasted, but to go to his political party to help elect another MK on behalf of his party under the PR (proportional representation) system. So he is sending two messages with one vote.

13.3 To redistribute the results to produce Constituency and Party Members of the Knesset (CMKs and PMKs) Dr Yuval spliced the country from north to south geographically, without regard to the composition of the population, and ignoring ethnic and religious make-up – as TR stipulates. Quite deliberately, no consideration was given to population mix or local interests.

13.4 The simulated results were based on the votes cast at real elections that took place under the present PR system. Naturally, once TR is introduced, voters and parties will position themselves to take account of the bigger groupings, and they may use tactical voting to take advantage of the new situation. So these simulations have to be treated with caution; they serve only as illustrative indications, and not as forecasts. However, buried in them are the future directions of voting trends.

13.5 Tables 1, 3 and 9 show that after a hypothetical introduction of TR, the big parties would benefit, and the smaller parties would lose out – with the exception of the Arab and certain Jewish religious parties which are concentrated in certain localities: for example, the Arabs in Galilee, and the Jewish religious in Jerusalem and Bnei Berak. In fact, Torah Judaism, an ultra-orthodox religious Jewish Party would keep its strength in the Knesset according to the simulations. Under TR, it takes advantage of its concentration in these localities while at the same time continuing to pick up individual supporters or adherents in the rest of the country. To close ranks under TR, some ultra-orthodox elements in Shas may seek to amalgamate with Torah Judaism to keep their joint strength by setting up a joint Party of Jewish Democrats. Such a new party might prove to be successful if it opens its doors (as Shas does today but not Torah Judaism) to membership of traditionally religious rather than strictly orthodox religious.

13.6 There is a similar trend among Arab voters. Hadash (an Arab/Jewish Party) is similar to Torah Judaism in that its Arab supporters are geographically localised, while its leftist Jewish supporters are spread countrywide. It is the only party in Israel that is trying to build its message on Arab/Jewish cooperation based on the reality of having to live together in Israel. It is the only Arab party that counts a Jewish MK as its number two on its list. This is unlike Meretz, whose ideology is built on pure socialism. The difference between the two is causing Meretz – basically a Jewish Zionist Party – to continuously haemorrhage to the rest of the left, while Hadash – essentially an Arab party – is gathering momentum. Hadash could increase its strength significantly under TR, because in addition to its localised Arab vote, it has added supporters countrywide both amongst Arabs and Jews. Therefore it should be a potential supporter of TR.

13.7 Dr Yuval and I re-arranged the results into bigger groupings, and recast the figures for the different parties to depict future trends (Table 2 for the 16th Knesset, and Tables 4, 5 and 8 for the 17th Knesset.) Although there is some logic in grouping certain parties together in these tables, these are for illustration only, and no claim or forecast is intended. However, the results are revealing and will no doubt give the various parties food for thought. The groupings for the 18th Knesset of 2009 are even more interesting because they set the scene for a struggle between Kadima and Labour for the soul of the progressive left in Israel..

13.8 It is clear that under TR in the first two elections, two dominant groups led by Kadima/Likud/Beitenu on the one hand, and Labour/Meretz on the other, would emerge and could each lead strong coalitions or rule alone as a group. In this respect it is interesting to note that with Kadima going it alone without Likud in the 2006 election, if Labour had at that time united with Meretz and the Pensioners under a regime based on TR, Labour might have then led the government. These assumptions will no doubt concentrate the minds of different parties and groups when it comes to understanding the undercurrents of politics in Israel based on real election voting, rather than on voting intentions depicted in the ephemeral results -- here today, gone tomorrow -- of public opinion polls.

13.9 The sad withdrawal of Prime Minister Arik Sharon from politics due to his sudden illness left Kadima an orphan before the 2006 elections, and the internal civil war between the factions that followed weakened the party. The 2009 election to the 18th Knesset threw out a new trend which could prove to be *life or death* for one or the other of Kadima or Labour, as Likud re-established itself as the main centre party of the right. Before the 2006 elections, Prime Minister Sharon set up Kadima to replace Likud as the right-of-centre party, but the results of the 2009 elections suggest that, on the contrary, Kadima is set to replace Labour as the left-of-centre party if it succeeds in attracting enough Labour MKs. This will depend on the position of the "Histadrut" trade unions. An analysis of this phenomenon is added in the conclusions at the end of this chapter.

13.10 Two of these tables (6 and 7) compare the results of two possible compositions of the 16th and 17th simulated Knessets based on two different ratios of regional Constituency Members of the Knesset (CMKs) to proportional Party Members (PMKs). The two ratios under consideration are 60:60 and 90:30. Here we see that a 60:60 split, as recommended by the Draft Law of 2nd April 2008 mentioned in the previous chapter, leads to even more fragmentation by drawing in smaller parties. The 90:30 split, on the other hand, gives the biggest party even more seats. The choice is there between more representation with the first ratio of 60:60 and more stability with the second of 90:30. Legislators have to decide – and they may settle on an 80:40 split. However, it is clear from the simulations – and they are only simulations – that, for the purposes of change, the 60:60 division is not a serious option.

13.11 The accusation is levelled against TR that under the 90:30 regime – as mentioned above – one party becomes too dominant and, on the face of it, there is no hope for any other party to catch up to replace it. This conclusion is false. A change in the comparative popularity of the two big national parties (say Likud/Labour in the past, and Likud/Kadima now) could dramatically shift the results of the Constituency Members of Knesset (CMKs) – and hence the fortunes of the second party. Lessons can be drawn from what occurs, for example, in the UK, where a small swing in popularity between the first and second parties (Conservative and Labour) can be translated into a major swing in the number of parliamentary seats – bringing the alternative government-in-waiting into office. The election of CMKs is based similarly on first-past-the-post, but of course under TR such dramatic swings are tempered and moderated to a degree by the election of the PMKs. Hence it is not the first-placed party which wins the major number of PMKs, but the second-placed party, because the first has already won so many CMK seats that it has depleted the aggregate votes left for it to win PMK seats. This is the balancing factor that TR provides.

13.12 In Israel, as in many Western democracies, the party leader is the biggest factor in deciding its electoral fortunes. This is due to the power of spin of the modern media that tends to convert parliamentary elections into quasi-presidential ones based more on the popularity of the leader than on the ideology or policies of his/her party. In this respect, elections are becoming presidential-style contests; and even more so in Israel. The effect of this trend on the results is that a leader who is popular nationally tends naturally to be automatically popular in each constituency. That of course helps to reinforce the swing between one leading party and its alternative.

ELECTORAL SIMULATIONS

Simulations applying TR to the 16th, 17th and 18th Knesset (2003, 2006, 2009)

TABLE 1
Simulation of the results of general elections to the16th Knesset (2003) if they had been carried out under TR with a 90:30 split
of CMKs to PMKs

Party/list	CMKs (out of 90)	PMKs (out of 30)	Total (simulation)	Total (actual results)
Likud under Sharon	68	2	70	38
Labour	11	5	16	19
Torah Judaism	3	2	5	5
Hadash	6	0	6	3
United Arab	1	0	1	2
Brit Leumi	1	1	2	0
Shas	0	4	4	11
Shinui	0	6	6	15
Mafdal	0	1	1	6
Echud Leumi	0	3	3	7
1 Nation Am Ehad	0	1	1	3
Meretz	0	3	3	6
Balad	0	1	1	3
Be'Aliya	0	1	1	2
Total	90	30	120	120

This simulation based on real figures taken from each electoral area shows a sweeping victory for Likud, because Prime Minister Sharon was very popular at the time and conducted a presidential-style campaign which suited his personality and appealed to an Israeli public yearning for a dominant leader to achieve peace. The simulation accentuates this result because the popularity of Sharon swept the country and was naturally reflected in the make-up of every constituency.

TABLE 2

Simulated grouping of the parties in the 16th Knesset (2003) if elections had been carried out under TR with a 90:30 split of CMKs to PMKs

Name of party/list	CMKs (out of 90)	PMKs (out of 30)	Total under TR (simulation)	Total MKs (actual results)
Likud, Israel Be'Aliya, Brit Leumi	69	4	73	40
Labour, Am Ehad, Meretz, Shinui	11	15	26	43
Shas, Torah Judaism, Mafdal Echud L	3	10	13	29
Balad, Hadash, United Arab	7	1	8	8
Total	90	30	120	120

This grouping of the parties shows how the actual centre-left and centre-right are balanced. Under the simulation, Prime Minister Sharon would have tipped this balance towards the right, recalling the personal success of Menachem Begin in 1977, when his personality wrenched political power for the first time from the successors of Ben Gurion's Labour Party. It suited Sharon to include Shinui in the coalition to give it a secular flavour. Under PR, by joining Sharon, the floating Shinui shaped his coalition at the time. Under the simulation, Sharon's Likud could have formed a government on its own.

TABLE 3

Simulation of the results of general elections to the 17th Knesset (2006) if they had been carried out under TR with a 90:30 split
of CMKs to PMKs

Name of party/list	CMKs (out of 90)	PMKs (out of 30)	Total (TR simulation)	Total (actual results)
Kadima under Olmert	61	2	63	29
Labour	5	6	11	19
Mafdal	4	3	7	9
Torah Judaism	5	1	6	6
Hadash	4	1	5	3
United Arab	2	0	2	4
Beitenu	4	3	7	11
Pensioners	0	2	2	7
Shas	4	4	8	12
Likud under Netanyahu	0	4	4	12
Greens	0	1	1	0
Meretz	0	2	2	5
Balad	1	1	2	3
Total	90	30	120	120

Here Kadima emerged as the centre-right party, pushing Likud to the margins of the extreme right. However, once Olmert succeeded Sharon, he could not fill his shoes; and the popularity of Kadima, -- call it New Likud – weakened. Olmert found it impossible to form a government on his own even though by now Netanyahu's Old Likud was almost pushed out of the race. The simulation again accentuates both trends. Beitenu emerges as a powerful force. The Russian immigrant bear who went to sleep under idealist Sharanski's Be'Aliya has woken up under wily and savvy Avigdor Lieberman.in Beitenu. So even under the simulation it keeps its strong position.

TABLE 4

<u>A</u>ssumption 1 of party grouping for 17th Knesset (2006) if elections had been carried out under TR with a 90:30 split of CMKs to PMKs

Name of party/list	CMKs (out of 90)	PMKs (out of 30)	Total (TR simulation)	Total (actual results)
Group 1 Kadima, Likud	61	6	67	41
Group 2 Israel Beitenu	4	3	7	11
Group 3 Labour, Meretz, Pensioners, Greens	5	11	16	31
Group 4 Shas, Torah Judaism, Mafdal	13	8	21	27
Group 5 Balad, Hadash, United Arab	7	2	9	10
Total	90	30	120	120

Here, in the actual results, Kadima without Likud has only 29 MKs and its support in the Knesset is therefore fairly balanced with Labour, which has 31 MKs together with its natural allies, Meretz and the Pensioners. Under simulations, the Sharon momentum would have continued because Likud under Netanyahu did not have enough time to recover. Israel Beitenu – basically a secular party – has established its position holding the balance of power between left and right. In fact, Beitenu has more in common with the centre-left than with the centre-right. Between Likud and Kadima, whichever can tempt Beitenu into its orbit will emerge stronger. Netanyahu understood this underlying trend and subsequently exploited it. Tsipi Livni's advisers initially misread this analysis of the situation.

TABLE 5

Assumption 2 of party grouping for 17th Knesset (2006) if elections had been carried out under TR with a 90:30 split of CMKs to PMKs

Name of party/list	CMKs (out of 90)	PMKs (out of 30)	Total (TR simulation)	Total (actual results)
Group 1 Sharon Kadima, NetanyahuLikud, Israel Beitenu,	65	9	74	52
Group 2 Labour, Meretz, Pensioners, Greens	5	11	16	31
Group 3 Shas, Torah Judaism, Mafdal	13	8	21	27
Group 4 Balad, Hadash, United Arab	7	2	9	10
Total	90	30	120	120

Here again, it is easy to see how pivotal Beitenu is becoming. Under the actual results, if it had supported and been accepted by Labour, the left-of-centre grouping would have had 42 MKs against Kadima's 29. At this juncture, it would have been impossible anyway for Kadima to gain the support of Likud – the party it had just split from. The situation under the simulation is different because it basically strengthens the big parties at the expense of the smaller ones. There was no way that Netanyahu – the leader of what remained of old Likud – would have accepted joining the government and thereby committing political suicide

TABLE 6

Comparison of two different splits between CMKs and PMKs (60:60 and 90:30) for the results of general elections to 16th Knesset (2003) if they had been carried out under TR

Party/list	60 Constituency : 60 Party seats			Actual results	90 Constituency : 30 Party seats		
	Constituency seats (out of 60)	Party seats (out of 60)	Total		Total	Party seats (out of 30)	Constituency seats (out of 90)
Likud	50	2	52	38	70	2	68
Labour	4	11	15	19	16	5	11
Shinui		11	11	15	6	6	0
Shas		7	7	11	4	4	0
Torah Judaism	2	2	4	5	5	2	3
Echud Leumi		5	5	7	3	3	0
Democrat Front Hadash	4	1	5	3	6	0	6
Mafdal		4	4	6	1	1	0
AM Echad 1 Nation		3	3	3	1	1	0
Meretz		5	5	6	3	3	0
Be'Aliya		2	2	2	1	1	0
Balad		2	2	3	1	1	0
Arab List		2	2	2	1	0	1
Herut		1	1	--			
National Brit Leumi		1	1	0	2	1	1
Greens		1	1	--			
Total	60	60	120	120	120	30	90

This table shows that the 60:60 split envisaged in the Draft Law of 2nd April 2008 creates even more splintering among the parties than that prevailing under the present PR regime. On the other hand, under the 90:30 simulation, the charismatic leadership of Prime Minister Sharon and the power of his then-party, Likud, are accentuated even more. That should not worry those who oppose TR based on 90:30. Because this result reflected as much the strength of Sharon as the weakness of Netanyahu in the country at large, and therefore in each constituency.

TABLE 7

Comparison of two different splits between CMKs and PMKs (60:60 and 90:30) for the results of general elections to 17th Knesset (2006) if they had been carried out under TR

Party/list	60 Constituency : 60 Party seats			Actual results	90 Constituency : 30 Party seats		
	Constituency seats (out of 60)	Party seats (out of 60)	Total		Total	Party seats (out of 30)	Constituency seats (out of 90)
Kadima under Olmert	36	5	41	29	63	2	61
Labour	7	10	17	19	11	6	5
Likud under Netanyahu		7	7	12	4	4	
Shas	3	7	10	12	8	4	4
Torah Judaism	4	2	6	6	6	1	5
Israel Beitenu	4	6	10	11	7	3	4
Hadash	2	2	4	3	5	1	4
Mafdal	2	5	7	9	7	3	4
Pensioners		5	5	7	2	2	
United Arab	1	2	3	4	2	0	2
Meretz		3	3	5	2	2	
Balad	1	2	3	3	2	1	1
Arab		1	1	--			
Herut		1	1	--			
National		1	1	--			
Greens		1	1	--	1	1	
Total	60	60	120	120	120	30	90

This table show the same trends with 60:60 and 90:30, but the weaker popularity of Ehud Olmert has diminished the support for Kadima, which has 63 MKs under the simulated 90:30 split for the 2006 election, as opposed to 70 using the same split for the 2003 election. This change in the popularity of Kadima helped Netanyahu to lead the remnants of the old Likud to survive to fight another day.

TABLE 8

Assumption 3 of party grouping for 17th Knesset (2006) if elections had been carried out under TR with a 90:30 split of CMKs to PMKs

Name of party/list	CMKs (out of 90)	PMKs (out of 30)	Total (under simulation)	Total (actual results)
Group 1 Kadima under Olmert	61	2	63	29
Group 2 Likud under Netanyahu, Israel Beitenu	4	7	11	23
Group 3 Labour, Meretz, Pensioners, Greens	5	11	16	31
Group 4 Shas, Torah Judaism, Mafdal	13	8	21	27
Group 5 Balad, Hadash, United Arab	7	2	9	10
Total	90	30	120	120

This grouping in these actual results shows the battleground for the subsequent 2009 election. The three top groups were fairly balanced, being led by Tsipi Livni, Netanyahu and Ehud Barak. Once Tsipi Livni alienated Shas, her party was unable to form an interim government and had to go to the country. Netanyahu pounced on the opportunity to court Shas at any price during the campaign. But Tsipi Livni jeopardised her chances further by attacking Avigdor Lieberman, the leader of Beteinu, as fascist, instead of trying to court him and his essentially secular party Beteinu on to her side. Lieberman, an intensely secular person, looks at Shas as the enemy, especially on civil marriage issues. Instead of dividing and ruling, Tsipi Livni closed the door in the faces of both of these antagonistic parties, so her able PR advisers had no option left but to move her away from her right-wing Likud roots and towards championing progressive pro-Palestinian and feminist causes. That stance helped Kadima make inroads into Labour, Meretz and other leftish pro-feminist movements, and made it inevitable that the results of the 2009 election would produce two new forces: Kadima on the left and Likud on the right. Netanyahu gained 15 new seats (12+15 = 27), thus recovering back from Kadima most of the votes lost at the time to Sharon. Kadima lost only one seat (29-1 = 28), making it still the biggest party in the new Knesset, perching high on the ruins of, Meretz , Labour, the Pensioners' Party and other leftish and secular voting groups. Meretz was weakened considerably. Labour saved its bacon by getting a helping hand from the trade unions. The

Pensioners disappeared completely. Post-election, Netanyahu managed to unify the support of Shas and Beitenu in a reluctant marriage of convenience under his government umbrella.

The 2009 elections showed yet again the stability of the religious and Arab parties, while the supporters of the governing establishment kept floating in all directions.

TABLE 9 (A)
Actual voting figures from elections to the 18th Knesset (2009)

Total votes:	3,416,587
Invalid votes:	43,097
Valid votes:	3,373,490
Unsuccessful votes blocked by threshold:	103, 904
Successful votes cast for 120 Seats:	3,269,586

TABLE 9 (B)
Comparison of actual results of elections to the 18th Knesset (2009) with results from simulation under TR

Name of party/list	Number of votes	Knesset seats (actual results)	Knesset seats (TR simulation)
Kadima	758,032	28	45
Labour	334,900	13	4
Echud Leumi/ Mafdal	112,570	4	2
Jewish Home	96,765	3	1
Torah Judaism	147,954	5	5
Hadash	112,130	4	6
United Arab	113,954	4	5
Beitenu	394,577	15	9
Pensioners	--	--	--
Shas	286,300	11	6
Likud	729,054	27	35
Greens	--	--	--
Meretz	99,611	3	1
Balad	83,739	3	1
Total	3,269,586	120	120

The simulation under TR shows that a left Kadima is stronger than right-wing Likud. However, the country at large was on the right. It was clear that only Netanyahu could form a coalition. Beitenu asserted its position as the joker in the pack. The game of forming precarious coalition continued waiting and crying out for electoral reform

TABLE 10

Comparative TR simulations of results of elections to the 18th Knesset (2009) and the 17th Knesset (2006)

Party/list	90 Constituency : 30 Party seats 18th Knesset 2009			Actual results		90 Constituency : 30 Party seats 17th Knesset 2006		
	Constituency seats (out of 90)	Party seats (out of 30)	Total			Total	Party seats (out of 30)	Constituency seats (out of 90)
Kadima	41	4	45	28	29	63	2	61
Labour	0	4	4	13	19	11	6	5
Likud	30	5	35	27	12	4	4	
Shas	2	4	6	11	12	8	4	4
Torah Judaism	3	2	5	5	6	6	1	5
Israel Beitenu	4	5	9	15	11	7	3	4
Hadash	5	1	6	4	3	5	1	4
Mafdal	1	1	2	4	9	7	3	4
Pensioners	--	--	--	--	7	2	2	
United Arab	4	1	5	4	4	2		2
Meretz	0	1	1	3	5	2	2	
Balad	0	1	1	3	3	2	1	1
Jewish Home	0	1	1	3	--			
The Greens						1	1	
Total	90	30	120	120	120	120	30	90

Analysis of the simulation shows the sources of support for the parties in localised constituencies on the one hand, and their wider, diffused support in the country on the other. Support for an unpopular party melts away quickly in the constituencies. Likud had no chance of recovering after the 2006 elections. It disappeared in the constituencies, was only kept alive by a weak Kadima under Olmert, and revived following the dictum that oppositions don't win elections; it is governments that lose them. The position of Labour after the 2009 elections is similar to Likud before them. Except that here the wider safety net of the trade unions kept Labour alive. Unlike his opponents inside Labour, Ehud Barak understood this and exploited it to the full. He enlisted the backing of the trade unions to bargain a strong place for Labour inside the coalition. Its leader, Offer Eini, emerged as the future strongman of Israeli politics and may very well – together with wily Labour veteran Ben-Eliezer – lead the revival of Labour. But that depends as much on the cohesion of Kadima, which is torn from the inside between left and right.

TABLE 11

Simulation of party groupings for 18th Knesset (2009) if elections had been carried out under TR with a 90:30 split of CMKs to PMKs

Name of party/list	CMKs (out of 90)	PMKs (out of 30)	Total MKs (under simulation)	Total MKs (actual results)
Group 1				
Kadima,	41	4	45	28
Labour,	0	4	4	13
Meretz	0	1	1	3
	---	---	---	---
	41	9	50	44
Group 2				
Likud,	30	5	35	27
Beitenu	4	5	9	15
	---	---	---	---
	34	10	44	42
Group 3				
Shas,	2	4	6	11
Torah J,	3	2	5	5
Mafdal,	1	1	2	4
Jewish H.	0	1	1	3
	---	---	---	---
	6	8	14	23
Group 4				
Hadash,	5	1	6	4
Utd. Arab,	4	1	5	4
Balad	0	1	1	3
	---	---	---	---
	9	3	12	11
Total	90	30	120	120

Here, the simulation shows that Kadima could easily come first, leading the centre-left (50 MKs), and Likud would come second even without the support of Beitenu (together they have 44 MKs). Then, however, the Jewish religious and the extreme right come into the game and would give Likud the advantage (of 44+14= 58

MKs), which is indeed an alliance that Netanyahu cleverly cultivated before the 2009 elections and harvested when the results came in.

In this table, we also see the trend of the Arab groups becoming stronger (even without the addition of four Druze MKs elected by national parties), and the Jewish religious groups weakening both in the real results and in the simulation.

TABLE 12
Comparative simulations

Party orientation	Party/list	16th Knesset (2003) Actual	16th Knesset (2003) Simulation	17th Knesset (2006) Actual	17th Knesset (2006) Simulation	18th Knesset (2009) Actual	18th Knesset (2009) Simulation
Floating	Shinui	15	6	-	-	-	-
	Pensioners	-	-	7	2	-	-
	Be'Aliya	2	1	-	-	-	-
	Kadima	-	-	29	63	28	45
Sub-totals		17	7	36	65	28	45
Centre-left	Labour	19	16	19	11	13	4
	Meretz	6	3	5	2	3	1
	Am Ehad	3	1	-	-	-	-
	Greens	-	-	0	1	-	-
Sub-totals		28	20	24	14	16	5
Centre-right	Likud	38	70	12	4	27	35
	I.Beitenu	-	-	11	7	15	9
	Brit Leumi	0	2	-	-	-	-
Sub-totals		38	72	23	11	42	44
Right	Shas	11	4	12	8	11	6
	Torah Judaism	5	5	6	6	5	5
	Mafdal	6	1	9	7	4	2
	Jewish Home	-	-	-	-	3	1
	Echud Leumi.	7	3	-	-	-	-
Sub-totals		29	13	27	21	23	14
Arab	Hadash	3	6	3	5	4	6
	United Arab	2	1	4	2	4	5
	Balad	3	1	3	2	3	1
Sub-totals		8	8	10	9	11	12
	Total	120	120	120	120	120	120

This table shows the impending struggle between Kadima and Labour. I have designated Kadima as a floating party because it is not clear what shape it is going to take in the near future. The old Likudniks within Kadima – led for the time being by retired army Chief of Staff Shaul Mofaz – might break away from what has become a left-orientated party led by Tsipi Livni. Netanyahu has already piloted a new law in the Knesset (nicknamed the "Mofaz Law") to facilitate such a breakaway of at least seven MKs, while preserving their state financing allocation that otherwise would have been lost as a result of breaking away from Kadima. Another scenario could be played out by Mofaz, or another die-hard rightist, challenging Tsipi Livni for the leadership. Her leftist supporters will then have to decide what to do. That would be the last chance for Labour. The big question is: would Labour exploit this division in Kadima or lose time and disappear? That depends to a great extent on the trade unions led by Offer Eini.

TABLE 13
Comparative simulations

Party orientation	Party/list	16th Knesset (2003) Actual	16th Knesset (2003) Simulation	17th Knesset (2006) Actual	17th Knesset (2006) Simulation	18th Knesset (2009) Actual	18th Knesset (2009) Simulation
Fluid parties	Shinui	15	6	-	-	-	-
	Pensioners	-	-	7	2	-	-
	Be'Aliya	2	1	-	-	-	-
	Beitenu	-	-	11	7	15	9
	Meretz/Greens	6	3	5	3	3	1
	Am Ehad	3	1	-	-	-	-
	Brit Leumi	-	2	-	-	-	-
Sub-totals		26	13	23	12	18	10
Solid central parties	Labour	19	16	19	11	13	4
	Likud	38	70	12	4	27	35
	Kadima	-	-	29	63	28	45
Sub-totals		57	86	60	78	68	84
Solid right parties	Shas	11	4	12	8	11	6
	Torah Judaism	5	5	6	6	5	5
	Mafdal	6	1	9	7	4	2
	Jewish Home	-	-	-	-	3	1
	Echud Leumi.	7	3	-	-	-	-
Sub-totals		29	13	27	21	23	14
Solid Arab parties	Hadash	3	6	3	5	4	6
	United Arab	2	1	4	2	4	5
	Balad	3	1	3	2	3	1
Sub-totals		8	8	10	9	11	12
	Total	120	120	120	120	120	120

Conclusions

In order to point out some trends and draw some conclusions, in the above table I grouped the parties into four categories.

- The Fluid parties seem to come and go. Each starts with a flourish and a fanfare, only to disappear soon afterwards. They are mainly secular in outlook and centred in and around Tel Aviv. Apart from Beitenu, their voters have supported Kadima in the recent elections. Beitenu is the exception. Its voters, backed by Russian immigrants, have more in common with Likud. Without the leadership of Avigdor Lieberman, its members will gravitate mainly towards, or might merge with, Likud.

- The Solid parties are the old Zionist parties with ideologies and outlooks inherited from the two main streams of Zionism, led after the establishment of the State of Israel by the two flag-bearers Ben Gurion and Menachem Begin. Labour and Likud are well defined. It is Kadima that is left undecided after the 2009 elections to the 18th Knesset. Which side will it swallow or be swallowed up by? In this category of solid parties there are only two places. One of the three has to give way.

- Prime Minister Sharon set up Kadima to replace Likud. He then added a sprinkling of Labour leaders to facilitate his then-impending evacuation of Gaza, and in order to pave the road for peace with the Palestinians. He looked upon Tsipi Livni as a potential successor in the distant future. So the Kadima -- call it New Likud under Sharon – that he created was a right-of-centre party. Sharon's untimely withdrawal from politics was followed by an internal civil war between Tsipi Livni and Ehud Olmert, and later on at the party primaries between her and Shaul Mofaz – the hawk who was brought into Likud by Sharon. This has created a new situation that will force Kadima to fight to replace Labour as a new left-of-centre party. It will have no chance of replacing Likud, as the latter has already regained old Likud voters and consolidated its position in the Knesset, in the government and in the country at large as the right–of–centre party. The big question is: which party will lead the left-of-centre in the next general election? The fight for this position could prove to *be life or death* for one or the other of Kadima or Labour.

- The Jewish religious parties, with the exception of Torah Judaism, are weakening as their supporters move to the bigger parties. The same applies to the Jewish ultra-nationalist parties, Mafdal and Jewish Home. It is interesting to note in this table (13) that while the power of the Jewish religious parties is progressively weakening, that of the Arabs is strengthening both in the actual results and in the simulations.

- Shas, the Sephardic Party, has two sides to it. On the one hand, it is deeply religious. Rabbi Ovadiah Yossef is holding it together tightly in that position. Without his spiritual leadership, it is difficult to predict its future. It has another side to it, the welfare and socialist side. It is seen by the Sephardic community as the protector of their interests. But for how long? Unless it emphasises its social side and accepts traditional but not strictly religious voters, it will continue to weaken. In this context it is important to remember that there has always been a difference between Western Jewry and its counterpart in the East. In the West, the dichotomy between religious and secular had a longer history; in the East, this division was never felt. Jews were Jews, because oriental Jews never wanted to be anything else and had no desire to assimilate. This oriental/Sephardic view of Judaism as a culture and a way of life carried on into Israel. How long will it last? It is one thing to assimilate into Arab culture; it is of course different in Israel, where they are being assimilated into other Jews. So the melting-away of Shas as a religious party is only a matter of time.

- The power of the Arab vote has to be taken together with the Druze vote. The Druze have secured four seats out of 120, almost 4%, far beyond the proportion of their numbers in Israel's total population, which is only 1.6 per cent. The reason for this is that they serve in the army and have no problem swearing allegiance to the state. Their communities are used to this in Syria and Lebanon. Moreover, while Muslim and Christian Arabs in Israel distance themselves from the Zionist Jewish parties, the Druze don't have any qualms about that. In this Knesset, the Druze ran with the rabbits and hunted with the hares. They won one MK in Balad (a Muslim Party) and one MK each in Kadima, Likud and Beitenu.

- The support of Muslim Arabs for Zionist Jewish parties disappeared in the 18th Knesset. In the 17th Knesset of 2006, the following two candidates were elected as Labour MKs: Ghalib Majadle, a Muslim who was appointed by Olmert to the post of full cabinet minister, and Nadia Hilou, a Roman Catholic. Neither succeeded in surviving among the dwindling number of Labour MKs in 2009. This trend should worry equally both Jews and Muslims in Israel.

- The Arab, mainly Muslim parties, on the other hand, are becoming stronger as independent groupings. That is fine and is what democracy is all about. The problems will start when Islamist elements infiltrate and take over one of them, which would sharpen the conflict with the main Jewish Zionist parties and could lead to conflict and even violence. Political leaders in Israel need to wake up in time to bring about internal reconciliation and pave the way to integrate all their Arab citizens inside Israel into the social and political fabric of the country. ***The introduction of TR can help in that direction.***

PART FOUR

CROATIA– THE HISTORY OF ELECTIONS

Ivo Škrabalo

COMMENTARY
by Christopher Cviić, OBE
THE POWER OF ELECTIONS

IN the opening chapter of this book, Aharon Nathan writes that the strength of a democracy is not purely a function of its method of carrying out elections. He is right. For those living in normal democratic countries, elections are a matter of routine, and as such, for an average citizen, not an object of special attention. However, it is important not to take them for granted. Indeed, for me, every trip to a polling station is a privilege and also a sacred obligation. My passionate attitude towards elections is easy to explain.

I spent my youth under a series of undemocratic regimes: first, there was the dictatorial regime of royal Yugoslavia; then, from 1941 to 1945, came Croatia under the quisling Ustasha regime of Ante Pavelić, followed by the return of Yugoslavia in 1945, but this time under Communist rule. What all of them had in common was not only the fact that they denied their citizens free elections, but also the way they spat at "rotten" Western democracy, caricaturing its allegedly free elections, depicting them as a travesty, a mere mask for the power of plutocrats and imperialists over working people. All those harangues had the reverse effect on me; they led me to imagine that there could be something really worthwhile about democracy.

It took me a long time to confirm this in practice. Only in 1964, at the age of 34 – here in the United Kingdom, as a freshly naturalized British citizen – did I have the opportunity to vote at real, democratic elections. Five and a half decades have passed since then, and I have never missed an election – whether local, regional, national, or European.

No wonder then that, as an "election fanatic", I instantly recognised in Aharon Nathan – the author of this book – a soulmate and a profound thinker who was seeking ways of perfecting elections as the key instrument of democracy. We met (and instantly became friends) as postgraduates at St. Antony's College in Oxford, in the autumn of 1959; he was then 28 and I, 29.

He came to Oxford with rich political experience, having already been actively involved in the young Israeli democracy, which had been born under dramatic circumstances eleven years earlier. He and his family had arrived there in 1949, only a year after the creation of the State of Israel, having fled from Iraq to save their lives, which were endangered because they were Jews. He graduated in history at the Hebrew University in Jerusalem and then served as a close adviser to David Ben Gurion – the prime minister from 1948 to 1963. At the end of the war with Egypt in 1956, Ben Gurion appointed Nathan Civil Governor of the occupied Gaza Strip. Because of his close knowledge of Arabs, their culture and language, Nathan was later appointed – also at the wish of Ben Gurion – leader of the Arabs' section of the Israeli trade union, Histadrut. In order to widen and deepen his knowledge on current problems in the Arab world, he was then sent to Oxford to study Social Anthropology.

During our first talks in Oxford, our very different experiences in the *milieux* we had frequented came to light. For instance, for me – who in the harsh late 1940s and early 50s of communist Yugoslavia had been excluded from political life because I was considered politically and ideologically non-correct – the elections there were nothing but a series of carefully directed *political shows*. Under communist rule, the electoral system guaranteed the continuity and stability of power, and the Communist Party behaved as if it was to rule for ever and ever. What was missing was free competition between political programmes, without which any society atrophies and perishes.

Completely different, but also in its own way negative, was the experience that my new friend Aharon brought with him from Israel to Oxford. He explained to me his deep disappointment with the Israeli electoral system based on the principle of proportional representation – even though it had been attractive at the first sight. In its Israeli variant, this system – by which MPs are elected strictly on the basis of the number of votes cast for the party lists – is really *very representative*. It takes into account all the votes cast and gives them equal weight. At the same time, by favouring the small parties, it creates *political instability*.

As confirmed to me also by other Israelis with whom I had the opportunity to speak, in Israel's notoriously unstable coalition governments – composed of small parties and governed by narrow interests – the parties imposed their own priorities, very often to the detriment of vital national interests. This hindered the government from solving burning national problems. All my interlocutors agreed with the view that the present electoral system was a cancer on modern Israeli democracy. Indeed, Nathan's previous boss, the Prime Minister Ben Gurion, had already tried to reform it, but without success. Nathan took the problem to heart as a personal challenge and a stimulus to continue – even after his Oxford years – studying politics, and particularly electoral systems. His successful business career and his long residence in the UK enabled him to follow at close quarters the way the system functioned in the "mother of parliamentary democracies".

The British system of elections, with single-member constituencies decided by a plurality of votes, is called – by analogy with horse races – the *first-past-the-post system* (i.e, the first one to reach the finishing line). In each of the 600-plus constituencies, the candidate wins if he gets a simple majority. The advantage of the British system is that it guarantees *stability of power*. The very next day after the election, it is usually clear who the prime minister is going to be, and who will make up the new government. But the disadvantage of this system is that it is *not sufficiently representative*. All the votes cast for the unsuccessful candidates are worthless, despite the fact that their combined total is often greater than that of the winner.

After years of study, and numerous consultations with political scientists, politicians, psephologists, experts in constitutional law and many others, Nathan created a system, which he called "Total Representation" (TR). He has already published some other books on the subject, in English, Hebrew, Arabic and Croatian. TR combines the high level of *representation* which is achieved in proportional electoral systems (Israel, EU) with the *direct bond* between individual MPs and their voters which is characteristic of the simple majority system in single-member constituencies (Great Britain). However, he adds to it a significant *new dimension*. In the book you are now holding in your hands, there are some chapters about Croatia. You have probably already asked yourself why a book by an Israeli electoral expert includes some chapters on Croatia, and is being published with a Croatian co-author, Ivo Škrabalo. I am in a position to be able to give you an informed answer to these questions.

Aharon Nathan and Ivo Škrabalo met here in Britain in the mid-1980s, and their acquaintance of many years has made this jointly-authored book possible. Aharon Nathan, who has lived in the same London neighbourhood as me for the past 40 years, had heard plenty about Croatia from me, but he wished to learn more from someone living over there. At the time, he already had well-established business connections with a number of companies in different parts of the former Yugoslavia, but he was less acquainted with Croatia. My first thought was to put him in touch with Škrabalo, which I did.

I had known Škrabalo since 1971, when I became a subscriber to and reader of the politically increasingly outspoken *Hrvatski Tijednik* [*"Croatian Weekly"*] from its first issue onwards and, at a distance, recognised in him one of the keenest political minds among the editors. Because of his work on the *Hrvatski Tjednik*, Škrabalo became a political pariah after Tito's crackdown on Croatia in December 1971 and was silenced as a journalist. But he used his "internal exile" very constructively. Already a law graduate, he now concentrated on the study of international law, and obtained a master's degree on the subject of self-determination and secession, His thesis was based on the then-current and fresh case of Bangladesh, which was potentially relevant for Croatia – by now feeling increasingly uncomfortable in Yugoslavia (although no-one was allowed to say so in public). Škrabalo's second university degree had been in film, and this now enabled him to earn a living for himself and his young family as an expert adviser to the Croatia-Film company. In this capacity, he had the opportunity to travel regularly to London for the selection and purchase of foreign films.

Some time in the second half of the 1970s, on the occasion of one of his brief business visits to London (always accompanied by a "politically correct" minder), I had the opportunity to meet him. At the time, I was barred from travelling to Yugoslavia, because of my critical writing in *The Economist* on Yugoslav political affairs (particularly on Croatia, after the suppression of the 1971 democratic movement popularly known as the "Croatian Spring"). My acquaintance (which soon developed into friendship) with this very well-informed and wise political analyst became a great professional advantage to me. From my point of view, he had also an additional value. Unlike the majority of my "Croato-centred" friends and acquaintances in Croatia, he also followed closely and insightfully events in Serbia, on which I wrote regularly in *The Economist*, and he shared his opinions with me. In return, I supplied him from my home – for reading behind locked doors in his London hotel – with bundles of *Nova Hrvatska* [*"New Croatia"*], a democratic opposition journal published in London. I also lent him some other *emigré* publications – also Serbian ones – which for understandable reasons could not be obtained at home.

When, in 1979, I was allowed to travel to Croatia as a journalist again, I met Škrabalo regularly. To these sessions over many cups of coffee, which for me represented real briefings, he used to bring armfuls of clippings from various Croatian publications, plus some from Belgrade like the daily *Politika* and the weekly *NIN*. I still have some of those papers today, with detailed annotations, under the label 'IŠ': for example, notes about the important and politically explosive leaked 1986 Memorandum by the Serbian Academy of Arts and Sciences (SANU). When, during the 1980s, I was producing a couple of documentaries on Yugoslavia for the BBC Radio Four series *Analysis*, Škrabalo assisted me. His penetrating and witty observations were noticed and remembered at the BBC in London, so that after the beginning of the war in 1991 he was regularly called on to participate in programmes by telephone.

The Škrabalos' apartment in Zagreb was not only a place for political debates but also, at least symbolically, for *political activity*. A tradition developed that, every four years, on the day of the US presidential election, a simulated, parallel poll would take place at the Škrabalos' house. This was where the family as well as close friends would cast their votes. These simulated private elections helped me understand that Ivo Škrabalo was not only a brilliant analyst of political events in Yugoslavia and the world, but also a politician-in-the-making. An opportunity to come out of the "making" stage became available when, in the early 1990s, the Communist rulers of the Socialist Republic of Croatia, under Ivica Račan, decided to allow the first free elections in recent Croatian history. For this decision, Račan will be remembered as a man deserving the utmost credit among the founders of modern Croatian democracy. Ironically, at the first free elections, in April 1990, it was not Račan, leader of the reformed Communist SDP that won, but Franjo Tuđman, the former Partisan general under Tito and now leader of the Croatian Democratic Union (HDZ).

In 1989, on the eve of historic changes in Croatia, the Croatian Social-Liberal League was founded; later, it was renamed the Croatian Social-Liberal Party (HSLS). Ivo Škrabalo was among the first people to join; he soon established himself as one of the most prominent members of the HSLS inner circle. In the 1992 elections, he was elected an MP for the HSLS, which was then the strongest party opposing the HDZ. In October 1995 he was again elected as one of the MPs for the city of Zagreb. However – as he explains in one of the chapters in this book – he did not return to Parliament. After the Electoral Commission concluded that Škrabalo had won the majority of votes – and even after the HDZ's candidate, Branko Mikša, had conceded Škrabalo's victory – a mysterious consignment of votes from abroad brought an additional number of votes for the HDZ, and Mikša, not Škrabalo was declared the winner.

Very soon afterwards, Škrabalo once again suffered the consequences of the electoral manipulation which characterised President Tuđman's time in power. After a great victory of the opposition parties in elections for the city of Zagreb, also in October 1995, the City Council elected as mayor one of the leading members of the HSLS – then the strongest opposition party. President Tuđman annulled the outcome, as he did also for the next appointed mayor from the same party. The third appointed mayor was Ivo Škrabalo, but Tuđman "discarded" him as well, as also happened to the fourth elected after Škrabalo. Totally illegally, Tuđman himself then appointed a female HDZ member as mayor.

Škrabalo was elected MP again in elections in January 2000. During his term, and also after his retirement in 2003, he continued to work on the problem of electoral reform in Croatia, on which issue he had already made a number of significant interventions in Parliament. Three years ago, Nathan resumed his visits to Croatia. He and Škrabalo started conducting regular correspondence on the subject of electoral systems, and the idea of publishing a jointly-authored book came up. The idea was presented to Slavko

Goldstein, the prominent publisher and a fervent advocate of liberal democracy. In Nathan's TR system, Škrabalo recognised a system that was also potentially relevant for Croatia. In fact, electoral reform has been a more-or-less permanent subject of debate in Croatian politics since 1990 – for many reasons. As was the case in other post-communist countries, progress towards democracy in Croatia after the first elections in 1990 was neither steady nor easy. Here, Škrabalo describes this progress and the subsequent changes to the electoral system in Croatia, putting the process into a wider historical context.

Every country has its own historical traditions and its specific political circumstances that affect how it votes. So, present-day Croatia does not suffer from the same problems as, for example, Great Britain, with its system of simple majorities in single-member constituencies, widely regarded as unfair. Nor are Croatia's problems identical to those of Israel, with its pure proportional representation system, which generates fragmentation and instability. All those who are searching for solutions should of course bear in mind that no shoe fits all sizes. With this necessary caveat, Škrabalo maintains that Nathan's system of Total Representation brings new possibilities for solving specific problems in the working of a democratic system. Consequently, he evaluates the TR system by two main criteria: first, it ensures true *political representation*, without which no democracy is worthy its name; the second criterion is *political stability*, without which no state can function successfully. In his last chapter, Škrabalo concludes that Nathan's system satisfies both criteria, and he demonstrates with examples how its application can help the current Croatian electoral system to be improved.

I warmly recommend the English version of this book by two highly qualified authors, confident that it will encourage a fruitful public debate in the United Kingdom as it has done in Croatia.

Chapter 14
THE HISTORICAL BACKGROUND TO CROATIAN DEMOCRACY

14.1 Throughout centuries of history, the **Croatian Parliament** (*Hrvatski sabor*) – in spite of its changing structure, irregular sessions and lack of a permanent residence – has been a central institution of political representation. At various times, it has performed all or some of four key functions: legislative, administrative, electoral and judicial. And this has been the case both during Croatia's periods of autonomy and independence, and during eras of domination by foreign powers or federation with neighbouring states. Indeed, Croatia has had an unbroken historical sequence of sessions and operations of different sorts of national or regional parliaments, whether these were people's assemblies, "estates" representations or modern representative bodies. This fact has been one of the main arguments in proving the continuity of Croatian statehood through the last ten centuries.

14.2 Our country's historical memory goes back as far as the 9th century AD, when Vladislav was elected Prince of "Littoral" Croatia (including part of the coastline). Despite the doubts of some historians, no patriotic account of the history of Croatian statehood can overlook the coronation of King Tomislav at a parliament session in Duvno Field in 925 A.D. There were also two later "coronation assembles" for rulers of domestic blood: King Dmitar Zvonimir in 1075 A.D. and Stjepan II in 1089 A.D. Subsequent assemblies which took place in order to crown and/or elect rulers from foreign dynasties add even more weight to the argument in favour of the centuries-long continuity of Croatian statehood. The thesis that there was a personal union between Croatia and Hungary is corroborated by the historical fact that King Coloman/Kálmán from the Hungarian dynasty of Arpads (*Árpádház*) was given a separate Croatian crown at a parliament of Croatian noblemen in 1102 in Biograd, and took the title of "King of Croatia and Dalmatia".

14.3 The acquisition, maintenance and, finally, forfeit of the right of the Habsburg dynasty to the throne of the Kingdom of Croatia (which also included a titular right to Slavonia and Dalmatia) were linked to decisions by the Parliament, as it was constituted at various historical moments. On New Year's Day 1527, at the Croatian Parliament in Cetingrad, noblemen elected the Austrian Archduke Ferdinand of Habsburg as ruler, and solemnly swore allegiance to him and his successors. This decision was made autonomously, two weeks after the Hungarian Parliament in Pressburg had elected the same monarch for the Kingdom of Hungary. Two centuries later, on 9th March 1712, the Croatian Parliament held a session, and – independently of its Hungarian counterpart – accepted and confirmed the *Pragmatic sanction on the succession of the Illustrious Archducal House of Austria*, by which the right of succession to the throne was conveyed also to the female line of the Habsburg dynasty. The Hungarian Parliament confirmed this new internal law of the Hapsburgs in 1723 – that is, eleven years later – which made it possible for the Empress Maria Theresa to accede to the throne.

14.4 Having looked at the role of Croatian representative bodies in electing monarchs, we return now to the earliest period of the Croatian state in the Middle Ages. At that time, parliaments were known as "people's assemblies", where rulers were elected and crowned, lawsuits resolved, and kings' decisions on administration and life confirmed. These bodies began to appear from the early 9th century onwards, and gradually grew into "estates" assemblies, representing noblemen and other citizens. These acted as a brake on the arbitrariness of princes or kings, and became the supreme legislative, administrative, elective and judicial bodies of the principality or kingdom respectively. From the late 13th and 14th centuries onwards, two distinct parliaments operated in the areas of Croatia and Slavonia, and the first joint parliament of the Kingdoms of Croatia and Slavonia was held in 1533.

14.5 For several centuries, the Parliament took this form of an "estates" representative body. Those who participated in deliberations included: Catholic bishops and abbots (the prelature); peers of the realm (viceroys, lords-lieutenant, counts and barons); representatives of the gentry from the various counties; and representatives of royal free cities and districts. The high clergy and nobility came to parliament personally, while the gentry were represented by their elected county members. Verdicts of the Parliament (laws of the country) were submitted to the ruler for confirmation. It was always a unicameral political body; it also elected two special envoys for the joint Hungarian-Croatian Parliament. The last Croatian estates parliament held session in October 1847.

14.6 The history of Croatian civil parliamentarianism began amidst the revolutionary turmoil of 1848. In that crucial year, the body changed its character, turning partly into a modern people's assembly: i.e. an elected, representative body. More specifically, according to the new electoral system – decreed by an injunction from the Viceroy's Council – it was to consist of 192 elected MPs (58 sent by the counties, 44 by the Hapsburg-administered border regions, 77 by free royal cities and a few MPs representing seven chapters of the Catholic Church and three consistoriums of the Eastern Orthodox Church). However, some features of the estates parliaments were preserved, because the status of the so-called "virilists" was maintained: these were persons called because of their birthright (important male members of the high nobility), or because of their high rank in the state and church hierarchy (bishops and high officials in the Viceroy's administration). It must be borne in mind that the right to vote was restricted by property and education. It must also be emphasised that suffrage was accorded only to men, which was also true elsewhere in the world at that time. Because of such restrictions, only around 2.5% of the total population had the right to vote.

14.7 In 1848, the Parliament made several historic decisions. It confirmed the decision by Viceroy Jelačić to cancel all political and legal links with the revolutionary Hungarian government which had rebelled against imperial rule from Vienna, and it assigned dictatorial powers to the same Viceroy because of the imminent war against the Hungarians. Earlier, it had made the decision to abolish serfdom, bringing to an end centuries of feudal relations in the countryside.

14.8 Over the next 20 years, up until the 1868 Hungarian-Croatian Settlement, the Parliament held two more sessions (in 1861 and 1865) under a somewhat modified electoral system, but without significant changes to the restrictions on the right to vote. Some prominent political figures from Dalmatia were also invited to join. But in fact, from 1861 onwards, a distinct Dalmatian Parliament operated (it consisted of 41 MPs elected from four blocs: wealthy taxpayers, the guild of crafts and trades, cities, and rural counties – plus two "virilists"). This Dalmatian parliament sent a delegation to the Imperial Council in Vienna.

14.9 After the Hungarian-Croatian Settlement came into force, between 1868 and 1918 the Croatian Parliament was a pivotal place for the country's intense political life, where factions favouring closer relations with either Austria or Hungary confronted advocates of an independent state: that is, advocates of the establishment of a state of the "Yugoslav nation" (as it was called in that period) inside or outside the Habsburg monarchy. In this period, parliamentary elections were held some ten times, and the Viceroy's government even changed electoral legislation in order to prevent the victory of the opposition. Viceroy Khuen's "electoral order" of 1888 was particularly rigid: under this, only a *"clean-living man of at least 24 years"* had the right to vote, but with additional restrictions concerning his domiciliary status, profession and education. The annual census tax of at least 15 forints (or 30 crowns in the Austrian currency) was considered extremely high, and a political battle for its discontinuation, or at least reduction, was waged. This campaign eventually achieved success in 1910, when the census tax was decreased to 10 forints (20 crowns). How large a move in the direction of universal suffrage this was can be seen from the following figures: under the earlier law, the total number of voters was 50,000 (out of 2,250,000 residents, i.e. around 2.2% of the population), while the lessening of the census tax increased the number of voters to 190,000, i.e. 8.8% of the population.

14.10 Towards the end of World War I, on 29th October 1918, the Croatian Parliament made a decision to dissolve *"all previous relations and links between the Kingdoms of Croatia and Slavonia, on the* *one hand, and the Kingdom of Hungary and the Empire of Austria, on the other hand"* – and the Hungarian-Croatian Settlement was also cancelled. At the same time, *"Dalmatia, Croatia, Slavonia with Rijeka are pronounced a completely independent state with respect to Hungary and Austria"*, which *"joins the common people's sovereign State of Slovenes, Croats and Serbs in the whole ethnographic area of this people"*. In a completely euphoric mood, at the same session, Parliament dissolved itself with the decision that *"it recognises the supreme authority of the National Council of Slovenes, Croats and Serbs"*.

14.11 Croatian parliamentary history after 1918 continued through the National Assembly of the Kingdom of Serbs, Croats and Slovenes (known from 1929 onwards as the Kingdom of Yugoslavia) – until Hitler's Germany, along with its allies Italy, Hungary and Bulgaria, occupied Yugoslavia and broke up its national structure in the April 1941 Blitzkrieg.

14.12 The first Yugoslavia (from 1918 to 1941), which was a centralised, unitary monarchy, spent eight years (1921-29) under a system of parliamentary representation limited by the King's will. This period was ended by the assassination of two Croatian MPs and the wounding of three more during a parliamentary session. There then followed six years (1929-35) of a military-monarchical dictatorship, and then – after the 1931 Decreed Constitution and the King's assassination in Marseilles in 1934 – six more years (1935-41) of a re-established quasi-parliamentarianism. During this period, elections were held twice (in 1935 and 1938); they were, to be fair, direct and multi-party, but women were excluded from public voting.

14.13 After the collapse of the Kingdom of Yugoslavia, Croatia was left to the Ustasha regime, with its extreme Nazi-Fascist orientation. On 10th April 1941, the new government promulgated the nominally Independent State of Croatia (*Nezavisna Država Hrvatska, NDH*). However, this totalitarian quasi-state was in fact under the political and military domination of the Third Reich and Fascist Italy. With the intention of making it appear that the NDH represented continuity in Croatian statehood, the Ustasha leader

(*Poglavnik*), Dr Ante Pavelić, decided to re-establish the Croatian National Parliament. Those invited to take part in the assembly included not only unelected, high-ranking Ustasha officials and two representatives of the German national minority, but also representatives of the last (1918) Croatian Parliament, Croatian representatives elected in 1938 to the last Yugoslav parliament, and some politicians from the Croatian Party of Rights (*Hrvatska stranka prava, HSP*). The new assembly held three sessions during 1942. However, after a group of representatives asked for the dissolution of prison camps and the discontinuation of the persecution of Serbs and Jews, the Parliament was no longer called into session until the end of the war and the defeat of the Ustasha government.

14.14 At the same time, during World War II, Croatian statehood was being restored in a different way under the auspices of the anti-fascist movement. Meeting in Jajce on 29th November 1943, in the area controlled by opposition forces, the Anti-Fascist Council of the National Liberation of Yugoslavia (*Antifašističko vijeće narodnog oslobođenja Jugoslavije, AVNOJ*) re-established Croatian statehood within the federal arrangement of the restored Yugoslavia. Elementary organs of the state government were also formed in the same geographical area. In Topusko, on 8th and 9th May 1944, at its third session, the Anti-Fascist Council of the National Liberation of Croatia (*Zemaljsko antifašističko vijeće narodnog oslobođenja Hrvatske, ZAVNOH*), constituted itself as a "*supreme legislative and executive people's representative body and the supreme organ of state government in democratic Croatia, a bearer of sovereignty of the people and state of Croatia*". Communists predominated in the composition of ZAVNOH, but there were also some members of the Executive Board of the Croatian Peasant Party (*Hrvatska seljačka stranka, HSS*), as well as the Serbian Club and some non-party anti-fascist figures. During its fourth session, which took place in the historic chamber in liberated Zagreb on 21st July 1945, ZAVNOH changed the assembly's name to the "People's Parliament of Croatia" (*Narodni sabor Hrvatske*).

14.15 "Democratic Croatia", as it was described in ZAVNOH's solemn document, soon proved to be only a nominal federal unit within the undemocratic Yugoslavia, under the *de facto* and later even the formal domination of the Communist Party as the only political grouping, The country changed its name several times and its attribute from "democratic" into "people's" and, finally, "socialist" – and elections were frequently held in it for federal, Republic and local representative bodies. These "elections" were – it must be pointed out – general and secret, but in a single-party system they were never competitive. Therefore, despite numerous, frequent, constitutional and systemic changes, and the introduction of what was called "socialist self-management", the period of communist government between 1945 and 1990 can be regarded as a period of complete stagnation in the development of representative democracy in Croatian parliamentary history.

14.16 It might sound paradoxical, but only the last election for the Parliament of the Socialist Republic of Croatia – held in two rounds in April and May 1990 – embodied all those features which qualify elections as being general and free. More specifically, it was only at this last election called by the outgoing communist government that the electorate, for the first time in Croatian history, was *general*, with no discrimination on the basis of property, education and gender; the election was *competitive* in a recently-established multi-party system where political parties could be freely set up and promoted; and voting was *secret* and predominantly *direct* (except for one of the parliamentary chambers, which was a relic of the self-management system that was soon discontinued).

14.17 The Parliament elected in 1990 changed the name "Socialist Republic of Croatia" into "Republic of Croatia", and voted in a new, democratic Constitution which was a basis for a referendum on the future organisation of the country. This referendum was held on 19th May 1991: more than 90% of voters declared themselves in favour of independence and sovereignty, and against *"the permanence of the Republic of Croatia within Yugoslavia as an integral federal state"*. Therefore, on 25th June 1991, the Parliament enacted the *Declaration on the establishment of the sovereign and independent Republic of Croatia* and started the process of disassociation from the Socialist Federative Republic of Yugoslavia. Finally, on 8th October

1991, it enacted the *Decision on the cancellation of all public-law links of the Republic of Croatia based upon which it constituted – together with other Republics and Provinces – the earlier Socialist Federative Republic of Yugoslavia.* The Decision came into force the very same day.

14.18 Having broken the bonds with Yugoslavia and the socialist single-party system, Croatia opted for a system of a free market economy, the rule of law and representative democracy – and this also meant free, secret, direct multi-party elections based on universal and equal suffrage. However, almost all countries in transition from totalitarianism into democracy – with no tradition and experience of free elections – have inevitably had to engage in a search for the best, simplest and most effective electoral system appropriate for the specific challenges faced by each one of them.

Chapter 15
ELECTORAL SYSTEMS: 1990-2007

15.1 In the period between 1990 and 2007, parliamentary elections were held seven times in Croatia (five times to the Chamber of Representatives, i.e. the unicameral parliament, and twice to the Chamber of Counties, which was discontinued in 2001) – almost every time according to different rules. In other words, almost all the basic electoral systems known in the world were applied during this time. Perhaps it seems logical that a country without a tradition of free competitive elections should have, in its own practice, tested out not only the simple-majority electoral system (otherwise known as **first-past-the-post** or **FPTP**) and **proportional representation**, but also mixed electoral systems of various sub-types. However, there are good reasons to believe that these changes were not the result of an effort by the legislature to find and establish the fairest way of representing the voters' will, but were largely the product of the ruling majority's intention to ensure landslide victories for itself and the preservation of its power, through electoral engineering. This lack of a stable system has led to uncertainty among voters about the fate of their own vote, which has, in turn, diminished their interest in going to the polls. It has also, over the long run, brought about an increase in political apathy and a lack of trust in the legitimacy and effectiveness of the long-wished-for system of representative, multi-party democracy.

1990: Parliament of the Socialist Republic of Croatia – two-round electoral system

15.2 In order to enforce the decision of the 11th Congress of the League of Communists of Croatia (*Savez komunista Hrvatske; SKH*), held on 11th-13th December 1989 in Zagreb, on the introduction of a multi-party system and its call for free elections, certain modifications to the 1974 Constitution of the Socialist Republic of Croatia had to be made. Once this decision had been taken, everything was done to speed the process up as much as possible. This was probably because the Communist Party believed that new political groups would not have enough time to find their feet in the changed circumstances – and thus the communists themselves could capitalise on the shift and do well in the elections. Passing the necessary series of nine emergency constitutional amendments (LIV-LXII) presented no problem for the submissive single-party parliament, and these in turn did not interfere with the system of self-management and the organisation of Parliament itself, which was at the time made up of three Councils.

15.3 The new amendments legalised political parties and paved the way for the enactment of an electoral law for competitive elections. The earliest non-communist political parties were registered on 5th February 1990, and as an oddity of the Croatian transition it should be noted that, on this occasion, a monopolistic communist party which had previously exercised power but had had no formal legal status, was now officially registered by a name which paved the way for its own transition: League of Communists of Croatia – Party of Democratic Changes (*Savez komunista Hrvatske – Stranka demokratskih promjena; SKH-SDP*).

15.4 Interestingly, for the first free, multi-party election, the ruling SKH-SDP opted for the single-member plurality system (essentially, FPTP), under which the voter had to cast ballots for individual candidates for all three Councils (next to whose names it would be noted which political parties they belonged to). It was probably calculated that there were more publicly-known personalities among the candidates of the former political establishment, and that the relatively unknown candidates of the newly-founded opposition parties would fare worse. In order to make their path to gaining seats in parliament even more difficult, a two-ballot system was introduced, so that if the ex-communists did not do so well first time around, the party would have a chance to mobilise itself for the second round. To win in the first round, an absolute majority of votes cast was necessary (and the total for the winning candidate had to be no fewer than one-third of all the registered voters in his or her respective constituency). If no-one won a seat in this way, all candidates who had won at least 7% of the vote would enter a second round; however, final victory now required only a simple majority! Each voter had one vote for each of the three Councils of the Parliament.

15.5 The mastermind of this electoral system was a professor of constitutional law and Dean of the Faculty of Law in Zagreb, **Dr Smiljko Sokol** (born 1940). He was also a committed member of the SKH and an official on various Communist Party committees. Later, during the 1990s, Dr Sokol carried on providing professional assistance in a loyal and expert fashion, when he occupied several important posts in the new government: minister without portfolio; President Tudjman's adviser for issues of constitutional law; member of parliament and vice-president of the Committee on the Constitution, Standing Orders and the Political System. The apex of his career came when he was elected for an eight-year term at the Constitutional Court, where he also occupied the post of chairman from 1999 to 2003. His name has been linked with all subsequent changes in Croatian electoral systems, because he created them – either by himself or as a member of a multi-member expert commission. Even when one of his own systems was changed (often very radically), Professor Sokol still played a crucial background role.

15.6 The Parliament of the Socialist Republic of Croatia was made up of three chambers with separate areas of responsibility and with different numbers of members. The number and areas of their electoral constituencies were defined by special laws for this election. In fact, the most important of the chambers was the **Social-Political Council** (*Društveno-političko vijeće, DPV*), to which 80 members were elected from the same number of single-member constituencies. The number of registered voters in each DPV constituency varied in a ratio of 1:4 (so Gospić had 21,802 registered voters, and Susedgrad 80,220). Next came the **Council of Municipalities** (*Vijeće općina, VO*), which had 116 members, one for each municipality of the period. All citizens aged 18 or over with permanent residence in the area of their constituency had the right to vote for these two Councils. However, the election of all 160 members of the **Council of Associated Labour** (*Vijeće udruženog* *rada, VUR)*, which was an institutional expression of the system of workers' self-management, was held only at work-places such as offices and factories, and the right to vote was granted to all full-time employees.

15.7 After a brief official election campaign, notable for the generally correct behaviour of national television and radio, elections for the DPV and VO were held on Sunday, 22nd April 1990, and for the VUR on Monday 23rd April (on a working day, because the election was held at "labour organisations"). Citizen participation in the election was high – with a turnout of no fewer than 84.54% of all registered voters. This showed just how enthusiastic the populace was about being able finally to participate in genuine elections. The level of interest was all the greater because political relations within Yugoslavia were very strained, and throughout Eastern Europe – in what had been a zone of unquestioned communist and Soviet dominance – countries were casting off their totalitarian systems one after another. At the same time, the USSR was facing collapse, with the prospect of a large number of Soviet republics becoming independent.

15.8 The second round of the election in Croatia was held two weeks after the first one (6th and 7th May 1990), and it merely confirmed what had been a foregone conclusion after the first ballot – the landslide victory of the nationalist movement, the Croatian Democratic Union (*Hrvatska demokratska zajednica, HDZ*) over both the incumbent SKH-SDP and the third force, a joint initiative of centrist parties known as the Coalition of People's Accord (*Koalicija narodnog sporazuma, KNS*) – which suffered a complete debacle. This was a confirmation of the experience of many countries which use pure first-past-the-post elections: they tend to over-represent the dominant party and lead to a two-party system. Thus, in the elections for the 80-member Social-Political Council (DPV), the HDZ won 1,196,059 votes (41.61% of the total) but 55 seats (68.75% of those available). Also a surprise in its own way was the performance of the incumbent SKH-SDP: it received no fewer than 1,015,895 votes (35.34% of the total), but this was sufficient for the victory of only 20 representatives – that is, it won 25% of the seats in the chamber.

The KNS candidates were the favourites among urban voters and received 15.29% of the vote, but this brought them only a miserable three seats, i.e. 3.75% of the total number.

15.9 The percentages in the Council of Municipalities (VO) were almost the same, so the HDZ won 71 seats (61.74%), the SKH-SDP 36 seats (31.3%) and the KNS only 5 (4.35%). The results for the Council of Associated Labour (VUR) were also similar: here, the HDZ won 83 out of a total number of 156 seats (53.2%).

15.10 Thus, in the founding Parliament of the Socialist Republic of Croatia, the HDZ, a movement led by **Dr Franjo Tuđman**, had a strong absolute majority, with a total of 209 representatives across all of the three Councils (59.5% of the total seats), which gave it plenty of scope to get down to the business of carrying out its nation-building vision without much regard to the views of other non-communist and anti-totalitarian political groups. Nor did the HDZ need to accommodate differing views on defence tactics, or on its approach to the process of disassociation from Yugoslavia and obtaining Croatian independence (on which goal there was a nationwide consensus).

15.11 Having been elected in such a way, the founding parliament could have faced procedural complications in its proceedings because of its tri-cameral structure: each of the three Councils had separate (but sometimes overlapping) powers. However, even without new constitutional amendments, this problem was summarily overcome in the Parliament itself by a mere modification to the Standing Orders. The changes made it possible to hold joint sessions where laws could be enacted and other decisions made without regard to the division of powers between the chambers. This dramatic alteration to the Standing Orders abolished Parliament's self-management organisation. The assembly then went on to enact a variety of important laws before its eventual dissolution: these included what was known as the Christmas Constitution, and basic laws for Croatia's transition from a federal unit into a sovereign and independent country – as well as for the functioning of multi-party democracy.

15.12 All this was taking place in the shadow of the war which was gradually flaring up in different parts of Croatia. Hostilities took the form of direct aggression by the federal Yugoslav People's Army (*Jugoslavenska narodna armija, JNA*), and by paramilitary forces (armed from the JNA's sources) in a number of districts with a Serbian ethnic majority, as a result of which some 27% of the territory of the Republic of Croatia was put under occupation in the course of 1990-92. These were difficult circumstances for the country's peculiar three-way transition: from totalitarianism to democratic pluralism; from a constitutive unit of a multi-national federation to a sovereign state; and from war (which had to be ended successfully in order to maintain the territorial integrity within the existing borders mapped out at the end of the Second World War) to a state of peace that would enable hundreds of thousands of displaced persons and refugees to return to their homes.

1992: Chamber of Representatives – a combination of the first-past-the-post system and proportional representation

15.13 The 1990 Christmas Constitution stipulated that the Parliament of the Republic of Croatia (*Sabor Republike Hrvatske*) should have two chambers – but in fact the new assembly was established only gradually. This was because a sizeable part of Croatia was at that time beyond reach of the government, having been occupied by the entity known as the "Republic of Srpska Krajina". Thus, circumstances were unfavourable for a definite administrative division of Croatia into counties, which was a prerequisite for calling elections to the Chamber of Counties. So elections to the more significant Chamber of Representatives were held first, in August 1992, with elections to the Chamber of Counties being held only in the spring of 1993 (these will be discussed separately in a later chapter). The electoral law for the Chamber of Representatives opted for a combination of the first-past-the-post system and proportional representation in a single constituency encompassing the whole country, with the ratio between the number of seats elected on the basis of each system being 60:60 (i.e. half-and-half).

15.14 Interestingly, from the standpoint of the system presented and recommended in this book, some of the crucial elements of Total Representation can be recognised here. Although the 1992 mixed system was later abandoned, it can be seen as an attempt to combine the advantages of the British first-past-the-post (FPTP) method with those of Israeli-style proportional representation (PR) – while avoiding the disadvantages of each. The truth is that in a new democracy like Croatia, after several decades of totalitarian monism, the introduction of multi-party democracy without major preparations presented a certain shock for political life, because there was no identifiable political class adept at parliamentarism (except, to some extent, the former communist "nomenclature"). Thus, voters needed to be given an opportunity to choose between different political options, but also a chance to recognise new political personalities within them. Therefore, neither the total personalisation of elections (as in the single-member plurality system of 1990) nor a predominant role for parties under PR (which, almost inevitably, leads to *partitocracy*) were favourable to the gradual development of a democratic consciousness in society, which is a necessary precondition for all segments of the electorate to be represented in Parliament. From this perspective, the 1992 system made sense, despite some of its disadvantages, which will be discussed later.

15.15 For the **1992 election**, members of parliament were to be elected by all Croatian citizens aged 18 or above in the constituency of their permanent residence. Each voter had two votes: one for a candidate (and his deputy) in a single-member constituency, and one for a national list of some of the proposed parties. The lists were closed, which meant that the composition and order of candidates were decided by party leaderships or proponents of independent lists, and the voter could only vote for the whole ticket, with no influence over who would eventually be elected from it. He/she did have a way of expressing split preferences: this could be done by casting his/her first vote for a candidate of a party different from the one for whose national list he cast his/her second vote. There were significant variations in the number of voters per constituency, ranging from 30,872 in Valpovo to 109,697 in Split 2.

15.16 Candidates in single-member constituencies were elected by a simple majority, no matter how large or small it was in relation to the number of voters who took part. If exactly the same number of votes were cast for two or more candidates, it was foreseen that the election in that constituency should go to a second round (though this never actually happened). Translating votes into seats in the PR segment of the election was a bit more complicated. In order to obtain any seats at all, a national list had to obtain at least 3% of the total votes cast. From there, the calculation to translate votes into seats was performed in two stages. In the first stage, the total number of votes received by each national list (*the electoral mass of a list*) was divided by numbers ranging from 1 to 60 (which was the number of MPs elected by proportional representation). From all obtained results, the sixtieth largest result became *a common divisor* used in the second stage of the calculation. In the final calculation, each national list's total tally of votes was divided by the *common divisor* – with that number giving the number of seats won. The result was calculated to two decimal places, where numbers ranging from 1 to 4 were rounded to the nearest lower percentage number, and those ranging from 5 to 9 to the nearest higher percentage number. This procedure was changed in 2003, when the D'Hondt method was legally introduced, with the series of divisors ranging from 1, 2, 3, 4, 5… to the number of seats allocated.

15.17 The first election to the Chamber of Representatives after the enactment of the Christmas Constitution was held on 2nd August 1992, the same day as the first direct election of the President of the Republic (by the majority electoral system, with a possible run-off in the second round). The Republic of Croatia had already received widespread international recognition; it had been admitted to membership of the United Nations; and there was a state of "neither war nor peace" in the country, because the cease-fire on the fringes of the four so-called UNPA zones (under the effective control of Serbian rebels) was being supervised by the international peace forces of UNPROFOR (the United Nations Protection Force), for which approximately 39,000 soldiers from various countries were deployed during a three-year period, from February 1992 to March 1995.

15.18 In this atmosphere of recently-gained national independence, combined with uncertainty regarding the war, a landslide victory was secured by Dr Franjo Tuđman as President of the Republic (he won 56.73% in the first and only ballot), and by his nationalist movement, the HDZ, for the Chamber of Representatives. Despite the competitive conditions of the election, the result – the absolute dominance of a single political option, with no relevant or effective political opposition – can be blamed on the euphoric, but at the same time anxiety-ridden, mood of the country. It turned out that the FPTP system (which applied to one half of the seats) had not succeeded in helping some of the better-known and stronger political figures make their way into Parliament, regardless of their party affiliation. Nor did it create a two-party balance of power – which is its usual outcome. And as a whole, the mixed system (with two votes per elector) led to a significant imbalance between the proportion of seats that each party won compared with its share of the vote.

15.19 The upshot of this was that the ruling party was strikingly over-represented compared with other groups. Thus, in the PR segment, the HDZ won 44.71% of the votes, which translated into 31 places in the chamber (equivalent to 51.67% of the seats elected from national lists). At the same time, however, in the FPTP part of the poll, the HDZ won 38.29% of the votes, which provided it with no fewer than 54 seats – in other words, 90% of the spaces in the chamber elected under this system! All together, having won 1,176,437 votes for its lists (44.71%) and 978,538 votes for candidates in the FPTP segment of the election (38.29%), the HDZ won a total of 85 seats or, in other words, 61.59% of all the seats in the Parliament.

15.20 As for the second-placed political option, the Croatian Social Liberal Party (*Hrvatska socijalno-liberalna stranka, HSLS*), it won 17.72% of the votes in the PR part of the poll, which provided it with 12 seats (20% of those from national lists). However, in the ballot for individual candidates, it won 13.67% of the votes, but secured a plurality in only one constituency, and therefore won just one seat in the FPTP segment. Thus, the HSLS won a total of 13 seats (though this was in fact 14, because one additional seat from the list of minority representatives should also be counted – this will be discussed in a separate chapter).

15.21 Because of the 3% electoral threshold in the PR part of the poll, only five more political groups managed to send representatives to Parliament – and, of these, only the candidates of the regional parties the Istrian Democratic Assembly (*Istarski demokratski sabor, IDS*) and the Rijeka Democratic Union (*Riječki demokratski savez, RiDS*) managed to win any seats at all in the FPTP part of the election. Only one independent candidate won a seat under FPTP (Count Jakob Eltz in Vukovar), but the HDZ never put up a candidate there anyway. The reformed communists abandoned the first part of their two-part party name (SKH-SDP) – the abbreviation SDP now no longer meaning "Party of Democratic Changes" but "Social Democratic Party of Croatia" (*Socijaldemokratska partija Hrvatske*). But unlike in the election of 1990, where they constituted a strong opposition, this time they polled only 5.53% in the PR segment, which provided them with three seats, and 7.54% in the FPTP segment, which left them with no seats at all.

15.22 From the point of view of the voters who participated in the election (turnout was 75.61% -- a drop of nine percentage points from the first free election), results suggest that many of these votes were effectively wasted, and therefore a fair part of the electorate was left unrepresented in Parliament. The consequence of the 3% threshold in the PR segment of the election was that 10.86% of the total votes were left unrepresented. The calculation for the FPTP part of the election was even more drastic. Here, 978,538 (38.29%) of the votes cast won no fewer than 54 out of 60 seats (90% of them), while the remaining six seats (10% of the total) were elected by 441,472 voters (33.02%)! This meant that one seat for the ruling party required, on average, 18,121 votes, while the average number of votes for the remaining seats was no fewer than 73,578. On top of this, one must take into account the fact that candidates from four parties did not win a single seat even though they polled 760,210 votes between them. Behind these figures lay a huge number of unrepresented voters – a fact which should lead to thorough and accountable reflection on the suitability of such a mixed system for a fair and just system of representative democracy.

1995: Chamber of Representatives – a revised combination of proportional representation and the first-past-the-post system

15.23 In late September 1995, the Chamber of Representatives elected in August 1992 made the decision to dissolve itself before the end of its term, and an **early election** was announced for **29th October 1995**. In order to achieve this, electoral legislation was amended (using an emergency procedure which allowed the HDZ to pass the proposal, using its absolute majority, within the prescribed 24-hour period). The mixed electoral system was retained, but with a significant change to the ratio between PR and FPTP. Instead of half-and-half, the balance was tilted in favour of PR (60 MPs), while only 28 MPs were to be elected on the FPTP basis. In addition, a distinct "list for the diaspora" was established, from which Croatian nationals with permanent residence abroad would elect 12 MPs by PR in a separate constituency (this aspect of the Croatian electoral system deserves, and will receive, separate treatment). The electoral threshold for being able to win seats in parliament was raised to 5% for individual parties, 8% for two-party coalitions and 11% for coalitions of three or more parties – and the same two-stage procedure as in 1992 was to be applied in translating the PR votes into seats. Separate constituencies for the election of MPs by national minorities were also created – this, too, will be discussed in a separate chapter.

15.24 The incentive for holding this parliamentary election one year early can be put down to President Tuđman's intention to take maximum advantage of positive public sentiment after his quick, effective and victorious military operations *Bljesak* (*Flash*) and *Oluja* (*Storm*) in the spring and summer of 1995. By means of these operations, the para-statal entities in the sectors known as "West", "North" and "South" were eliminated, while gradual and peaceful integration was agreed for Eastern Slavonia (sector "East"). In this way, the authority of the Republic of Croatia was re-established throughout its national territory, and the uncertain state of "neither war nor peace" was put to an end. There was not much public knowledge about the improper criminal acts carried out on the Croatian side after the liberation of the formerly occupied areas, and they were barely discussed in the public arena. Meanwhile, the mass exodus of the Serbian population from these zones met with little sympathy among the Croatian public, probably because it called to mind the mass expulsion of Croatian and non-Serbian residents from these same areas during the first stages of the war in 1991.

15.25 Apart from this political calculation about national euphoria, another incentive for amending the electoral legislation (if one interprets it as a way of ensuring an even larger HDZ majority) was the outcome of the first election to the Chamber of Counties, held in 1993 – when it first became apparent that the opposition was strengthening itself and becoming more intelligent in its approach. Then, the strongest opposition party, the HSLS, won 16 seats, compared to the HDZ's 37 seats (i.e. the HSLS won more than 25% of the 63 vacancies for MPs), even though the electoral system in this chamber was also designed to favour disproportionately the party with the greatest number of votes. This made the HDZ feel that the existing balance in favour of FPTP in the Chamber of Representatives was a danger to it, since it was likely that the opposition would unite around single candidates in each constituency. Thus, the system was tilted more towards PR.

15.26 In fact, although the outcome of the 1995 election was another HDZ victory, it showed that the party would have been better off sticking with the previous balance of PR and FPTP, since in the FPTP segment of the election, it won 21 seats (i.e. 75% of those available) with 1,055,448 votes (44.87% of the total), while in the PR part of the poll, it won 42 seats (52.50% of those available) with 1,093,403 votes (45.23% of the total). So, in all, it won 63 seats in Parliament in this way. However, when we add to that 12 additional seats obtained through the list for the diaspora, Tuđman's mass movement once again obtained an absolute majority, with 75 seats (out of a total of 127).

15.27 Under the FPTP rules, the HSLS won two seats, and other opposition parties managed to win five seats in total. In the

PR segment, the opposition New Parliament 1995 coalition, which brought the Croatian Peasant Party (*Hrvatska seljačka stranka, HSS*), together with four other minor parties, did unexpectedly well – receiving no fewer than 441,390 votes (i.e. 18.26% of the total) and 16 seats. Outside the coalition, the HSLS polled 279,245 votes (11.55%) with 10 seats, and the SDP recovered noticeably from its performance in previous elections, its 215,839 votes (8.93%) giving it 8 MPs from its list and two more from the FPTP segment. Meanwhile, the radical nationalist Croatian Party of Rights (*Hrvatska stranka prava, HSP*) received 121,095 votes (7.09%) for its list and thus gained four MPs.

15.28 It is interesting to note that under FPTP, parties which agreed to oppose the HDZ with only one candidate per constituency received 917,252 votes, which provided them with no more than seven seats (25%). This was the case even though they lagged barely 125,000 behind the votes which provided the HDZ with three times more seats. By and large, the HDZ accomplished the intention behind its redesign of the mixed electoral system, and obtained an almost two-thirds majority (75 MPs out of 127). By expending just a little more effort to win over MPs from minor parties, the party could then go on to enact legislation of all kinds without difficulties – even, if necessary, constitutional amendments.

15.29 One of the problems with free elections in countries which had not until that point been acquainted with the basic practice of representative democracy was a general lack of experience in managing electoral bodies and procedures properly and impartially – though this could sometimes also be put down to a lack of political will. Above all, the voting process was not sufficiently regulated or supervised at all its stages so as to render impossible fraud at polling stations or at the count. In fact, the Croatian experience shows that, within an electoral system already designed to favour the ruling party, it is possible to increase this advantage even more by drawing constituency boundaries in a particular way – gerrymandering – and making it impossible for party representatives and NGOs to monitor and supervise the poll thoroughly.

15.30 Here I will take the liberty to recount a little of my personal experience from the October 1995 election. Within the ranks of the opposition, we were aware that, given the euphoric climate of public opinion after the military triumph, we stood more chance of getting into Parliament in the PR segment of the election than we did in the constituencies, where a simple majority without a second ballot was necessary and sufficient for election. However, even though I had a virtually guaranteed place among the top ten candidates on my party's list (having already served as an MP), the leader of the HSLS made a personal request that I should stand for election in the FPTP segment (replacing one of the party's other leading figures, who had stood down at the last minute). My candidacy was to be in what was known as the 26th constituency, which included the centre of Zagreb. This constituency was considered rather sensitive because – for the sake of its prestige – the HDZ felt it needed a victory in the heart of the capital. So it put up as its candidate none other than the then-mayor of Zagreb, Branko Mikša. In addition, this was precisely the constituency where the opposition had been unable to reach a consensus about putting up a single candidate, because the Action of Social-Democrats (*Akcija socijaldemokrata, ASH*) insisted on putting up Silvije Degen, who was the popular president of the "Zagrebers' Club" (*Klub Zagrepčana*), while the HSLS, as the strongest opposition party, also wanted to appear in this central constituency.

15.31 So, aware of the financial advantage that the city budget put at the service of my opponent from the HDZ, I resorted to a rather cheap and basic campaign. For instance, one night just before the weekend, my party volunteers stuck our yellow-and-blue posters so high up on the lamp-posts that the city cleaners took three days to remove them. On another occasion, I announced that I would set up a table in the street at a certain place and at a certain time in order to talk to passing voters. This unusual approach obviously had some effect, because in the early hours of the morning after the election, an unofficial report from the Electoral Commission listed me as a winner, admittedly by an unusually narrow margin – and my challenger Mayor Mikša personally congratulated me on the radio. The tiny difference in the number of votes led to suspicions in our party that the ballots had not been counted properly, because where we had election monitors at polling stations, they had informed us that I was leading by a margin of 3 to 2. However, after the votes from all 147 polling stations had been counted, it was announced that Mikša and I had received around 32,000 votes each (with a victory margin for me of just 172 votes), while the third-placed candidate, Degen, had received 14,500 votes. But my joy did not last long. Later that day, the president of the Electoral Commission, Dr Krunislav Olujić, announced that around a thousand votes had arrived later from "diplomatic missions abroad, from deep-sea ships, from barracks and from polling stations in jails" – so Mikša prevailed by a margin of some 400 votes. This caused indignation, mockery and mistrust – and led to a strong, widespread, public belief that there had been electoral fraud. One piece of evidence for this came from the fact that, out of a total of about 100,000 votes cast, Mikša and I had been practically at level-pegging, but that when another 1,000 votes came in, the ratio was suddenly 7 to 3 in favour of him.

15.32 We appealed to the Electoral Commission, to no avail. But when our representatives, Vlado Primorac and Hrvoje Kraljević, examined election materials from 19 randomly selected polling stations, they found irregularities in no fewer than 16 of them. The most common form of manipulation took the form of invalidated votes. It only took someone from the electoral board to circle one extra candidate on a ballot paper for that vote to become invalid. The most suspicious case was at one polling station where, on no fewer than 50 out of 52 invalid ballots, one of the circled names was – mine! As for the additional votes from prison and abroad, we also investigated those, but the late Primorac told me, laughingly, that these ballots were so perfectly in order that this was itself an indication that they had been carefully faked. We came to the conclusion that the additional votes had been requested overnight, at the last minute, after the ruling party's combined efforts at minor vote-rigging in various city polling stations had not produced the desired effect. So it turned out that I did not enter Parliament that year, although I *was* described as "a moral victor of an immoral election" (a quotation from a greeting card). I came to realise that, in politics, morality in general – even a moral victory – cannot be put to any real use...

15.33 In all the new Eastern European democracies, after their initial electoral experiences, it soon turned out to be necessary to establish preconditions so that multi-party elections would be simultaneously *free* and *fair*. At Croatia's first election in 1990, there were initial doubts about whether the political will existed for the election to be orderly – but, in the end, few people complained about incorrectness at polling stations, where all parties had the right to send their representatives to the electoral organising committees. At the next election (1992) it was stipulated that these committees should be composed of non-party people, but the parties did have the right to send monitors. However, although the organising committees were supposed to be non-partisan, in practice they were full of relatives and other people close to HDZ members – and even though parties had the right to send monitors, the minor, and even the major, opposition groupings did not have enough people at their disposal, and many of them did not want to be publicly associated with the opposition. In the 1995 election, there was a rule that there could only be one monitor from the ruling party and one other representing all the opposition parties; these had to agree who it would be and where he or she would be stationed. However, as the official opposition included some parties who were, in practice, close to the HDZ, there was mistrust about the scrutiny and correctness of the election.

15.34 In the elections after 1990, other questions of irregularity were raised, mainly because of out-of-date voter registers (with their proverbial "departed souls") and the discontinuation of the practice of sending registration reminders to potential voters, encouraging elderly and uninformed voters to exercise their right to vote. There were also objections to the composition and workings of electoral committees, as well as to the decision not to allow the participation of independent, impartial monitors. In the 1995 election, international monitors did appear, either from certain countries' diplomatic missions, or as special envoys of inter-governmental organisations like the Council of Europe and the OSCE. However, they usually arrived just two or three days before the election, and left the day after, even before the announcement of the first provisional and unofficial results. Their reports usually confirmed the correctness of the electoral procedure, with possibly some parenthetical and minor objections.

15.35 In Croatia, there is no record of any really major scandals regarding electoral irregularity – a few isolated cases of discarded boxes full of ballots being found near polling stations, or almost inexplicable results from late-arriving votes, such as in my own case, hardly count as such. However, things started to improve after the setting up of a non-party civil society association which aimed to encourage citizens to participate more actively in political processes: its name was GONG (originally, the acronym for *Građani organizirano nadziru glasovanje*). During presidential elections, and despite resistance from the government, GONG sent its volunteer monitors to polling stations. Then, in 1999, the right of non-governmental organisations to be accredited, to monitor the whole electoral process, and especially to observe the conduct of elections was legalised, as long as they applied in advance and received accreditation. Since the simplest and probably the most widespread form of minor fraud in elections was the transformation of a valid vote into an invalid one by circling an extra candidate on the ballot paper, it is significant that from 2000 onwards and after GONG came on the scene, there was a fall in the number of invalid ballots registered in all elections (from 1.66% in 2000 to 1.48% in 2007). During the 1990s, these figures were significantly higher (3.85% in 1990 and 3.31% in 1995). In any event, even leaving to one side the increased activity of NGOs, Croatia's political culture and democratic standards improved slowly but gradually, so there was less and less room for vulgar incorrectness at elections.

15.36 As for impartiality, it should be emphasised that in Croatia, in the past 10 years, there has been no public challenge to the overall result of any election using judicial mechanisms – but one still finds cases which question the full political impartiality of electoral bodies. Many things in electoral management and the behaviour of the media are not regulated properly yet, and the difficult task of strengthening the transparent funding of parties and electoral campaigns has yet to be completed. The media (both public and commercial) also need to do more to develop general democratic awareness among voters, and fight indifference – which can also be interpreted as a reflection of disillusionment with the system of representative democracy.

2000: Chamber of Representatives – 2003 and 2007: Parliament – proportional representation

15.37 In its difficult transition, burdened by war, from a half-century-long single-party totalitarian system towards multi-party democracy, Croatia also went through a detrimental but relatively short-lived decade-long regime which deserves the inherently contradictory name of *multi-party autocracy*. More specifically, the 1990 Christmas Constitution established a structure of semi-presidential government (similar to De Gaulle's Fifth Republic) in which the predominant features were the constitutional – and in practice additionally increased – powers of the President of the Republic. He became virtually an omnipotent head of state upon whose will, and sometimes mood, many important national political decisions depended. The first President of the Republic, Dr Franjo Tuđman, must be credited with the establishment of the state for which, while waging war, he procured independence and international recognition. However, at the same time, he was not the architect of democracy; nor did he successfully carry out the economic transition from a system of self-management to an open market.

15.38 During the second half of the 1990s, it was clear that Tuđman's authoritarian system was becoming weaker and weaker. In late 1996, it was announced that the president was seriously ill. Almost simultaneously, there was a mass demonstration by more than 100,000 people in central Zagreb in support of the radio station known as *Radio 101* – and, contrary to his orders, this was not broken up by the police. This led to a *dismantling of fear*, which is always a precondition for the withering away of strict personal regimes.

15.39 In February 1998, at the call of the trade unions, almost 80,000 people tried to break through to the same square, but they were stopped by 8,000 policemen. Tuđman called the protestors a mob, but on 1st May, during the celebration of the workers' holiday, he was hissed down. Afterwards, his mainstay, the Defence Minister Gojko Šušak, died, and there were many scandals and a crisis in the banking system, during all of which the president's health was deteriorating. The HDZ and the whole country were preparing for the post-Tuđman period. Fortunately, democratic institutions already existed; they only needed to be improved and put into full effect. Aware that they would be deprived of Tuđman's charisma at the next election, leading figures in the government became uneasy about losing support within the existing electoral system, so they made the decision – this time by means of a consensual method – to change it. The idea was that the new system would nullify the opposition's objections about a lack of proportionality between votes and seats, and would still give the leaderless HDZ a chance of victory – even though it was now becoming a classic political party, with internal quarrelling and factional feuding.

15.40 In March 1999, the chairman of the parliamentary Committee on the Constitution, Standing Orders and Political System, Vladimir Šeks, appointed a working group to draft a broad proposal on the principles of electoral legislation. In addition to the inevitable Professor Smiljko Sokol, this was made up two professors from the Political Science Faculty who were also leading psephologists – Mirjana Kasapović and Ivan Grdešić – and two of Sokol's fellow-teachers from the Constitutional Law Department at the Zagreb Faculty of Law, Branko Smerdel and Mario Jelušić. The group completed its task within two weeks, issuing the document *"Basic principles of legislation for the election of representatives in the Croatian State Parliament – a proposal"*, in which they opted for the application of PR with a fairly large number of constituencies and a legal electoral threshold. The working group emphasised that the new electoral legislation should be based on a consensus among parliamentary political parties, which would be a guarantee of the continuity and stability of the electoral system; they argued that after ten years of democratic changes, it was high time that a more durable and stable system was institutionalised.

15.41 Starting from "the principle of fair political representation of all segments of the electorate", the proponents asserted categorically that this principle "can only be realised through proportional representation". However, taking into account the need for effective political authority, they advocated a reasonably large number (10) of multi-member constituencies (with 10 MPs being elected in each), but that the number of residents in each constituency must not differ by more than +/- 5 per cent. Furthermore, they proposed a legal electoral threshold of 5% for parties and 8% for electoral coalitions. Lists would be closed, and the electoral lists of the same party in different constituencies should have different people's names at the top (contrary to the earlier practice, when Tuđman was the name at the top of all the HDZ's lists, even though he could not, as President of the Republic, be nominated for the parliament). The proposal asserted that PR is a simple system, easily understandable to voters, who thus feel that their votes "are not wasted". It should also be noted that in the part of the proposal for the election for the Chamber of Representatives, the veteran architect of Croatian electoral systems, Dr Sokol, entered the qualification that "even though he still considers the combination of PR and first-past-the-post the most appropriate", he was willing to accept PR in ten constituencies as a joint proposal. But he accompanied this with a significant remark: *"He does not do this just for the sake of the consensus, but also because this form of proportional representation – because of its index of proportionality and its likely political consequences – is close to his variant of the mixed system"*

15.42 As for the touchy subject of the election of representatives of the diaspora, the working group confirmed the voting rights of all Croatian nationals, even those without permanent residence within Croatia, and also the need to ensure their appropriate representation. They suggested that the majority party and the opposition should reach a compromise settlement on the mode of this "diaspora" election and the number of its representatives. Dr Kasapović and Dr Grdešić also entered certain qualifications in this part of the Proposal which will be discussed further elsewhere. Regarding the *"politically very sensitive and disputed question of the representation of national minorities"*, the working group recommended that the majority party and opposition parties should also reach their own agreement on that.

15.43 Based on this Proposal, in late October 1999 a new package of electoral legislation was passed more or less consensually, by which the already well-established (but often criticised) mixed system was replaced by proportional representation in 10 large constituencies. Within each constituency, 14 MPs would be elected based on closed and blocked lists. To translate votes into seats, the law stipulated the same method as in 1992 and 1995. In addition, a separate 11th constituency for voters with no permanent residence within the Republic of Croatia was envisaged, popularly called the "list for the diaspora", which would also have 14 candidates, but the number of actual seats would vary according to a "non-fixed quota", and would be decided with reference to the number of valid votes required to elect an MP in the ten constituencies for voters with permanent residence in Croatia. A single 5% electoral threshold was introduced for all lists (party lists as well as coalition lists). The same package of electoral legislation also introduced some changes into the previous system for the election of representatives of national minorities.

15.44 This new system has been in operation up until the present day, because it has achieved widespread public acceptance, is simple and understandable to voters, and has led to a greater level of representation in the ratio between the number of votes and parliamentary seats won by individual parties. During this period, there have been significant improvements in the political culture of campaigns, though the media tends to interpret legal requirements for balance and equal airtime in a rather strict and formal way, which has restricted journalists' freedom and led to dry, boring debates which lack real conflict and controversy.

15.45 At polling stations, there has been a general move towards correctness and transparency. This has taken place both because of the presence of electoral committees whose membership gives equal representation to majority and minority parties, and because it is now legally possible for there to be independent, accredited monitors. So there have been no significant protests about irregularities, and the proportion of invalid ballots, compared with previous elections, has been halved (1.66% compared with 3.31% previously). Nevertheless, even under this system, there is well-used room for manipulation when it comes to drawing the boundaries of constituencies. Although the provision of the electoral law that the number of voters per constituency must not vary by more than +/– 5 per cent has been largely observed (which means there are around 360,000 voters per constituency), less attention has been paid to another legislative instruction: that "attention must be paid, as far as possible, to the legally defined areas of counties, cities and municipalities in the Repub lic of Croatia". In fact, the way that boundaries have been drawn suggests that gerrymandering is never far from the minds of those doing the drawing. This can be can be seen most obviously in the case of Zagreb, the capital, with an approximate population of 770,000, which would logically imply that it should be divided into two constituencies. However, contrary to any logic, some parts of the city have been divided into no fewer than four constituencies, which tie in with the neighbouring counties. Blending the urban with the rural electorate in this way has given the ruling party some extra chances, and weakened the opposition's hand in its urban strongholds. I can say, from my own personal experience that I did not know who I was actually representing, because my own 7th constituency extended from the southern part of Zagreb city, over the south-west part of the County of Zagreb (including lake Jarun) and the whole County of Karlovac to the eastern part of the County of Primorje and Gorski Kotar, finally emerging on the seaside at Novi Vinodolski. I used to say as a joke that I represented voters "from Jarun to the Adriatic" ("*od Jaruna do Jadrana*")

15.46 The first **election** under the new system of proportional representation was held, exceptionally, on **Monday, 3rd January 2000** (in order not to interfere with the celebration of the New Year and of the New Millenium). Since the head of state, Dr Franjo Tuđman, had passed away on 10th December 1999, three weeks before the election, campaign activities were suspended for a three-day morning period. Then, after the funeral, they were extended, as were all the other deadlines, but nobody complained about this because it is always expedient to find pragmatic solutions for unpredictable situations, even though they deviate from the letter of abstract rules.

15.47 As for the outcome of the election, it brought about the first **change of government** since the establishment of the democratic political system. This change of administration also marked the end of the period of government by President Tuđman, which had been largely autocratic despite the multi-party system. The former opposition, which ran together in two blocks, won a landslide victory over the HDZ. The greatest number of votes (1,133,136) was received by the Social-Democratic-Liberal coalition of SDP/HSLS (40.84% of the vote, which provided them with 71 seats, i.e. 50.71%), while the four parties of the so-called Poreč Group (HSS, IDS, HNS and LS) received 431,484 votes (15.55%) and won 24 seats. Meanwhile, the hitherto unbeatable HDZ received 676,264 votes and 40 seats (plus six more from Croatian expatriates), with the right-wing HSP/HKDU coalition – which barely passed the threshold with 5.28% of the vote (and five seats) – joining them in opposition. The other four party lists and independent candidates did not pass the electoral threshold, so that their 207,294 votes (or 7.47% of the total) were left unrepresented, or, in common parlance, were wasted.

15.48 The coalition government of six, and later five, parties did not change the electoral system during its term, so elections were held twice more under the same system and, on both these occasions, victory went to the HDZ. In the election of 23rd November 2003, it received 800,503 votes (33.23% of the total), thus winning 62 seats plus four more from the diaspora. The SDP (together with the IDS, Libra and LS) received 560,593 votes (23.26%) and won 43 seats (of which 34 were the SDP's alone). The HNS (with the PGS) polled 198,781 votes (8.25%) and won 11 seats (10 HNS + 1 PGS), but other parties also received some votes and seats: the HSS 7.26% of the vote and nine seats; the HSP 6.46% and eight seats; HSLS/DC 4.13% and three seats; HSU 4.08% and three seats. So although certain parties fell below the 5% threshold nationally, they passed it in particular constituencies, and were thus able to win seats. In this way even one representative of a minor party, the HDSS, entered Parliament.

15.49 The **most recent election**, which was held on 25th **November 2007**, showed support for the minor parties falling away, and a concentration of political power in two centres – the right-wing one (HDZ+HSP+HSS and their satellites), and the left-wing one (SDP+HNS and regional parties) – while the once strong liberal option has almost disappeared from the political horizon, and what is left of it has edged towards the ruling parties. The HDZ received 834,203 votes (34.91%), and won 61 seats (plus four more from Croatian expatriates – 73,446 votes); the SDP polled 776,656 votes and won 56 seats; the second-ranked opposition party, the HNS, received 168,439 votes (7.05%) and won seven seats; the joint HSS/HSLS list received 161,813 votes and won eight seats (HSS six and HSLS two), while two minor parties, the HSP and the HSU, won one seat each. This electoral system (of PR in geographical constituencies) proved helpful to regional parties with strong local support: thus, the IDS in Istria and the HDSSB in Slavonia each won three seats. Other parties and independent candidates which did not reach the threshold in any constituency received a combined total of 151,412 wasted votes (which amounts to 6.34% of the total number of valid votes).

15.50 The outcome of the election showed that the current electoral system in Croatia encourages *partitocracy*; reduces the importance of the candidate's personality (except, to some extent, for the "leader" of the list, who does not have to be a candidate!); and encourages the existence of fewer, larger parties. Interestingly, the 5% electoral threshold is not a totally decisive factor in excluding minor parties from Parliament because they may have strong support in certain parts of the country, enabling them to win seats. But they can still be eliminated by the *natural threshold*. This is because in a PR-based constituency system, depending on the balance of forces in a given area, you still need a certain number of votes to win even one seat. For example, in the 2007 election, the cases of the HSP in the 5th constituency and the HNS in the 8th constituency showed that both parties reached the 5% electoral threshold, but nevertheless did not participate in the allocation of seats because of the natural threshold, which exceeded 5%.

Chapter 16
CROATIAN EXPATRIATES – THEIR RIGHT TO VOTE AND SPECIAL REPRESENTATION

16.1 During the war years of the early 1990s, **Croatian expatriates** provided valuable moral and material assistance to their homeland, which was being forced to obtain its independence and existence as a sovereign country by armed resistance. This undeniable fact was used as a justification for what happened in the autumn of 1995, when the electoral system was amended in such as way as to provide the HDZ with additional safe seats. The thinking went as follows: there were about 400,000 Croats living permanently outside Croatia who had already easily obtained Croatian citizenship – this figure represented about 10% of the electorate in Croatia itself. Since voters in Croatia were to elect 120 MPs, the conclusion was drawn that 10% of parliamentary seats should belong to expatriates. It was therefore stipulated that the **"diaspora"** should **elect 12 MPs** from a separate list.

16.2 This electoral legislation was enacted in a hurry in the Chamber of Representatives just before its self-dissolution – and then a new election was called. The 1995 vote was held in a strongly patriotic atmosphere, in the aftermath of Operations "Flash" and "Storm" – effective military victories over insurgent Serb forces, which rather than resisting the well-equipped and trained Croatian Army, ended up mostly fleeing (together with almost all the civilian population of the occupied areas). Among the Croatian opposition and the public as a whole, the move to change the electoral law was denounced as an attempt by the ruling party to gain extra profit from this situation. It was certainly not seen as an opportunity for true representation of the diaspora, i.e. Croatian expatriates. There was particular questioning of the fact that Croats in **Bosnia-Herzegovina** had been given the right to vote in Croatia, as under most definitions they did not fit the criteria for true expatriates, since they were native residents in their own homeland, which was an independent, sovereign neighbouring country, and they also paid taxes and had civil responsibilities there, which they did not do in Croatia. Above all, they had the right to vote in Bosnia.

16.3 But, in fact, a law had already been passed which granted **dual citizenship**, i.e. a certificate of Croatian citizenship (*domovnica*) and a Croatian passport, to anyone outside the country who could prove his/her Croatian ethnic origin, even in the second generation. Numerous overseas expatriates and their descendants had taken advantage of this, but citizenship was granted in even larger numbers to Croats from Bosnia-Herzegovina, even while war was still being waged there and there was no final solution on the horizon to the new status of this multi-nationa1 former Yugoslav republic. It is worth nothing that under the Dayton peace agreement of 1995, the Croats of Bosnia-Herzegovina obtained the status of one of three constitutive nations of that republic.

16.4 At first, political arguments against the voting right for Croatian expatriates and the election of their special representatives were ignored by the government, but in time public opposition to this move became louder and louder. So in 1999, during the reform of the electoral system, changes were made to the method of calculating the number of these special representatives. But not enough was done to clarify the situation at the constitutional level, and more harmonisation is required.

16.5 The Constitution of the Republic of Croatia, Article 45, clearly states in the first paragraph that *"Croatian citizens aged 18 and above have universal and equal suffrage in accordance with the law"*. However, in the second paragraph, the Constitution stipulates the responsibility of the state to *"ensure, even to its nationals who happen to be outside its borders at the election day"*, that they can use their right to vote *"so that they can vote even in countries in which they find themselves or in any other way stipulated by law"*. I emphasise the word *happen* in the quotation because it implies that the voting right is dependent upon one's usual residence being within Croatia. However, since a large number of citizens with permanent residence *outside* Croatia had already been created by the policy of dual citizenship, in the 1992 election there had been two different types of voting abroad.

Voters with permanent residence within the Republic of Croatia, but who *happened* to be abroad on election day, voted at Croatian diplomatic and consular missions, with two ballots: one for candidates from their respective local constituencies, and one for national lists. Voters with no permanent residence in Croatia had only one vote: for 60 candidates from the proposed PR lists (as the constituency in the PR segment incorporated the whole of Croatia and all its voters).

16.6 This logical solution, however, was not preserved in the 1995 parliamentary election. Since diaspora Croats generally saw loyalty to President Tudjman and the HDZ as an expression of true patriotism, the HDZ tried to find a way of translating this sentiment into an increased number of safe seats for itself. Thus, voters who did not have permanent residence within the territory of the Republic of Croatia were to elect 12 MPs based on special lists using the proportional formula, with a 5% electoral threshold. The number of MPs was justified by the supposed number of expatriate voters (close to 400,000), which amounted to around 10% of the total electorate, though this was all based on very unreliable and out-of-date voting registers. It also ignored the fact that the turnout among Croatian expatriates was significantly lower than the domestic one – which made these MPs less representative than those elected within the country. In 1995, there was also a departure from the rule that voting could only be carried out at diplomatic and consular missions – so polling stations were opened everywhere: for instance, at Catholic missions, in emigrant clubs, even in Croatian restaurants abroad! Moreover, the candidates for the "constituency for the diaspora" did not have to have permanent residence outside the Republic of Croatia, so as a rule they were residing within the homeland and were in no way representative of the electorate that voted for them: i.e. the expatriates!

16.7 It must be remembered that the Constitution does not refer to a **special right to representation** of any segment of the electorate anywhere, except for **national minorities** – and therefore the idea that diaspora voters should be able to elect their own special representatives is not consistent with its provisions. In fact, the outcome of the 1995 election showed that 90,012 voters from the diaspora voted in 12 HDZ MPs from the special list, which means that 90% of those who actually voted supported the ruling party, demonstrating exactly why the HDZ had pushed for this new provision. But each victorious diaspora candidate was elected with, on average, just 7,501 votes – a much smaller number than was required to win a seat within Croatia itself. Indeed, although there were 398,839 registered voters without permanent residence within the Republic of Croatia, only 109,389 of these actually voted: that is, only 27.43%.

16.8 When this new experience was taken into account in the revision of electoral legislation in 1999, a new, different solution for the number of MPs elected by Croatian expatriates was reached. This new arrangement for such voters specified that they would have a distinct (11th) constituency, where, using the *non-fixed quota* method, the number of seats would depend on the average number of valid votes per seat cast in the other 10 constituencies – in other words, those belonging to voters who had permanent residence within the Republic of Croatia. The maximum number of seats within the extra, 11th constituency would be 14 – just as in the homeland constituencies. The procedure for calculating the number of MPs that would be elected in the 11th constituency by the *non-fixed quota* method was specified in Article 41, paragraph 2, of the Electoral Act: *"The total number of valid votes of voters in the ten constituencies of the Republic of Croatia will be divided by 140, which is the number of MPs elected in these constituencies. The number of valid votes in the special constituency will be divided by the result obtained in this way (a quotient). The result that will be obtained is the number of MPs elected in the special constituency. If the result is not a whole number, it will be rounded up to the nearest whole number from 0.5 and above, and rounded down to the nearest whole number from below 0.5".* This formula has been used three times up until the present day, and the earlier number of 12 MPs for the diaspora has been shown to have been unrealistic. In the 2000 election, in the 11th constituency, 126,841 voters (or 35.22%) voted, which provided six seats (all for the HDZ); the next time, in 2003, the turnout fell to 70,527 voters (17.78%), which provided four seats (again for the HDZ), and in

2007, the votes of 22.32% of the diaspora electorate were translated into five seats. Although this change in the electoral legislation paid more attention to the principle of equality of suffrage and gave the diaspora MPs greater representative authenticity, the fundamental question of whether there is any justification for nationals without permanent residence within Croatia to be able to elect special representatives remains.

16.9 The special voting right awarded to Croatian expatriates has led to profound theoretical and practical debates in other countries which have a significant diaspora. Its advocates have put forward various arguments: that expatriates have an interest in helping to shape governments in the countries from which they originate; that they are intimately tied to their old homelands; that they are interested in the future and well-being of their parent countries; that they provide financial assistance to those countries; and that they are keen for their parent countries to maintain and foster national and cultural identity etc. Opponents, on the other hand, suggest that voting rights for expatriates and emigrants must not be awarded as a *quid pro quo* for economic benefits, political support or emotional attachment. The right to vote should belong only to those who live within the same legal system, so voters must be both subjects and objects of legislative authority. Voting should not be reduced to the simple homesickness of expatriates, because it establishes a government which can give people money and take it away from them, affect their private lives, commit them to prison, send them to war, and sometimes even take their lives or put them in danger. Under the Croatian system, expatriates can participate in the formation of a government, but evade all its actions. The fact that Croatia (like some other countries, among which it, unfortunately, is prominent) easily grants citizenship to ethnic Croats, no matter where and for how long they have lived outside Croatia, and even provides them with the right to elect special MPs, does not make a big difference to such an understanding of the problem.

16.10 A few other European countries with numerous expatriates have introduced the concept of special "diaspora" MPs, but only in very small numbers, so that they cannot affect the balance of power in parliament. In **Portugal,** the European diaspora elects two

MPs, and the non-European diaspora elects another two. In **Italy**, in each of its two chambers there are five or six such MPs (which amounts to only around 1-2% of the legislature). Compared with the above-mentioned countries, **Croatia's** 1995 law leads the way in granting extensive power to voters without permanent residence in the homeland. And the 1999 reform only partly reduced the impact this can have on the balance of power between different political groups.

16.11 To look at another example: **Israel**, with a huge ethnic and religious diaspora all over the world, has a completely different approach. Even though virtually the entire Jewish population of Israel is made up of migrants (and their descendants) who have come from abroad, Israeli citizenship has been never been granted indiscriminately just because someone belonged to the Jewish religion or nationality. Only a person of Jewish origin who has settled in Israel and performed some civil duties for the country can obtain the status of a citizen (for example, he/she has to master the language, pay taxes, and the youth of both sexes have to enlist for military service). And even though suffrage is granted to each and every Israeli national no matter where his/her permanent residence is, it can be exercised only within the territory of Israel (which also includes the premises of diplomatic and consular missions). This means that whoever wishes to vote abroad must, on election day, be in an overseas country or city where there is an Israeli embassy or consulate. Even though a sort of a new diaspora has emerged during the six decades of the existence of the state of Israel (it is estimated that around a million Israeli nationals have permanent residence abroad), no-one has ever contemplated the possibility of giving them special representatives.

16.12 In March 1999, there was some disagreement within the Croatian working group which drafted the proposal for the reform of electoral legislation about the right to vote and election of expatriate representatives. As a whole, the group agreed that under the Constitution as it stood, the diaspora did indeed have the right to vote and the right to special representation; it also recommended their method of election and the number of their representatives should be decided through a compromise between the majority party and opposition parties. But like Professor Sokol, who had noted his reservations regarding the introduction of PR, on this occasion two highly-regarded professors from the Political Science Faculty – **Dr Mirjana Kasapović** and **Dr Ivan Grdešić** – found it necessary to insert their own **qualification**, i.e. *Napomena* (Note), which is worth quoting in its entirety: *"While acknowledging the stated interpretation of the respective constitutional provisions and the views of the working group, Dr Mirjana Kasapović and Dr Ivan Grdešić emphasize that these are contrary to their understanding of political representation. They deem that the division of Croatian nationals into those who have constitutional rights and duties (citizens residing in the Republic of Croatia) and those who only have constitutional rights but no duties (nationals without permanent residence within the Republic of Croatia) is unacceptable. Therefore, they think that the framers of the Constitution should give some thought to changing the existing constitutional provisions and finding other ways for Croatian nationals who do not reside in Croatia to participate in the political life of the country".*

16.12 In fact, every time Croatia has a parliamentary or presidential election, this issue of whether citizens who do not have permanent residence should be allowed to vote is the cause of renewed public debate This brings an element of unease into the campaign, along with unfortunate doubts and controversies, even about the very meaning of general elections as a fundamental institution of representative democracy. These controversies have become more intense because of the specific role of the large number of voters from the ranks of the Croatian population in neighbouring Bosnia-Herzegovina: in 2007 they made up the majority of the 404,950 names on the National Electoral Commission's voter register for the 11th constituency. But Croats in Bosnia did not migrate there from what is today the territory of Croatia, and they were never emigrants in the classical sense, not even of the foreign worker (*Gastarbeiter*) type in the modern era. On the contrary, in previous centuries, whole families of them actually immigrated to war-ravaged areas of Croatia, as demographic reserves of the Croatian nation; and, in modern times, numerous foreign workers (*gastarbeiters*) moved from Bosnia to other European countries, even to Croatia, in search of jobs. Croats in Bosnia-Herzegovina are, in short, a **native population** residing in their own home, who by the twists of historical changes have stayed outside the borders of today's independent and sovereign state of Croatia, and now live within the newly established state of Bosnia-Herzegovina, where, according to the provisions of the Dayton Constitution, they have the status of a constitutive nation. Croats in Bosnia should, therefore, seek to achieve their vital interests through legislative bodies in their own country, where they have active and passive suffrage and where they perform their civil duties (above all, paying taxes). Voters from Bosnia constitute a large majority in the electorate of Croatia's 11th constituency, and as often as not the proximity and easiness of crossing the Croatian border (added to what we know about messy voter registers) raises doubts about possible double voting (once at an *ad hoc* polling station in BH, and then at the nearest polling station on the Croatian side of the border). Therefore, the conclusion can be drawn that switching the election to the *non-fixed quota* method has only partly reduced conflict and controversy about this issue – and has certainly not got rid of all the problems.

16.14 The question of whether Croatian expatriates should be able to elect their own representatives at all still remains, especially when these representatives do not live abroad, do not live with their voters and do not share their circumstances and needs. It is a moot point how much, and in what way, Croatia, as a parent country, should do for its expatriates. Representatives of the diaspora should not simply be there to act as reserve MPs for a single party, i.e. the Croatian Democratic Union, or to tip the scales in tight inter-party outcomes. It would be advisable to consider this whole issue again and even to follow the suggestion of the two reputable professors, as outlined above. Indeed, there needs to be a political consensus that the framers of the Croatian Constitution should find some other way for expatriates to participate in the political life of the country that would serve to maintain and strengthen cultural and economic bonds between the diaspora and the homeland. Expatriates should not be able to affect decisions on the duties and affairs of citizens resident in Croatia.

Chapter 17
NATIONAL MINORITIES AND POSITIVE DISCRIMINATION

17.1 Article 5 of the **2002 Constitutional Act on the Rights of National Minorities** stipulates that a **national minority** is *"a group of Croatian citizens whose members traditionally inhabit the territory of the Republic of Croatia, its members having ethnic, linguistic, cultural and/or religious characteristics different from those of other citizens and are led by the wish to preserve these characteristics"*. Even though the confusing description of *"autochthonous"* national minorities had been maintained in the preamble to the Constitution from 1990, this definition from the Constitutional Act left no room for doubt, and put the rights of the members of all minorities, both old and new, on an equal footing. In this way, Croatia committed itself to guaranteeing cultural, social and even political rights to the members of all national minorities within its territory. This has been particularly reflected in their right to participate in government, which has been the subject of electoral legislation.

17.2 I will now explain the background to this. On **25th June 1991**, the Croatian Parliament passed the Constitutional Decision on the Sovereignty and Independence of the Republic of Croatia, thus launching the process of disassociation from the other republics and from the Socialist Federative Republic of Yugoslavia. This was also the beginning of the process whereby the newly-proclaimed sovereign country sought international recognition. On that very day, in the same solemn session, the Parliament passed two more important documents: the Declaration on the Proclamation of the Sovereign and Independent Republic of Croatia, and the **Charter on the Rights of Serbs and Other Nationalities in the Republic of Croatia**. These texts put forward some solemn historical arguments in favour of the independence of Croatia, defined procedures for disassociating from the federal bodies of the SFRJ, and emphasised the principles for *"a just solution to the issue of Serbs and other ethnic groups in the Republic of Croatia"*, because this was *"one of the important* *factors for democracy, stability, peace and economic progress, as well as for collaboration with other democratic countries."*

17.3 But in fact, at that very moment, in Belgrade, the federal bodies of state power and the federal army, the JNA (Yugoslav People's Army; *Jugoslavenska narodna armija*) – under the effective control of Slobodan Milošević – were preparing armed action in order to prevent Slovenia and Croatia from gaining independence. This was because if these republics left Yugoslavia, they could take the others with them, which would necessarily lead to the collapse and final dissolution of the socialist federation, most of whose power and benefits went to Serbia. The main propaganda tool used by Milošević and the media linked to him was the accusation that Croatia was reviving the notorious Ustasha regime from the World War II, which criminally persecuted Serbs and Jews by Holocaust methods, modelled on those used in Hitler's Third Reich. Even though the Second World War partisan movement, which put up resistance against the so-called Independent State of Croatia (*Nezavisna Država Hrvatska, NDH*), had attracted mass support from the Croatian population and the significant participation of active combatants, this anti-Croatian propaganda from Belgrade managed to trigger a certain response within the international community. Unfortunately, this was helped by some tactless and furious nationalistic statements by President Tuđman, as well as by the unpunished crimes of some of his henchmen and local bigwigs in the field.

17.4 For all these reasons, there was a logical need for a solemn commitment in a distinct Charter, simultaneous with the proclamation of the independence of the Republic of Croatia to the effect that: *"Serbs in Croatia and all nationalities have the right to proportionate participation in bodies of local self-government and appropriate government bodies."*

17.5 But the JNA was soon launching attacks on various cities in Croatia and encouraging the rebellion by parts of the Serbian population in less developed regions of the country (sometimes even handing out weapons). Meanwhile, the Croatian government was having to wage a defensive war under unfavourable circumstances, because the UN Security Council had imposed an embargo on deliveries of weapons to all warring parties (thus treating the heavily armed aggressor and the unarmed victim in the same way). At the same time, Croatia was engaged in diplomatic activities to obtain international recognition for itself. International mediators and politicians were also seeking a cease-fire in Yugoslavia. In order to achieve this, they made it a condition of their sponsorship of a cease-fire and armistice that the Croatian state should guarantee to fully respect the political rights of Serbs in Croatia, and even strengthen them with respect to the above-mentioned Charter.

17.6 Following the adoption of the Vance Plan in Geneva on 23rd November 1991, an armistice was finally signed in Sarajevo on 2nd January 1992; this was to be monitored and enforced by UNPROFOR (the United Nations Protection Force). Since the cease-fire was also a self-explanatory precondition for the international recognition of Croatia (which was carried out by the European Union on 15th January 1992), one can easily see why, on 4th December 1991, Parliament passed the **Constitutional Act on Human Rights and Freedoms and on the Rights of Ethnic and National Communities or Minorities in the Republic of Croatia**. This gave the status of law to some far-reaching minority rights at the constitutional level: not only the right to cultural autonomy, but also in the field of political rights, where it gave special self-governing status to municipalities where particular minorities constituted most of the population. What is most interesting for our present discussion is Article 18 of the Constitutional Act, which stipulates in its first paragraph: *"Members of ethnic and national communities or minorities which have a share in the population of the Republic of Croatia of more than eight per cent are entitled to be represented, in proportion to their share in the population, within the Parliament and Government of the Republic of Croatia and bodies of the supreme judicial authorities.*

17.7 Such a definite provision, with the force of constitutional law, doubtless caused the designers of the electoral system a lot of trouble on the eve of the first parliamentary election in the independent Croatia, because they had to find a way of fulfilling this commitment, even though it was in practice hardly reconcilable with the fundamental principle of equality of suffrage. In fact, this constitutional-law provision continued to cause trouble even in subsequent reforms of the electoral system, because circumstances changed (the number of members of the Serbian minority was dramatically reduced) – but it is in Croatia's own interests to respect certain acquired rights permanently. Hence, the designers of all electoral systems up until the present day have resorted – to a greater or lesser degree – to the *principle of positive discrimination*. In order to achieve a more important purpose – the adequate representation of national minorities – they have departed from the principle of avoiding discrimination, because, in this case, it was thought to be good for social peace and political order. The idea is that this sort of discrimination does not lead to any reduction of anyone's rights; on the contrary, it leads to some additional rights for a group that should feel safe and equal. In practice, though, it caused a certain departure from the principle of equal suffrage (detailed in Article 45 of the Constitution), i.e. the principle that each vote must have equal weight (*one person – one vote* and *one vote – equal weight*). Members of minorities were granted the right to elect their representatives with a significantly smaller number of votes than were required by others, and to this end different systems were applied at different elections.

17.8 In the **election** held on **2nd August 1992**, the first one after the enactment of the above-mentioned Constitutional Act, the first-past-the-post system was applied for the following, special, non-geographical constituencies for members of national minorities: **Italian** (1), **Hungarian** (1), **Czech and Slovak** (1) and the **German, Austrian, Ruthenian and Ukrainian** minorities (1), which meant that there would be a total of four such representatives. It must be borne in mind that there was also a provision stipulating that members of national minorities could choose whether to vote in their territorial constituencies or in the special constituency for their group. However, the main point is that, under this system, the commitment that the **Serbian minority** would be represented proportionally would not be automatically fulfilled because they did not – for a mixture of practical and political reasons – have their own special constituencies So the electoral law specified that, if the Serbs were not represented in proportion to their share in the total population, members of that minority would be elected to the Chamber of Representatives from national party lists in accordance with the success of these parties in the election.

17.9 On this occasion, it was calculated that the Serbs should have up to 13 representatives (out of 120), because according to the last census in 1981, 11.6% of the population of Croatia were Serbs. In fact, eight unelected candidates of Serbian ethnic origin were listed on the SDP list and two more on the HNS list, which was not sufficient to meet the required quota. So, in order to fulfil it, a subsequent ruling by the Constitutional Court included the Serbian People's Party (*Srps ka narodna stranka, SNS*) in this, even though it had not passed the electoral blocking threshold – so three of its candidates became MPs anyway. However, the SDP, which had only just (with 5.53% of the vote) passed the electoral threshold and therefore won three seats from its list in the normal way, did not want to admit all its own subsequently confirmed Serbian representatives into the SDP parliamentary club (in order not to be denounced as a "Serbian party" in the period of the armed rebellion); so it ended up admitting only three of them, while the remaining five appeared in the Chamber of Representatives as independent MPs. Also, according to another ruling by the Constitutional Court, a representative of the **Jewish** community was elected to the Chamber of Representatives in the very same way (from the HSLS list), and this increased the number of representatives of other national minorities, besides those four elected in special constituencies, to five, as was specified by the electoral law. The electorates in the special constituencies were significantly smaller than those in the territorial constituencies. There were 9,590 registered voters in the Italian constituency (75.84% of whom actually voted), 6,139 in the Hungarian constituency (the turnout was 38.52%), 8,258 in the Czech and Slovak constituency (71.42% voted), and no more than 985 voters in the fourth constituency for four national minorities (only 358 voted, or 36.35%). This proved that the proportional representation of the Serbian ethnic community using the subsequent selection of non-elected candidates from party lists was neither practical nor fair.

17.10 The segment of the electoral law dealing with national minorities had already been amended before the election to the Chamber of Representatives held on 29th October 1995. The four special single-member constituencies for these minorities were preserved. However, when it came to the Serbs, there was some departure from literal proportional representation, because there were no longer any exact figures. This was because Croatia's Operation "Storm" – the military liberation of the occupied areas in the summer of 1995 – had led to the mass exodus of a sizeable chunk of the Serbian population. It was therefore decided – without any exact statistical basis – that the Serbian minority should elect three representatives in a special three-member constituency with an unlimited number of votes, so that each voter in this constituency had as many votes as representatives to be elected. The rule that members of national minorities could choose whether to vote in their own single-member territorial constituency or the special constituency for their group was also preserved (which meant that they had to publicly declare their ethnic affiliation). An examination of the data for the 1995 election – the number of registered voters and their turnout in the special constituencies – reveals sharp differences in the level of voter participation between the different minorities.

The greatest interest was generated in the constituency for the Czech and Slovak minority, where 10,216 voters actually voted (66.43%), while 17,439 voters were registered in the Italian constituency, of whom 10,436 of them actually voted (59.84%). Somewhat less interest was seen in the constituency for the four minorities with the smallest number of registered voters (2,578), because only 1,389 of them turned out at polling stations (53.88%), while the turnout in the Hungarian constituency was less than half (out of 6,938 voters, 3,292 actually voted, or 47.45%). The election for the three-member constituency for the Serbian minority attracted the least interest: out of 174,611 registered voters, only 55,013 voted, or less than one third (31.51%). In response to these figures, some voices were raised among the public challenging the representativeness of MPs elected by only a few hundred votes, compared with those elected under the normal procedure.

17.11 On the eve of the next **election,** held on **3rd January 2000,** new modifications were made to the system for electing minority representatives. Five special, single-member constituencies were established, which meant that even the Serbian minority was entitled to only one seat. At the same time, one more group – the Jewish one – was added to the list of the four minorities (the German, Austrian, Ruthenian and Ukrainian minority) which elected their common representative in a special constituency, but this did not lead to a significant increase in the number of registered voters in that particular constituency (the number increased from 2,578 to 3,224). The turnout was quite similar to that in the previous election (ranging from 63.71% among the Italians to 18.96% among the Serbs), and the representatives of particular minorities also varied in the number of votes they polled. It should be remembered that members of these groups could still choose whether they to vote in a special constituency, or in a territorial constituency, just like other citizens. In this election, the opposition formed two coalitions and scored a crushing victory over the hitherto unassailable HDZ, so it can be assumed that a significant number of Serbs opted to vote at the country-wide level in order to help the opposition win. The largest number of votes won by any minority candidate (12,396) were received by the representative of the Serbs, Milan Đukić, even though he polled only 47.72% in his special constituency, while the representative of the Italian minority, Furio Radin, was elected by a significantly smaller number of votes (5,152), but this was equivalent to no fewer than 78.91% of the total number of votes in his constituency. The remaining representatives of the smaller minorities won seats based on a significantly lower number of votes: Tibor Santo (Hungarian) received 1,892 votes; Zdenka Čuhnil (Czech and Slovak) polled 1,401 votes, and the record for the smallest number of votes was captured by the representative of the five least numerous minorities: Borislav Graljuk (a member of the Ukrainian minority), with no more than 342 votes!

17.12 For the parliamentary **election** held on **23rd November 2003,** PR was once again applied in 10 nationwide constituencies, while the earlier system for the election of minority representatives was in fact modified only slightly. What happened was that on 13th

December 2002, Parliament passed the new **Constitutional Act on the Rights of National Minorities**, which states in its Article 19: *"members of national minorities which have a share in the total population of the Republic of Croatia of more than 1.5 per cent are entitled to at least one and no more than three parliamentary seats for the members of the respective national minority, in accordance with the law regulating the election of representatives to the Croatian Parliament"*, while members of the national minorities with less than 1.5% are – all together – entitled to elect at least four representatives in accordance with electoral legislation. Subsequent amendments in 2000 and 2003 were entered into the Refined Text of the 1999 Act on the Election of Representatives to the Croatian Parliament, so it was stated that *"members of national minorities in the Republic of Croatia have the right to elect eight representatives to the Parliament, elected in a special constituency made up of the entire territory of the Republic of Croatia"*. Article 16 stipulated that members of the Serbian national minority should elect three representatives (again, in a special three-member constituency by unlimited voting). For other minorities, it was stipulated that they should elect five representatives in a single constituency using FPTP, or one representative for each group: (a) the Hungarian, (b) Italian, (c) Czech and Slovak minority, (d) the "old" small minorities – Austrian, Bulgarian, German, Polish, Romany, Romanian, Ruthenian, Russian, Turkish, Ukrainian, Wallachian and Jewish – and finally, (e) the "new" minorities that emerged after the collapse of the SFR of Yugoslavia, in which they used to be part of the federation – Albanian, Bosniak, Montenegrin, Macedonian and Slovene. Since the reform of the 1999 electoral law (with additional amendments) had done the job of stabilising the electoral system, the method of electing minority representatives described above was also applied in the last **election** to the Croatian Parliament, held on 25th **November 2007**. The practice that members of national minorities could choose whether to vote in their territorial constituencies or in a special constituency for their group, was maintained.

17.13 In the period of the coalition government from 2000 onwards, several amendments to the Constitution were made which had the effect of abrogating Tuđman's semi-presidential system and strengthening the role played by the Parliament and the government elected within it. However, at the same time, the use of *positive discrimination* as a way of protecting minority rights was also formally reinforced. As for the electoral system, the new constitutional provision on the so-called *dual right to vote* was especially important, because it caused, and is still causing, political and even constitutional-law disputes. Specifically, Article 15, paragraph 2, of the Constitution states: *"Besides the general electoral right, the special right of the members of national minorities to elect their representatives to the Croatian Parliament may be provided by law"*. A logical and literal interpretation of this text should make clear and indisputable that universal suffrage (which belongs to all citizens) has primary significance and cannot be questioned, while the special right to elect representatives of national minorities is only optional, and dependent on special legislation, i.e. on the ever-changing political will of the parliamentary majority. However, and unfortunately up until this very day, no combination of dominant parliamentary forces has yet had enough political will to put this constitutional provision into force; it has been seen as merely optional, and primary significance has been given to the right to elect special representatives of national minorities, as guaranteed by the Constitutional Act on National Minorities and included in electoral legislation.

17.14 The effect of this is that if they choose to vote for their own ethnic representatives, national minorities have been denied the chance to participate in general suffrage at elections, which actually makes them disadvantaged in their undeniable constitutional rights as Croatian citizens. One could also draw the conclusion that this kind of implementation of constitutional provisions facilitates ghetto-isation, rather than social integration of minorities. Even the Constitutional Court gave a negative opinion about this problem in September 2003, while avoiding entering into the merit of the matter. Under the chairmanship of the omnipresent Smiljko Sokol, a proposal by the Italian and Serbian minorities to institute proceedings for the assessment of the accordance of Article 3, paragraph 2 of the electoral law with Article 15, paragraph 3 of the Constitution, was rejected. Nevertheless, minority representatives put this issue on the agenda time and again in each election, even as one of the conditions for their support for the coalition government led by the HDZ, whose prime minister promised to examine this issue during the second year of his term.

17.15 When this issue is finally seriously examined and dealt with, the parties involved in bargaining will face another old, unsolved problem. I refer to the fact that during the discussions prior to the passing of the Constitutional Act of 2002 which legalised the so-called *dual right to vote*, the view was also advanced that this provision should in no way cause the over-representation of national minorities, in the sense that their MPs should NOT play a decisive part in the formation of a parliamentary majority. If the constitutional rule of the dual right was actually applied, the number of minority representatives should only be token (in the sense that they should elect only one, or no more than two, representatives, the idea being that they should really be spokespersons of their groups' specific interests). Meanwhile, the normal electoral system based on universal suffrage should be adapted in such a way that it could favour national minorities: to the extent, anyway, that those of them who had passed the 1.5% threshold, could also win seats in Parliament within the regular electoral procedure. But this view, which has never been formalised in the form of an amendment, has not attracted a response from among the representatives of the minorities

17.16 Political inertia, which tends to respect *vested rights*, remains a serious obstacle to thoroughly modifying electoral legislation for members of minorities, because reducing the number of their representatives would probably provoke serious objections about a new kind of discrimination – negative discrimination. In fact, the proper interpretation of Article 15 of the Constitution suggests the *additional* (not dual) *right to vote*. Similarly, Article 19 of the 2002 Constitutional Act, which states that *"members of national minorities elect at least five and no more than eight of their representatives in special constituencies, in accordance with law"*, with the added statement *"by which the acquired rights of national minorities cannot be reduced"*, requires that the electoral system be reformed in order to stop the unconstitutional practice whereby members of national minorities can vote for their own representatives only if they give up their right to vote in general elections for representatives as all other citizens do. The conclusion is clear: there should be both the additional right to vote and positive discrimination in the election of minority representatives. I am sure that this will not shake the foundations of the legal system of the Republic of Croatia; on the contrary, it will help to politically integrate not only Croatia's traditional, but also its "new" minorities (with no intention of cultural or ethnic assimilation). The aim is to achieve increased harmony and to overcome the psychological consequences of their hard experiences in the wartime years. It is in the interests of the Republic of Croatia that members of national minorities should feel and behave as citizens of our country, and that they can maintain their special identity at the same time.

Chapter 18
A BRIEF HISTORY OF THE CROATIAN BI-CAMERAL PARLIAMENT

18.1 In line with its historical tradition, Croatia has always had a **unicameral Parliament.** However, during the final stages of the preparations for passing the Christmas Constitution, late in November 1990 – and after public discussion had ended – President Tuđman decided to go against the views held by his personally-chosen advisors, and the authors of the final draft of the Constitution, Vladimir Šeks and Smiljko Sokol. What happened was that at the last minute, he expressed the wish to have **two parliamentary chambers** in his semi-presidential system of government. In an interview in early 2008, Professor Sokol gave a colourful account of this episode, describing how – upon Tuđman's request that constitutional provisions for the Chamber of Counties should be drafted within just a few days – he impressed the President by dictating these provisions, on the spot, to the secretary who was in the room, and taking just 25 minutes to do it. In order that nobody would think that this was mere improvisation, Sokol said that, having already expected such a request, he "had taken a peek at the Spanish and French Constitutions" before coming to the President, knowing that Tuđman wanted the second chamber (with no real powers) just in order to make an ostensible concession to regionalism and the Serbian minority, and also because he wanted to have a place where he could place party associates who were no longer of any real use to him. Sokol sweetened this idea of a second chamber further for his master with another provision that the President of the Republic could personally appoint up to five representatives *"from the ranks of particularly meritorious citizens"*, and that he himself would become a life member of the Chamber of Counties on the expiry of his term of office.

18.2 Established as a regional representative body, the **Chamber of Counties** consisted of three representatives from each county (21

× 3 = 63), elected directly by the citizens of individual counties under a secret ballot – and an additional five representatives were appointed by the President of the Republic. Under the Constitution, its powers were more or less limited to the right of *legislative initiative* and *providing preliminary opinions* in the process of approving the Constitution and so-called organic laws regulating national and human rights, state administration and local self-government. In addition, the Chamber of Counties had the right to temporarily suspend laws passed in the Chamber of Representatives (within 15 days of them being approved); this was applicable to all laws except those requiring a two-thirds majority in the Chamber of Representatives. In practice, during the Chamber of Counties' two mandates, this temporary veto was exercised only once, but the assembly persisted in holding extensive debates about almost every bill and passed its opinions to the Chamber of Representatives, which noted them without comment or discussion. In this way, the second chamber became an insignificant copy of the first, with many fewer powers, and was therefore widely considered a second-class representative body which provided a home for relatively unimportant politicians who were nonetheless owed something by their party.

18.3 The **first election** to the new chamber was held on **7th February 1993**, after the counties had been established by law (20 counties + the City of Zagreb with the status of a county). The original plan was that there should be just one round of voting under the first-past-the-post electoral system in single-member constituencies. But the opposition was against this arrangement, and threatened to come to an internal agreement according to which only one candidate from a united opposition would stand against the ruling party's candidate in each constituency. The HDZ took this threat seriously, and the electoral law was therefore amended just a few days before the election, switching the system to proportional representation in three-member constituencies, with a single vote for party lists. There would also be a 5% *electoral threshold*, and votes would be translated into seats using the same method as in elections for the Chamber of Representatives. This ostensible concession to the opposition, which had requested either proportional representation or a two-ballot system, nevertheless served the HDZ well, especially because of a provision stipulating that the names at the top the lists (which appeared on the ballot papers) did not have to be candidates themselves (so Tuđman was the name on the HDZ list in all the counties!).

18.4 Anyone who has ever consulted theoretical texts on psephology knows that PR in small constituencies produces almost the same effect as first-past-the-post, and leads to huge disproportional effects in the correlation between votes and seats. This is exactly what happened with the application of the system described above, because the HDZ scored a landslide victory with 45.49% of the vote, which provided it with 37 seats (i.e. 58.73%). The HSLS emerged as the strongest opposition party in this election, winning 16 seats (one quarter of the total), while the HNS (which had rejected the proposal for a pre-election coalition with the HSLS) won just one seat, which was the same result as the SDP. The HSS, meanwhile, won five seats, and the regional IDS three seats. The reason for this outcome was not the 5% electoral threshold, but the *natural threshold* for small three-member constituencies, so that some of the lists polled as much as 18.8% of the vote in places, but were still left without any seats. In the final reckoning, there were 2,227,763 valid votes, but of these, 284,782 votes – or 12.78% of the total – were left unrepresented. President Tuđman then went on to appoint five of his modern "virilists": three were formally non-partisan, but the remaining two were overt HDZ members, and in this way, the ruling party increased the number of its seats to 39, or 57.35%.

18.5 The second, and last, **election** for the Chamber of Counties was held on **13th April 1997** using the same method as in the first, the only modification being that a differentiated electoral threshold was introduced: 5% for a single party, 8% for two-party coalitions, and 11% for coalitions of three or more parties. Although this system logically encouraged parties to make coalition agreements and for the opposition to put up one single, pooled list, two ad hoc opposition coalitions nevertheless stood against the HDZ (though not in all counties): the HSLS/HSS, which won 16 seats (with

23.04% of the vote), and the SDP/HNS, which received 16.42% of the vote, and thus won only four seats. Apart from these coalitions, among the rest of the opposition, the only other victory came from the regional IDS, which won its two safe seats in the County of Istria. In fact, because of the opposition's disunity, the HDZ increased its superiority in seats relative to the previous Chamber: having formed an undeclared coalition with the extremist right-wing HSP, it won 42.72% of the vote, and 39 seats (+ 2 seats for the HSP).

So it ended up with more than one-fifth of the seats. Again, President Tuđman used his right to appoint members of the Chamber of Counties, thus providing three more seats for the HDZ, and, in keeping with an earlier agreement, he also appointed two representatives from the ranks of the Serbian national minority in the Counties of Osijek & Baranya, and Vukovar & Syrmia. As for "wasted votes", the calculation is disturbing: out of 2,529,412 valid votes cast, 385,873, or 15.25%, were left without an elected representative, which means that every sixth or seventh voter made his/her journey to the polling station in vain.

18.6 The brief history of the Chamber of Counties starts and ends with arbitrary decisions on the establishment and discontinuation of this parliamentary institution, which was never intended to have a meaningful place and function in the Croatian system of representative democracy. Following the opposition victory in 2000, and in order to keep the new coalition's pre-election promises, Parliament made some thorough amendments to the Constitution, with the primary aim of replacing the semi-presidential system with a parliamentary one. In addition to the parliamentary Committee on the Constitution, Standing Orders and Political System (led by Mato Arlović), which prepared the draft of the constitutional amendments, the issue was also considered by a *"working group for the development of an expert basis for a possible draft of constitutional amendments"*, appointed by the President of the Republic, Stjepan Mesić. This working group was made up of respected professors and experts in constitutional law – Branko Smerdel, Arsen Bačić, Zvonimir Lauc, Jadranko Crnić, and Nikola Filipović – and was headed by the retired professor of constitutional law Veljko Mratović. In a text entitled *"Expert bases for the development of the draft of the* *amendments to the Constitution of the Republic of Croatia"*, the working group went on record as favouring the discontinuation of the Chamber of Counties on the expiry of its current term. However, Parliament, acting on the advice of the Arlović committee, did not accept this proposal, despite the sound, expert arguments set forth by the working group, which emphasised the manner in which Tuđman had insisted on establishing the new chamber at the very last minute. The group's final report said: *"The way in which the bicameral system was introduced into the Draft of the 1990 Constitution is a reflection of a form of political decision-making which has to be removed and prevented by constitutional amendments, for it ignores public opinion and expert arguments"*.

18.7 But despite this opinion, after the first constitutional amendments in November 2000, this *"weak second chamber, with unclear powers, which has not met the expectations of its proponents"* (in the words of the working group) continued to operate, the only difference being that the appointed representatives and the seat for the ex-President of the Republic were erased from the Constitution, while the poorly defined powers of this chamber were neither specified nor limited. However, the HDZ (which now found itself in opposition) had a large majority in the Chamber of Counties with which it could slow down and stonewall the legislative passage of the promised reforms in the Chamber of Representatives. As the constitutional deadline for the new election to the Chamber of Counties approached, this threat was quickly recognised, and thus, in late March 2001, barely four months after the previous changes, constitutional amendments were once again made using summary procedure, and the Chamber of Counties was abolished. Thus, the Republic of Croatia abandoned its unsuccessful, short-lived experiment in *asymmetric bicameralism* and returned to its tradition of a unicameral parliament, as befits a small, unitary European country.

18.8 The way in which the second chamber of the Croatian Parliament emerged and was then abolished, and the haggling over its electoral system, provide yet more testimony to the lack of maturity in the political culture of countries that tried to establish democratic institutions after their decades-long experience of totalitarian systems. Croatia is in no way an exception, because the fact is that fundamental institutional decisions were, for the most part, made for opportunistic reasons at particular moments, no matter which political group had a majority. Indeed, even allowing for the fact that during Tuđman's government in the 1990s, the criteria for virtually all decisions were opportunistic and aimed at helping the HDZ keep an absolute grip on power – even so, some of the decisions were contrary to the laws and regulations passed by that very same government. In the Croatian case, however, there was at the same time a gradual, growing awareness of the need to establish, elect and set in motion institutions in line with a long-term vision of a democratic system. The implication of this long-term view is that systemic reforms should not be approached merely in terms of the transient, temporary interests of a single political opinion (one's own), but attention should also be paid to expert arguments, and to experiences from other countries during the little more than 200-year-long history of modern democracy.

PART FIVE

CROATIA– ELECTORAL REFORM

Ivo Škrabalo

Chapter 19
TOTAL REPRESENTATION AND THE CROATIAN ELECTORAL SYSTEM

19.1 Between the first multi-party election, held in April 1990, and the most recent one, held in November 2007, Croatia tried three completely different electoral systems. However, latterly some stability has been reached, for the last three Parliaments have all been founded on the 1999 electoral law, and the same PR system – based on ten large multi-member constituencies – has been in operation. This solution was reached by adopting the proposals of a team of experts, which were the result of a consensus among parliamentary parties. And the system has been used three times without any fundamental or extensive alterations (though there have been some minor ones). So, among the virtues of the current system is its very stability, which has had a positive effect on voters' understanding of the electoral process, and on their trust in the legitimacy of electoral outcomes. Of course, this has helped the consolidation of democracy in transitional Croatia. But it is also true to say that after each election, there have been criticisms of certain aspects of this variant of PR. And as well as being virtues in themselves, the system's stability and its repeated applications provide an opportunity to analyse it thoroughly and uncover some of its deficiencies.

19.2 The world's most stable electoral system is the British one, the famous "first-past-the-post" (FPTP), which has lasted for more than a century. However, it is the object of much criticism because it leads to a vast number of "wasted" votes, which are left unrepresented in Parliament. It has also created a fairly rigid two-party structure, which has prevented other political options from articulating their views. Meanwhile, the main objection raised by critics against Croatia's existing PR system in 10 fourteen-member constituencies is that there is no strong bond between an MP and his/her electorate, and that, with respect to the list from which he/she was elected, the MP is permanently dependent on his/her political party, which leads to an unhealthy aberration of democracy known as *partitocracy*. In fact, all previous experiments with amending the electoral system in Croatia have been guided by the interests of political parties, especially the dominant one (which wanted to guarantee its continuous over-representation in the Parliament). Despite the smooth way the system has operated, therefore, there is some room to deliberate on possible reform, if a way can be found to bring it back closer to those for whom it exists: the voters.

19.3 As an MP from 2000 to 2003, I myself gave a lot of thought to necessary modifications to the existing PR system. I even came up with some solutions of my own when, as chairman of the parliamentary caucus of the LIBRA party (a small liberal grouping which emerged after 10 of us split from the HSLS) we joined the governing coalition's working group to help draft a proposal for electoral reform (though it was not, as it transpired, carried out during the lifetime of this coalition). What bothered me most was the fact that I did not know where my electorate was and who it was made up of, because I had been elected as the second-placed candidate on the SDP/HSLS coalition list in the 7th constituency, which extended from the western fringes of Zagreb around the city lake of Jarun, over the entire County of Karlovac and Gorski Kotar (where I have my weekend cottage!) up to Novi Vinodolski on the Adriatic coast. I had already been thinking about a return to the mixed system during the preparations for the electoral reform of 1999, because I felt that, on the one hand, in a country with no tradition of multi-party democracy, it was indeed necessary to create conditions for the emergence of many different political options through national party lists. But I felt at the same time that it was important to give voters a chance to vote directly for political personalities: i.e. recognisable individuals as representatives of local priorities. So in 2002, LIBRA proposed a mixed system (60 FPTP +60 PR seats).

19.4 In fact, I can see now that some of these elements were similar to the building blocks of the TR system, which Aharon Nathan has imaginatively tied together here in a coherent and completely logical entirety. Although I suggested a two-ballot FPTP system for one half of the election, I also proposed that in the second, PR, segment the final number of votes for the allocation of seats should consist of the votes received by a political party's list – but augmented by all the votes polled by non-elected candidates of that same party in the FPTP election. I also proposed that candidates should be allowed to compete simultaneously in both the PR and the FPTP parts of the election.

19.5 Thus, I am now approaching the point where I will describe the application of Nathan's TR system to our Croatian circumstances, well aware of the closeness between his views and my own, and also with a lot of background knowledge, since we in Croatia have accumulated significant experience during our frequent reforms of mixed systems, and in recent years of stable PR. To be fair, I should point out that I have no formal qualifications in political science, but as a Master of Law and a twice-elected MP, I will try to overcome this disadvantage through first-hand insights, since I took part in five elections in three capacities: as a voter; as a non-elected candidate (both on a list and in a constituency); and on two occasions as an elected MP.

19.6 Fortunately, any proposal for electoral reform in Croatia no longer needs to put most of its emphasis on the correctness of procedures at polling stations and on achieving credible methods of counting, because the problem of direct electoral fraud is behind us. The remaining unsolved problems of ordering voter registers and correct electoral geography (defining constituency boundary lines without gerrymandering) will probably be more easily solved now that we have had 18 years of pluralist democracy in an independent country. Bearing in mind that elections are an essential precondition and element of representative democracy, I am advocating the creation of an electoral system which will not only meet the essential features of free elections (which means that they should be *free, competitive,* with *equal rights* for all voters and candidates, *direct* and *secret*), but which will also be *credible* (meaning that elections should reflect the political will of voters as precisely as possible

– and provide *representation for each vote*). All this will be achieved if the electoral system is convincing and generally accepted, which requires that it should also be *clear, understandable, impartial, fair* and, as such, *stable*. I accepted the flattering invitation to contribute to this book by the author of the TR system, because I believe that his innovative marrying of the FPTP system with PR – the two basic electoral models used around the world – meets the above-mentioned criteria and provides an acceptable, maybe even the best, solution to some so-far-unresolved obstacles in Croatia's electoral path. Of course, there is no single, perfect system applicable to every environment, and even the implementation of TR requires certain corrections with respect to some specifically Croatian electoral issues.

19.7 How would the TR system look in Croatia? Individual elements of the proposed system will be discussed in more detail in subsequent paragraphs; here, the concept will be presented only in its broad outline. The idea is as follows. With a single vote and on a single ballot, the voter would elect his/her candidate in his/her local constituency, and thereby also his/her party in the list segment of the election. In this simple way, 120 representatives would be elected to the Parliament, out of which 84 would be elected within the FPTP system in single-member constituencies, while 36 of them would be elected from lists (either party lists or independent lists). This second part of the election would be decided by PR, using the mass of unsuccessful votes cast for non-elected candidates in the constituencies, with a low, 2% electoral threshold, so that the number of "wasted votes" would be negligible. In accordance with the existing Constitutional Act on the Rights of National Minorities, members of **national minorities** could elect eight additional representatives. Elections of minority representatives would be held according to the FPTP single-member model, because their small number of voters means that they hardly fit the TR system, and they are anyway an exception necessary because of Croatia's peculiar political circumstances and precedents. However, the TR system makes it possible that minorities who make up more than 1.5% of the population in particular constituencies or on a list (which is in fact only the Serbian minority) would be able to win a seat in the normal way – and therefore no electoral threshold will be specified for those parties. When everything is taken into account, under the TR system, the Croatian Parliament would consist of no more than 128 MPs, which is appropriate for the size of the electorate.

19.8 The country's territory would be divided into **80 constituencies,** whose boundaries would be defined by Parliament, based on proposals by the National Electoral Commission, and with the help of demographic and statistical experts. The criteria for drawing boundaries would be specified in the electoral legislation, because, given the size of the total electorate (around 3,600,000 voters) in the Republic of Croatia, each constituency could have around 45,000 voters, within a range of +/- 3 per cent. In addition, county boundaries would be respected wherever possible, and where they were not, attention would have to be paid to territorial entities at the regional or sub-regional level. Four additional constituencies outside the Republic of Croatia would be established for Croatian nationals with no permanent residence within the country, and these constituencies (encompassing groups of countries) would be drawn according to territorial and geographical criteria. For the PR segment of elections, as well as for the election of representatives of national minorities, the entire country would be a single constituency.

19.9 For nominations in single-member constituencies, a candidate would require the signatures of 400 citizens who had active voting rights and were permanently resident in the respective constituency (around 1% of voters). The list of a particular party or independent group in the PR segment of the election would be made up of all its candidates in the constituencies – any number up to 80 – and it would be possible to put forward a list even if one did not have candidates standing in all constituencies. The name at the top of the list would be listed on the ballot alongside the name of the party (or next to the chosen name of the list) as an identification sign for voters. This is one of the reasons why that name should be that of the party leader, because this person would then have a golden opportunity to enter Parliament even if he/she was not elected in his/her constituency, because he/she would be first in line for a PR seat. The general political interest, in other words, requires that the most important party leaders should be in Parliament so that they can directly participate in solving the issues of the day, first through dialogue and then by voting. The other list candidates would be arranged alphabetically by surname, next to the names of the locations of their constituencies. The list would be named after the party or party coalition, or the head of an independent list, respectively – or its name would be chosen in such a way that the list would be recognisable.

19.10 Once in the polling station, the voter would see the following on the ballot paper: first, the names of all the candidates in that particular single-member constituency, arranged alphabetically (alongside the name of their party or their list). Also appearing on the ballot paper would be the lists themselves, with the names of their leaders at the top, and then the other candidates in alphabetical order. (Voters would probably already have got to know about the lists and the names of their candidates through the media, electoral campaigning and posters at polling stations). People with permanent residence within the Republic of Croatia who found themselves outside the country on election day would be able to vote for candidates in their own constituency, at polling stations set up in the country where they happened to be – on production of a valid electoral ID. Some thought should also be given to the introduction of a permanent electoral ID card for all voters, which should be revalidated before each election.

19.11 In constituencies, the candidate who won the plurality of votes would be elected, and if two candidates polled about the same number, the election would be re-run within 15 days. Immediately after this first count, the National Electoral Commission (*Državno izborno povjerenstvo, DIP*), would announce the names of the victorious candidates and the number of votes cast for them. Then the DIP would rank all the candidates who were unsuccessful in the FPTP segment in order on all their lists (with the leader of the list – if not elected in his/her constituency – still at the top), according to the number of votes cast for each one. Then, in the PR segment of the election, the votes of all the unsuccessful candidates, by parties, would be added up, and the number of seats to go to individual lists would be reckoned from this *voting mass*.

19.12 It would be up to the parties themselves to think ahead and make sure that their unsuccessful votes were represented in the PR segment. For example, there could be a situation where a party received too few votes either to pass the 2% electoral threshold, or – because of electoral arithmetic – to win even one seat under PR. In order to avoid these votes being wasted, each list could – before the election – issue a statement, through its leader, before the National Electoral Commission that it was establishing a *connected list* with another party, so that when it came to the allocation of seats in the PR segment, one would transfer its surplus votes to another (of course, the one with fewer votes would transfer to the one with more). This is because after one round of PR calculations and allocations, there would usually remain a few unallocated seats, so connected lists could help and be decisive in this case. Such a statement could also be issued by an individual, independent candidate who was not taking part in the list competition, but was politically close to one of the lists in the PR segment. This would increase the level of representation of all the votes cast. However, in order to avoid extreme fragmentation in Parliament, a 2% electoral threshold would be stipulated, which means, for example, that if one assumed, say, competition between 15 lists, the 2% threshold would be close to the natural threshold. The electoral threshold would apply to all lists, except for the lists of parties declaring themselves as representatives of national minorities, for which there would be no such threshold, and possibilities would be opened up for larger minorities to win parliamentary seats in constituencies where they were more densely populated.

19.13 Translating votes into seats itself would be carried out by the National Electoral Commission. It would first deduct the total sum of votes for all 80 elected FPTP representatives from the total number of valid votes. The remainder would form the voting mass which would be distributed among lists. Then the number of seats going to each list would be calculated. The formula for calculating seats is pretty simple and easily understandable. The voting mass for the PR segment of the election (and this equals the sum of valid votes of all non-elected candidates in the constituencies) would be divided by 36 (the total number of seats in this segment), and the resulting *electoral quota* would represent the number of votes required for the election of one list candidate. Each list would be assigned a number of seats depending on how many times its total number of votes could be divided by this quota – and within the lists, the seats would be allocated based on how many actual votes each candidate won, with those who won the most coming first in the queue. It is to be expected that each list would then be left with a small surplus of votes (smaller than the electoral quota required for one seat). At this second stage, connected lists would play a significant role, because the remaining seats would be allocated by the largest remainder method. Thus, the list with the largest number of "surplus" votes (including votes added on from partners in the connected lists) would win a seat for its next-best-placed candidate. In the case of two lists having the same number of "surplus" votes, the seat would go to the list whose next-best-placed candidate received the most votes. If they were still impossible to separate even in this respect, the percentage of votes received by a particular candidate in his/her constituency would play a decisive role (because the same number of votes in two constituencies would not necessarily be the same percentage of all the votes in these constituencies.)

19.14 In the case of the termination of a candidate's term (because of his/her resignation, loss of legal ability, imprisonment for longer than six months, or death) there would be no by-election, because there is no such tradition in the Croatian electoral system; the vacancy – no matter whether the term being terminated was that of a candidate from a constituency or a list – would be filled by his/her deputy, i.e. the second-ranked non-elected candidate from his/her list ("the first below the line"). If there was no such candidate, the seat would remain vacant until the expiry of the term of the respective Parliament, i.e. until the next regular election. Filling the vacancy of a representative of a national minority would depend on which minority was in question: in the case of the three most numerous minorities (the Serbian, Italian and Hungarian ones), it would be filled by his/her elected deputy, while in the other categories, the first non-elected candidate with the largest number of votes would become the deputy.

19.15 The problem issue of the voting rights of Croatian nationals with no permanent residence within the Republic of Croatia – **the diaspora** – has been a source of serious political disputes ever since 1995, when the special procedure for the election of 12 such representatives in a separate constituency was suddenly introduced. The advocates, as well as the opponents, of this arrangement have based their arguments on the very same Article 45 of the Constitution. The first paragraph of this Article states: *"Croatian citizens aged 18 and above have universal and equal suffrage in accordance with law"*. This is where some people have found justification for the argument that the law guarantees this right even to Croatian nationals who have never lived in Croatia, but were granted certificates of citizenship when Tuđman's regime encouraged the acquisition of dual nationality by expatriate ethnic Croats and those who lived in the neighbouring republic of Bosnia-Herzegovina. This was despite the fact that those Croats had always lived in Bosnia, and were therefore not "expatriates". Since these privileged voters voted practically unanimously voted for the HDZ, the opposition parties had good reason to claim that the whole arrangement of the special electorate was devised in order to secure 12 additional safe seats for the ruling party.

19.16 The opposition found *its* argument in the next, second paragraph of the same Article 45 of the Constitution, which guarantees the exercise of the right to vote *"even to its citizens who, at the time of the election, happen to find themselves outside its borders"*, suggesting that this refers to citizens whose normal permanent residence is within the Republic of Croatia and who are abroad on election day by way of an exception. There thus appears to be no reason for a special constituency with additional seats. But this interpretation was not accepted in the reform of the electoral law in 1999 (even though two first-rate experts, Kasapović and Grdešić, disowned this decision). However, a compromise *was* reached, in the form of the "non-fixed quota", which has been applied in all elections ever since (thus halving the number of safe seats for the HDZ!).

19.17 My basic view is that the only logical and constitutionally reasonable solution is that permanent expatriates should not participate in parliamentary elections in their old homeland, or that their voting right should be recognised only if their permanent decision in which of the two countries they would like to enjoy their right to vote is determined by bilateral international treaties with countries where they live and whose citizens they are. This is because I believe that voters with no commitments toward Croatia, such as the payment of taxes, should not be able to influence the composition of the legislative body and, indirectly, the executive branch of government. However, after so many years and so many electoral cycles, this privileged status can nevertheless be considered a kind "acquired right", and its abrogation would perhaps bring unnecessary trouble and political disputes. So I propose that it be pragmatically incorporated into the TR system as a sort of *positive discrimination* in favour of this category of nationals. However, these elections for the diaspora should be set up in such a way that they provide an opportunity for expatriate voters to elect people who will genuinely express and represent their interests, and not just the interests of one homeland party or another.

19.18 First, I suggest that this category of voters should have an equal active and passive voting right. To explain: so far, these voters have lived abroad, but their candidates/representatives have had permanent residence in Zagreb or possibly in some other city in Croatia. But I propose that their candidates should also have had permanent residence *outside* the Republic of Croatia for at least one year before the election. Another point: under Croatia's electoral law (Article 9), there are certain posts which a candidate for MP in Croatia is not allowed to hold; this should also apply in the diapsora election, so that a representative of the Croatian Parliament must not fill any of these incompatible positions, whether in Croatia or in any other country (bearing in mind that in Tuđman's era there were some officials of the executive branch from Bosnia-Herzegovina in the Croatian Parliament). As for registration, voters with no permanent residence in the Republic of Croatia must have registered at one of the country's diplomatic or consular missions, by invitation and within a particular time before the elections. Polling stations would be established, through an arrangement with the host country, in the premises of diplomatic or consular missions, or in the premises of suitable, non-political, civil institutions of the local Croatian diaspora. Postal voting might also be introduced for the diaspora (via postal mail or e-mail), providing that a procedure is established beforehand which would render impossible any abuse. As for constituencies, they would be defined primarily on a territorial basis, without regard to the potential number of voters, because their representatives are meant to be in the role of spokespeople who express the particular interests of their voters – and these are undoubtedly different in Mostar and Vancouver! Therefore, under the TR system, the diaspora's four multi-member "external" constituencies could look something like this:

1. *European countries* (the 2007 election took place in 25 countries);

2. *Non-European countries* (the 2007 election took place in 22 countries);

3. *Bosnia-Herzegovina* (the 2007 election took place at 124 polling stations);

4. *Post-Yugoslav countries* (Montenegro, Kosovo, Macedonia, Slovenia, Serbia; the 2007 election took place in four countries at 21 polling stations).

VOTERS IN THE 11th CONSTITUENCY IN 2007

EUROPEAN COUNTRIES

Country	Number of polling stations	Registered voters	Valid votes
1. Albania	1	21	-
2. Austria	2	8,652	835
3. Bulgaria	1	40	3
4. Czech Republic	1	365	6
5. Denmark	1	442	8
6. Finland	1	-	-
7. France	3	1,826	108
8. Greece	1	51	9
9. Ireland	1	-	-
10. Italy	3	2,246	66
11. Hungary	2	650	20
12. Netherlands	1	1,045	14
13. Norway	1	216	3
14. Germany	23	38,233	2,135
15. Poland	1	59	5
16. Portugal	1	18	-
17. Romania	2	1,481	103
18. Russia	1	113	5
19. Slovak Republic	1	-	-
20. Spain	2	200	5
21. Sweden	3	2,096	120
22. Switzerland	5	8,350	509
23. Turkey	2	52	1
24. Ukraine	1	-	-
25. United Kingdom	1	515	8
TOTAL	**62**	**66,671**	**3,963 (5.94 %)**

NON-EUROPEAN COUNTRIES

Country	Number of polling stations	Registered voters	Valid votes
1. Afghanistan	2	-	-
2. Algeria	1	20	3
3. Argentina	2	2,909	185
4. Australia	12	4,781	748
5. Brazil	2	297	33
6. Chile	3	1,793	52
7. Egypt	1	67	2
8. India	1	7	1
9. Indonesia	1	10	1
10. Iran	1	-	-
11. Israel	1	61	14
12. Japan	1	-	-
13. South Africa	1	448	8
14. Canada	9	2,753	453
15. China	1	7	1
16. Libya	1	7	1
17. Malaysia	1	4	3
18. Morocco	1	-	-
19. New Zealand	1	487	1
20. Peru	1	1,410	64
21. USA	6	5,373	254
22. Venezuela	1	467	112
TOTAL	51	20,901	936 (9.26 %)

BOSNIA AND HERZEGOVINA

Number of polling stations	Registered voters	Valid votes
0124	287,136	80,261 (27.95%)

POST-YUGOSLAV COUNTRIES

	Country	Number of polling stations	Registered voters	Valid votes
1.	Montenegro	4	2,543	544
2.	Kosovo	-	-	-
3.	Macedonia	1	1,763	352
4.	Slovenia	1	4,376	92
5.	Serbia	15	23,716	1,067
TOTAL		21	32,398	2,055 (6.34%)

The data that I directly requested and kindly obtained from the National Electoral Commission reveals great differences in the number of voters in the proposed "external" constituencies, with this, such constituencies would ensure the representation of specific interests in mutually different environments. The tables above also show how much attention is paid to voters in Bosnia-Herzegovina, where 124 polling stations were opened, while in huge countries like Australia only 12 polling stations were opened, and only nine in Canada. In much the same way as in the homeland constituencies, the voter would vote for one of the nominated candidates, and in the case of that candidate not winning, the votes he/she received would be added to the list of his/her party. If the candidate did not belong to any party, he/she would have the opportunity to state in advance to which party list his/her votes should go.

19.19 The representation of **national minorities** in parliament has been a permanent peculiarity of the political landscape in all elections since Croatia gained independence and recognition. In accordance with my interpretation of the respective provisions of the Constitution and Constitutional Act on the Rights of National Minorities, as presented in Chapter 17, I propose that in any reform of electoral legislation for the introduction of TR, the dual (additional) right to vote should be asserted and procedurally regulated. Abolishing the electoral threshold for parties declaring themselves representatives of national minorities would open up the possibility that the Serbian minority (the only one exceeding 1.5% of the population) could win some constituency seats even within the general electoral sy stem. Therefore, the National Electoral Commission would have to resist pressures to divide the regions where the Serbian minority was more densely populated, while responsibly completing the task of creating the electoral geography it had been entrusted with. Under the circumstances, this would not be difficult, because since the war, and even though some of the Serbs who fled in 1995 have returned, there are no pronounced mono-ethnic regions of any minority in Croatia. However, respect should be shown to the regions or towns where they are more concentrated in number, and these should not be divided into several constituencies. If practice shows that this is a more effective way for national minorities to get their representatives into Parliament, electoral procedure could then be modified, without interfering with minority rights.

19.20 However, until such an optimal situation has been corroborated in practice, the existing, tested procedure should be applied. In the special constituency, encompassing the entire territory of the Republic of Croatia, members of national minorities would exercise their right to special representation by requesting the second ballot, where their candidates would be listed, arranged in six categories. C ategory (1) would be the Serbian minority, which would elect three representatives. All the other categories would elect one representative each. These are: (2) Italian, (3) Hungarian, (4) Czech and Slovak, (5) "old" minorities: Austrian, Bulgarian, German, Polish, Romany, Romanian, Ruthenian, Russian, Turkish, Ukrainian, Wallachian and Jewish, and (6) "new" minorities: Albanian, Bosniak, Montenegrin, Macedonian and Slovene. Forty signatures of members of national minorities would have to be collected for the nomination of each candidate. The previous system of voting for the Serbian minority would be preserved: under this, they would elect three candidates with the largest number of votes. Among the other minorities, victory would go to the candidate who won the plurality of valid votes in his/her category. If two or more candidates polled the same number of votes, the election would be repeated. In the categories of the Serbian, Italian and Hungarian minorities, a candidate for deputy MP would also be proposed, while in the other categories only a candidate for representative would be nominated, and if necessary, the candidate who won the second largest number of votes would become the deputy. It is true that in these elections, the votes of non-elected candidates would be "wasted" – i.e. they would be left unrepresented – but set against this is the fact that, according to the principle of positive discrimination, the minority representatives would be elected by significantly smaller numbers of votes than would be necessary for the average elected representative in the general elections. And indeed, because of the dual right to vote, members of national minorities would be able equally to participate in the general poll.

Chapter 20
WHY TR IN CROATIA? POINTS FOR DISCUSSION

20.1 I will now give a final analysis of the advantages and potential disadvantages of abandoning Croatia's existing electoral system in order to implement **Total Representation**, as so passionately advocated by the man who has devised it, Aharon Nathan.

20.2 But before embarking on this analysis, I would like to take the liberty of indulging in some political nostalgia worthy of a senior citizen. In the early 1990s, when I was elected to the (first) Parliament of the independent and sovereign Croatia, the position of MP was popularly perceived as one of the most reputable and respected public posts. Now, many years later, I am sometimes approached in the street by strangers who tell me that they remember that period and my appearances on the parliamentary rostrum. In those days, people used to actually sit and watch live TV coverage of parliamentary sessions and, in this way, we went through a kind of education for democracy, which we all badly needed after half a century of a regime that started off as hardline totalitarian, and then became softer at the edges. Of course, I am not arrogant enough to imagine that these speeches of mine were in any way crucial or impressive, because even these citizens do not recall what I was actually saying, but they obviously remember seeing me in the Parliament, which was then the most legitimate and supreme political institution of the new state – and its status was helped by its members. Unfortunately, today being an MP has turned, in the public's view, into one of the most despised posts – and some of today's members have actually contributed to this reputation, as has the entire so-called political élite of the country. For all that, the cause of the decline in Parliament's prestige is really to be found in the gradual erosion of trust in the very system of representative democracy itself; unfortunately, this has occurred after the system has been in operation – in a somewhat mediocre fashion – for only eighteen years.

20.3 I am a long-standing and almost fanatical supporter of the ideas of liberal democracy, and have been politically active since the crucial year of 1989; my aim during this time has been to help them become a reality in the practice of Croatian society, and to help the establishment and functioning of parliamentarism in a free Croatia. So I will now seek to examine the advantages and disadvantages of both electoral systems (the existing one and TR), taking account of our accumulated experiences – in other words, in an empirical, rather than a theoretical, fashion.

20.4 The development of Croatian parliamentarism during the 1990s was characterised by a sequence of big electoral wins for the Croatian Democratic Union (HDZ), which was (nonetheless) disproportionately well-represented compared with its support in the country. In the semi-presidential system, under the authoritarian President Tuđman, the HDZ played the role of a nationwide political movement, claiming exclusive credit for the establishment of the state and the victorious outcome of the war for independence. In this context, it was questionable whether we were operating in an environment of real parliamentary pluralism, because a series of adjustments to the electoral system enabled the HDZ further to cement its status as a single, superior, dominant party (and, in practice, it behaved as if its real aim was to become a *hegemonic* party, like the ruling communists back in the days of the nominally pluralistic communist Poland or the GDR, i.e. the former East Germany).

20.5 The HDZ used its dominant position to stir up discontent among the minor parties, which caused the party system to be fragmented; there was also a reduction in the range of the appeal of centrist parties with the potential to become stronger (the HSLS, HSS). After another ten years, this led to their being included in a grossly unequal coalition under the auspices of the post-Tuđman HDZ. Only two parties managed to resist such constant manoeuvring, and these today present the only real opposition to the governing – though no longer overwhelmingly dominant – HDZ. One of these is a political child of the 1971 "Croatian Spring", the Croatian People's Party – Liberal Democrats (*Hrvatska narodna stranka –*

Liberalni demokrati, HNS), which, despite the ambiguity of its name and agenda, and the profile of its membership (somewhere between populism and liberalism), seeks to occupy the political centre. The second one is the Social Democratic Party (*Socijaldemokratska partija, SDP*), which deserves particular praise for its role in the 1990 transition: despite the fact that Croatia was still then within the Socialist Federal Republic of Yugoslavia, the SDP held a smooth, free multi-party election and handed over power to the winners. Even though it was a legal successor of the League of Communists of Croatia (*Savez komunista Hrvatske*), it has, since its inception, proclaimed its commitment to the democratic transition. In the very first election it added the cunningly devised abbreviation SDP to its name, which first meant the Party of Democratic Changes (*Stranka demokratskih promjena*), and then soon turned into the Social Democratic Party. Although it barely passed the electoral threshold in the 1992 election, the SDP continued to gain strength, excluding from its leadership t hose who were conspicuously tied to their communist, i.e. Yugoslav, past and did not easily accept the mere role of being reformed communists acting as a constructive opposition.

20.6 The architect of this transformation of the Communist Party into a Social Democratic Party was Ivica Račan, who must be, in a certain sense, credited for the democratic transformation of Croatia as a whole, because although he was perceived as a procrastinator, he actually played a crucial role in several key moments of the transition. The first time he did this was at the 11th Congress of the SKH in 1989, when, as newly elected chairman, he advocated the passing of a decision on allowing a multi-party system; then again in 1990 when – together with the Slovene delegation – he led the Croatian (SKH) delegates out of the 14th Congress of the SKJ (League of Communists of Yugoslavia; *Savez komunista Jugoslavije*) in Belgrade because he opposed Milošević's attempts to make Yugoslavia resist the inevitability of democratisation and decentralisation. Finally, in 2000, Račan won the general election as the leader of the SDP/HSLS coalition – this put an end to the HDZ's absolute dominance, ended Croatia's unofficial but real international isolation, and eliminated some, though far from all, of the negative consequences and features of Tuđman's decade-long autocratic rule.

20.7 However, despite the positive contribution of the SDP to pluralism in Croatia, in practice, after the crucial election held on 3rd January 2000, the process of the crushing of minor parties continued. As for the two main political groupings, the 2003 election, when the HDZ won again and Račan's SDP handed over office without delay, led to a more even balance power of between them – and this grew still more marked after the 2007 election. The paradox lies in the fact that the Croatian Parliament's version of a two-party system emerged *after* the application of PR, which, in theory, tends to lead to parliamentary fragmentation.

20.8 The emerging two-party system in Croatia (though in fact there are more than 100 registered political groups!) is actually a picture of two major parties with almost equal support among the electorate, and this reflects the truth that there are deep divisions within Croatian society on a range of different issues. The rival parties include a few people who became rich as a result of the war and the transition, and a large mass of people who were society's victims of the same processes, but one can also observe a deep cleavage as a consequence of the excessive nationalist rhetoric and nation-building practice of the 1990s. On the one hand, there has been a growth of nostalgia for the Ustasha regime of the early 1940s among those who have not fully grasped the true horror of this criminal, Nazi-Fascist episode in recent Croatian history. These people are engaged in a confrontation with anti-fascism, which they equate in all respects with communism. On the other hand, because of current hard social circumstances, there are also those who occasionally manifest a provocative nostalgia for communist egalitarianism – a selectively warm memory of the guaranteed social security and relative openness of Tito's brand of "self-management socialism" in Yugoslavia.

20.9 But because of Croatia's long-awaited admission to the European Union, no-one on the parliamentary spectrum wants openly to take up a position on either the extreme Right or the extreme Left. In fact, extremist views in Croatia have no relevant political organisations of their own, and hence everybody jostles for space in the imaginary political centre. Even though in previous years the Croatian Party of Rights was recognised as an expression of the most right-wing views, today it is rather marginalised; the conservative HDZ and HSS pass themselves off as centre-right, and the SDP occupies the centre-left, although there is virtually no relevant party beyond it on the far left. The HNS is on roughly the same part of the political spectrum – on a case-by-case basis, it is slightly to the right or left of the SDP – but today, both these parties in fact fulfil the role of watchdogs of the fundamental tenets of liberal democracy. Meanwhile, the HSLS – once a natural home for moderate, sensible, liberal, urban voters – has got lost in the vast HDZ hunting-ground and, therefore, lingers on the fringes of the centre-right and indeed of any political relevance.

20.10 The public feels that this configuration of political options and the polarisation of party forces are not good for healthy parliamentarism; this can be seen from the total loss of trust in Parliament and in the entire political establishment. New elections have not been called, but *ad hoc* internet groups lead embittered people out on to the city squares with relative ease. This is particularly the case with young people (fortunately, for the time being not in large numbers) who shout furious slogans aimed at each and every political party. This dramatic reduction in trust in the institutions of liberal democracy leads to the growth of political apathy and resignation, because citizens do not view their elected representatives as people who can be entrusted with the task of expressing and promoting their genuine interests.

20.11 So, the existing system of PR has not enabled voters to have a closer bond with their representatives (and vice versa), and the consequences show that this is its major disadvantage. The *depersonalisation* of the entire electoral mechanism has given rise, inevitably, to another major drawback of Croatia's political set-up – *partitocracy*, in the sense that political parties and their omnipotent leaders dominate the constitutional bodies of the state. Under this system, MPs largely serve only to use their fingers on the electronic voting machine in Parliament as directed by their parties, without the opportunity to take a personal stand – not even on controversial issues of morality or habit, which are actually beyond the sphere of politics and belong strictly to the individual conscience (from abortion to euthanasia and same-sex communities, and from the prohibition of smoking in public places to specifying how much alcohol drivers are allowed to have in their bloodstream). The total predominance of the parties in parliament is also disastrous, because they are a mere consequence of the idea of representative democracy, a system whose basic purpose is to solve social conflicts by free competition between different views, and to make decisions on the principle that the majority opinion should prevail. In new democracies, like Croatia, *partitocracy* undermines the trust of citizens in Parliament and thus threatens the very essence of the system. Of course, this could have pernicious consequences for the development of the new country, which has only just emerged from communism; to create conditions for the revival of totalitarianism in any new form whatsoever would certainly not be good.

20.12 Aharon Nathan's refined TR system – Total Representation – is a lucid combination of the advantages of the well-known and well-established systems of first-past-the-post and proportional representation. It was devised with the intention, on the one hand, of correcting the disadvantages of Britain's ossified two-party system – the result of the pure application of FPTP. On the other hand, TR is also intended to overcome the fragmentation of the Israeli Parliament, with its fragile, fluctuating majority coalitions that have made every government permanently unstable and hence frequently inefficient. This is a consequence of Israel's system of pure PR, with virtually no functioning electoral threshold. However, even though TR was designed pragmatically, and on the basis of empirical experience, it has additional, advantageous qualities that may go unnoticed at first sight, but which make it usefully applicable even in situations remote from those of Britain and Israel.

20.13 This is the case of the Croatian Parliament, where the problems are different from those in the House of Commons or the Knesset. In Croatia, parliamentary dominance by two strong and almost equally matched parties has been gradually achieved through a long process of "the big fish swallowing the small fry". This has occurred precisely during the era of Croatia's third post-

1990 electoral system: PR in ten constituencies. But the division of the electorate and their representatives into two numerically equal halves is so marked that one side can threaten to paralyse a session by engineering or collaborating in a lack of a quorum, while the public gets the impression that all that is happening is a futile verbal competition, with no good results. Meanwhile, there are deplorable examples of conflicts of interest and abuses of representatives' privileges. This is where the rage against the entire political class and the loss of trust in the institutions of representative democracy stem from.

20.14 In order to solve this problem, it is necessary to persuade the electorate that their votes have some weight and that they do influence political life. This *personalisation* of the political class can be brought about using the TR system, which will certainly help to undermine and weaken the *partitocracy* that has evolved in Croatia over the last eighteen years. More specifically, TR is based on candidates' personalities, because the first segment of the election is conducted in constituencies where an individual with a name and surname wins with the help of his/her party (or without it), and not a party with a list of people who are more or less unknown to voters. The party, on the other hand, comes into its own in the PR segment, but even there it also depends upon individuals, i.e. those of its candidates who did not succeed in the constituencies. Each of these brings with him/her a certain number of votes, which provides him/her with a certain political weight. The number of ballots cast for each candidate in the FPTP segment is also precisely known. In this way, the level of voters' trust in each MP or party official is quantified on the political stage, which makes the weight of different members of the political class measurable – and the political arena is personalised. The parties will also benefit from this, because the introduction of objective measurement will ensure that it can no longer be said that one can move up only by currying favour with the leadership. This will encourage intra-party dialogue, and the parties themselves will become more attractive to potential new members and thus also voters.

20.15 If the application of TR leads to the personalisation of the political élite, this will certainly help to weaken the noxious *partitocracy*, and political parties will return to their original mission of assembling and organising like-minded people into potentially active participants in the legislative and executive branches of government. TR will also affect the internal lives of parties; in today's Croatia, they are dominated by autocratic presidentialism, which means that it is largely the decision of the party chairman or leader to distribute jobs to activists and appoint candidates to constituencies – the voters' opinion counts for nothing. Once the political value of each party member who has run for office is objectively measured, it will be impossible to preserve the current system whereby a party is totally dependent on its chairman or immediate leadership. This would be a contribution to the democratisation of political parties, which is one of the standard requirements cited at round-table discussions on the development of Croatia's political system. Another positive effect can be expected from the adoption of TR: it would reduce the current, excessive centralisation of political life, where the majority of representatives and officials come from the capital, Zagreb. Even within the existing PR system, there has been some effort to ensure that at least the name at the top of the list should come originally from the constituency he is running for. But under TR, serious competition for votes in the constituencies will make it even more necessary that reputable figures from each geographical environment should run for office; the positive consequence of this will be the revitalisation, but also the much-needed *decentralisation*, of political life, with each voter – wherever he/she lives – having increased influence on the political landscape as a whole.

20.16 More specifically, TR guarantees that there will be hardly any "wasted votes", and that the overwhelming majority of ballots will be represented in Parliament in some way, either by a local MP or by their role in selecting the Party MPs from the respective lists. As the voter will be quite familiar with the candidate for whom he cast his/her ballot, that voter will feel that he/she is electing a person who he/she can trust, and even if this candidate does not win a majority in the respective constituency, the voter will know that his/her vote has not been wasted, and that it does affect the outcome of the proportional election at the national level. A real bond between voters and their representatives is being established, and this kind of reform may even lead to a restoration of trust in the purpose of elections as fundamental levers in the functioning of representative democracy.

20.17 I believe that this reform of the electoral system could be adopted by consensus, because TR does not favour anyone at the starting line, and it would not be adopted in order to favour one political option or another; rather, it is intended to increase the trust of frustrated voters in the very institution of elections. The introduction of TR in Croatia would probably not significantly affect the relative strengths in Parliament of the parties as they are currently constituted under PR. In fact, the outcome of the 2007 elections has shown that under the current system there are no large discrepancies between the percentage of votes cast and the percentage of seats won, which means that the reasons for reform do not stem from the fact that the current system leads to allegedly unrepresentative voting outcomes. What *is* surprising, however, is that the continual strengthening of parliament's two largest parties has not created pre-conditions for stable government; at the moment, the administration is largely dependent on the party discipline of majority MPs and on votes from the representatives of national minorities. The electorate is deeply divided, but the TR system would open up the possibility of new, currently minor, political groups appearing in Parliament, which could eventually – at least to an extent – contribute to the much-needed sound of more voices being heard in parliament.

20.18 Of course, the current system has its benefits, and the application of TR does not eliminate these, but brings additional advantages. From the standpoint of the voter, the most important gain is the personalisation of elections and of the entire political environment, because the individual, both as voter and elected representative, becomes the centre of the political market-place. The number of votes cast for a particular candidate (whether they win or lose) becomes the measure of his/her political relevance, and this very measurability reduces the opportunity to indulge in the well-known practice of trading seats (through switching to other parties or becoming independent candidates). This personalisation of the new electoral system does not, however, lead to the weakening, but to the strengthening of political parties, because they always have objective criteria at their disposal even in internal elections (for example, when choosing the leadership or selecting candidates for various official posts). The creation of no fewer than 80 constituencies (instead of 10) is bound to decentralise politics, while the single constituency for the election of 36 PMPs will favour some proportionality in the results. Besides, TR is a transparent system, easily understandable to voters, and thus easily controllable at each stage of the electoral procedure. As for the virtue of stability that the current PR system has brought, that is beyond doubt, but the TR system could also become stable within two or three electoral cycles, provided that it is not easily modified in the interests of one political group or another. In any case, no human act lasts forever, so we can imagine that new circumstances in the future will require this electoral system to adapt to them.

20.19 The specific circumstances of the Croatian political landscape have dictated that even in this reform of the electoral system, solutions for two specific categories of voters should be found; these have already acquired the right to special electoral treatment under the criterion of positive discrimination. So, for these categories, the principle that every vote should be equal has been bypassed, consciously and deliberately, by political consensus. These categories are those of **national minorities** and **Croatian expatriates**. The rules of TR cannot be fully applied to these two distinct electorates. In fact, no idea in the field of social relations can be implemented totally consistently and at any cost, regardless of the consequences, without this extremism endangering the basic values and vitality of the idea itself. It is good that TR is a flexible system which recognises the realities and peculiarities of different social situations. In this way, it can exist fruitfully with exceptions if these are necessary for social stability.

20.20 Because they are small in number and are geographically dispersed, it is not possible to fit all of Croatia's national minorities into the TR system. For TR requires two electoral segments, and the small and dispersed minority electorate cannot be further broken down into special constituencies. Also, as most of them elect just one MP, there is no room for an additional PR segment. Although there are many minorities in Croatia, most are relatively small, while the Serbian minority, because of its greater size, and for historical reasons, is entitled to be represented in Parliament as an ethnic entity. (It is interesting to note that at one point in history, during the period of the Austro-Hungarian Empire, the Vice-Speaker and Viceroy were both Serbs.) Given the fact that Croatia has not yet got over the material and psychological consequences of the Serbian rebellion of the early 1990s (which was closely tied to the Yugoslav Army/JNA's attack on Croatia to prevent it from gaining independence), it seems best to preserve the current way of electing minority representatives on the principle of "if it ain't broke, don't fix it." At the same time, legalising minorities' constitutionally undeniable dual – or additional – right to vote for members of their own group could help integrate all of them into the civic body of the country.

And thus, with more harmonious inter-ethnic relations, we may see that, after four or five electoral cycles, members of these groups will gradually lose interest in electing special representatives (and their turnout in this segment of elections is already low). If conditions are created that enable members of the larger minorities to win seats at elections in the normal way (and the TR system gives this opportunity, provided that the electoral threshold in the PR segment is removed), and if the smaller minorities recognise that it is MPs, not voters, who benefit most from their own existence, one can expect in future that their special parliamentary representation will be reduced symbolically to just one or two MPs who function as spokespeople, or ombudsmen, for the interests of all minorities. However, until such time as this optimistic hope is realised, the existing legal arrangements for their representation meet all the necessary standards. Indeed, despite the obvious violation of the principle of equality of votes, the Croatian public has accepted the fact that minority MPs are typically elected by a smaller number of votes than others; people seem to be aware of the political benefits of positive discrimination, not only for minorities, but for the social stability of the country as a whole.

20.21 Within the proposed framework for the implementation of the TR system in Croatia, a place has been found even for the representation of Croatian expatriates in a new and untested way. As far as the number and geographical location of non-resident Croatian nationals is concerned, it has been possible to define logical constituencies on all continents for the election of the "diaspora" MPs. These members of parliament – being members of the diaspora themselves – would truly and publicly represent Croatian expatriates, so that they could establish at least a symbolic bond with their parent country. To be sure, even in the case of the diaspora, a certain departure from the principle of the equality of votes must be tolerated under TR. These constituencies differ significantly from one another in their number of voters, which is a consequence of having a disproportionally large number of privileged electors with dual citizenship in Croatia and Bosnia-Herzegovina. However, even though these people do not meet the true definition of expatriates (because they have never left their homeland), they do legally enjoy the special right to vote as non-resident citizens. For that matter, *positive discrimination* has been applied even to them, because the Croatian electoral system entitles them to the *dual right to vote*, considering the fact that they exercise their right to vote in both Croatia and Bosnia. Generally speaking, modern Croatia has respected the classical slogan of the founding fathers of American democracy in the late 18th century: *no taxation without representation*. However, in debates on the voting right of people with dual citizenship, the arguments advanced by the opponents of special rights for Croatian expatriates have been ignored, even though they originate from the very same slogan but in its logically inverse form: *no representation without taxation*.

20.22 In completing my contribution to the launching of this innovative idea by Aharon Nathan, I have not provided my description of the possible introduction of TR in Croatia merely as an example of the application of an intriguing theory – no, I have in fact become more and more convinced that such a reform of the electoral system would be very useful to Croatia. This is a country that has emerged out of the collapse of communist totalitarianism and stands on the threshold of accession to the European Union.

Once we have become a full member of the European family, the Croatian Parliament will once again – as it has through history – strengthen its mission to unify its legislative, supervisory and representative functions as the symbolic and most important bearer of the legitimacy of Croatian statehood. The majority of decisions by European legislative and bureaucratic bodies will be subject to the revision or ratification of national parliaments, and this will certainly increase the importance of electing suitably qualified representatives and of generating public trust in the Croatian Parliament. I believe that TR will greatly help to increase voters' interest in elections, and the increased personalisation of political competition may help block what is known as "negative selection" (where people get selected to important posts more on the basis of their political obedience than their real merit) for the most important state and social posts, which has been so noticeable in Croatia.

20.23 So I offer this presentation of electoral systems in Croatia and of a possible switch to the Total Representation system as an incentive for a broad, serious and well-argued public debate among all those who have the interest and knowledge to take part in it usefully and constructively. My response to possible objections that there is no point introducing an electoral system which has never been tested in practice anywhere, is that this is exactly one source of its appeal for us. As a transitional young democracy, we have persistently copied all sorts of arrangements from the wider world in various fields, and now we have the opportunity to enter the European Union with an electoral system not known in the EU, but which, I am sure, will soon be copied in other countries because of its undeniable virtues and advantages – albeit maybe with some minor adaptations to specific circumstances or different environments. Another quite personal remark: my support for TR has no motivation in terms of the current political situation in Croatia. I am no longer politically active or aligned, and I wish to remain so. I will continue to be permanently committed to liberal ideas of representative democracy, as *the worst form of government except all those other forms that have been tried from time to time*, as was so memorably expressed, in his characteristic style by Winston Churchill during his famous speech in the House of Commons in November 1947.

Therefore, I repeat: this call for a public debate on the reform of the Croatian electoral system by means of the application of the Total Representation system described in this book, comes from a former, no longer active, non-party politician, who defines himself as an *independent liberal Croatian post-nationalist*.

KEY TO ABBREVIATIONS IN THE TEXT

ASH   Action of Social-Democrats of Croatia (*Akcija socijaldemokrata Hrvatske*)

AVNOJ Antifascist Council of the National Liberation of Yugoslavia (*Antifašističko vijeće narodnog oslobođenja Jugoslavije*)

B&H   Bosnia and Herzegovina (*Bosna i Hercegovina*)

DC   Democratic Centre (*Demokratski centar*)

DIP   National Electoral Commission (*Državno izborno povjerenstvo*)

DPV   Social-Political Council (*Društveno-političko vijeće*)

GONG   Citizens Organised in Control of Voting (*Građani organizirano nadgledaju glasovanje)*

HDSS   Croatian Democratic Peasant Party (*Hrvatska demokratska seljačka stranka*)

HDSSB Croatian Democratic Party of Slavonia and Baranya (*Hrvatska demokratska stranke Slavonije i Baranje*)

HDZ   Croatian Democratic Union (*Hrvatska demokratska zajednica*)

HKDU   Croatian Christian Democratic Party (*Hrvatska kršćansko-demokratska stranka*)

HNS   Croatian People's Party – Liberal Democrats (*Hrvatska narodna stranka – liberalni demokrati*)

HSLS   Croatian Social Liberal Party (*Hrvatska socijalno-liberalna stranka*)

HSP   Croatian Party of Rights (*Hrvatska stranka prava*)

HSS   Croatian Peasant Party (*Hrvatska seljačka stranka*)

HSU   Croatian Party of Pensioners (*Hrvatska stranka umirovljenika*)

IDS   Istrian Democratic Assembly (*Istarski demokratski sabor*)

JNA   Yugoslav People's Army (*Jugoslavenska narodna armija*)

KNS   Coalition of People's Accord (*Koalicija narodnog sporazuma*)

LS   Liberal Party (*Liberalna stranka*)

NDH   Independent State of Croatia (*Nezavisna Država Hrvatska*)

ABBREVIATIONS

PGS   Alliance of the Littoral-Gorski Kotar (*Primorsko-goranski savez*)

RH   Republic of Croatia (*Republika Hrvatska*)

RiDS   Rijeka Democratic Union (*Riječki demokratski savez*)

SDP   Social Democratic Party (*Socijaldemokratska partija*)

SFRJ, SFRY   Socialist Federative Republic of Yugoslavia (*Socijalistička Federativna Republika Jugoslavija*)

SHS   [Kingdom of] Slovenes, Croats, and Serbs (*Slovenaca, Hrvata i Srba*) (State from 29/10 to 1/12/1918) or Serbs, Croats, and Slovenes (*Srba, Hrvata i Slovenaca*) (Kingdom from 1/12/1918 to 3/10/1929)

SKH   League of Communists of Croatia (*Savez komunista Hrvatske*)

SKH-SDP   League of Communist of Croatia – Party of Democratic Changes (*Savez komunista Hrvatske – Stranka demokratskih promjena*)

SNS   Serbian People's Party (*Srpska narodna stranka*)

TR   Total Representation

UN   United Nations

UNPA   United Nations Protected Area

UNPROFOR   United Nations Protection Force

VO   Council of Municipalities (*Vijeće općina*)

VUR   Council of Associated Labour (*Vijeće udruženog rada*)

ZAVNOH   Anti-Fascist Council of National Liberation of Croatia (*Zemaljsko antifašističko vijeće narodnog oslobođenja Hrvatske*)

ABOUT THE AUTHORS

AHARON NATHAN was born in Iraq in 1931. He read Middle East Studies at the Hebrew University in Jerusalem and Social Anthropology at Oxford. In 1953 he was appointed Senior Assistant Advisor on Arab affairs under both Prime Ministers Ben Gurion and Moshe Sharett. In that capacity he was secretary to the standing committee of the security services in the Arab sector.

In 1955 he was appointed by Ben Gurion as Secretary to Yohanan Rattner's Commission on Military Government which recommended a more open and fair administration of Arab areas in Israel. In 1956 he was appointed Secretary to Judge Azulai's fact-finding Commission on Kafr Qasim, which initiated the strict distinction between lawful and unlawful orders for future engagement rules for Israel's Defence Forces.

In the Suez War (1956) he was Deputy Military Governor (to Brig. -- later on General -- Mati Peled). He set up and headed the first civil administration in the Gaza Strip. In the 1960s he was in charge of integrating Arab workers as full members into the Histadrut Trade Unions and co-ordinated the election of the 4th Knesset in the Arab sector. In 2005, he was appointed by the President of Israel to a commission that examined the government and governance of the country. At the same time he joined the board of governors of the Citizens' Empowerment Centre in Tel Aviv.

Despite maintaining active links with Israel - including military service in the 1967 Six-Day War - he has, since the 1960s, lived in the UK from where he pursued a career in business and travelled extensively throughout the Far East and Eastern Europe. The experiences of different countries have continued to feed his passion for electoral reform and encouraged him to devise and refine "TR", the Total Representation system.

Professor Ivo Škrabalo was born 1934 in Sombor (then Yugoslavia, today Serbia) and has lived in Zagreb, Croatia, since 1952. He graduated at Zagreb University, first at its Law Faculty and later at its Drama Academy as a theatre director. He then went on to obtain a master's degree in International Law, with his thesis on the self-determination and secession of Bangladesh from Pakistan.

A great deal of his life has been devoted to cinema: he has directed a number of documentaries and acted as assistant director on several feature films; he is also the author of three books on the history of Croatian cinema. However, he has also played an active role in political and public life. In 1971, during the so-called "Croatian Spring" he was an editor of the short-lived, mass circulation *Croatian Weekly*. In 1989, on the eve of the end of communism, he became a co-founder of the Croatian Social Liberal Party, the country's first non-communist political party at that time. In the first democratic government, he served as assistant minister at the Ministry of Culture, Sports and International Cultural Co-operation. He served two terms as an MP in the Croatian Parliament (1992-95 and 2000-3), and at that time was a leader of the Committee for Inter-parliamentary Co-operation, as well as a member of the Permanent Mission to the Parliamentary Assembly of the Council of Europe.

In 2003, President Chirac made him an Officer of the Legion d'Honneur for his contribution to Croatian-French relations and for his role in the creation and consolidation of democracy in Croatia.